Also by Nell Frizzell

Fiction
SQUARE ONE

Non-fiction
THE PANIC YEARS
HOLDING THE BABY

CUCKOO

www.penguin.co.uk

CUCKOO

Nell Frizzell

bantam

TRANSWORLD PUBLISHERS
Penguin Random House, One Embassy Gardens,
8 Viaduct Gardens, London SW11 7BW
www.penguin.co.uk

Transworld is part of the Penguin Random House group of companies
whose addresses can be found at global.penguinrandomhouse.com

First published in Great Britain in 2024 by Bantam
an imprint of Transworld Publishers

Copyright © Nell Frizzell 2024

Nell Frizzell has asserted her right under the Copyright,
Designs and Patents Act 1988 to be identified as the author of this work.

This book is a work of fiction and, except in the case of historical fact,
any resemblance to actual persons, living or dead, is purely coincidental.

Every effort has been made to obtain the necessary permissions with
reference to copyright material, both illustrative and quoted. We apologize
for any omissions in this respect and will be pleased to make the
appropriate acknowledgements in any future edition.

A CIP catalogue record for this book
is available from the British Library.

ISBNs 9781787634343 hb
9781787634336 tpb

Typeset in 11.25 /15.75pt Sabon LT Std by Jouve (UK), Milton Keynes
Printed and bound in Great Britain by Clays Ltd, Elcograf S.p.A.

The authorized representative in the EEA is Penguin Random House Ireland,
Morrison Chambers, 32 Nassau Street, Dublin D02 YH68.

Penguin Random House is committed to a sustainable
future for our business, our readers and our planet. This book
is made from Forest Stewardship Council® certified paper.

To all my sisters.
And all their siblings.

1

I knew what he was as soon as I clicked on the photo.

Hair like black popcorn, nose like an axe, eyes the colour of milkless tea. It wasn't that he looked like my father – my dead father – although of course he did. It was that he looked like me. Staring into my phone at a picture of this stranger was like looking at myself, made man.

I put the phone on my bedside table, beside a glass of water speckled with air bubbles from several untouched nights. A strand of hair poked out from behind the prostrate phone and next to that lay an Allen key that I'd used weeks ago. There was also a photo of Clive, my father – my dead father – in a frame. He was staring at the camera, wearing a blue smock. He wore smocks because he couldn't bear the idea that anyone in the world might not immediately realize he was an artist. Dad had been the sort of man who actually put pencils behind his ear. The sort of person who sketched on the Tube. I adored him.

With slightly shaking hands, I picked up my phone again. The details about this man were lying there like cling-film-wrapped chicken: cold, pale, revolting. Oliver

Coburg. Male. Auckland, New Zealand. I felt guilty. I felt like the witness and the perpetrator all at once. I had found this man. I had spat in a tube and created him. I was Frankenstein.

This time, I pushed the phone under my pillow and walked out of the room. On the landing, a towel printed with small red flowers hung over the wardrobe door. Pulling it down, a full-length mirror appeared; and there I was. Flat feet. Three dark hairs sprouting from the knuckle of my big toe. Knees like russet apples. A pair of pyjamas bought under duress for someone's hen do about five years ago. I didn't even get to my face before turning towards the bathroom. Salty water was flowing into my mouth. I'm not the sort of person who normally vomits from shock but this was shock and guilt together. A combination like vinegar and baking soda. Expansive, stinging. I had done this and might never be able to undo it. I stood in front of the toilet and heaved three times. My stomach clenched. My eyes watered. But nothing else came up.

Stepping into the shower, I turned the tap and spat into the bath. That's the thing about living alone; I could behave like a feral beast. I could eat ham for breakfast and hide dirty plates in the oven and fall asleep to my dad's old answerphone messages and who would know? I was out of view. As the shower warmed up, I looked into the hole above the curtain rail. It had been there when I moved in, more than a year ago. A broken tile, presumably. This wasn't a luxurious flat. Even as I'd looked round it, still liquid with grief, flush with death money, I'd known that it needed work. I'd also known, with the certainty born of hopelessness, that I wasn't going to do any of that work. The agent had smiled the grinding, hysterical smile of the London estate agent and told me that it had 'literally mind-blowing potential', and I'd nodded. Because what was I going to do? Argue? Ask to see a different flat? Demand they do the work before I moved in? Of course not. I'd just agreed and put down a deposit. It was the first and only flat I viewed and I took it. I'd lied to Rita, of course. My sister still believed that I'd sat in a branded Mini Cooper and driven around North London all day inspecting the seven flats she'd researched, and had liked this one the best. Which maybe I would have.

Rita. Pushing the soap under my armpit, I flinched. What was I going to say to Rita? She'd know something had happened. I'm not a particularly good liar and, anyway, she was my sister. Well, half-sister. But sister, really. I'd just have to explain. It was sort of her fault, anyway. If she hadn't got a dog, none of this would have happened.

When I got back into my bedroom, I could hear the phone vibrating under my pillow. Gamar.

'Hello?'

'Nancy? Can you hear me?'

'Yes, where are you?'

'I'm in the office. In Khartoum.'

'Oh.' A second's pause. 'How long have you been back there?'

'Only since last night.' And, of course, he hadn't got in touch last night. Hadn't sent a message. He hadn't thought of me at all. 'But I went straight to the hospital as soon as we got back and have only just come off my shift.' Shame coloured my cheeks. Imagine being jealous of a hospital. 'How are you?'

'Oh, fine. Yes. I'm fine.'

'Sorry. There's a bit of a delay.'

'Yes.' Often our calls were like shouting down a well: the reply would be slow and echoey.

'Are you sure you're all right? You sound a bit ... um ...'

Suddenly, there were tears sliding from the corners of my eyes and on to my nose. I'm so inured to crying now that I'd hardly noticed.

'Nancy?'

'Do you remember that DNA test I did?' I let out a juddering sigh.

'Yes. What is it? You know, Nance, those things aren't accurate. If you're worried about inherited conditions you need to do a proper—' But I'd accidentally started to answer him, cutting off the sound of his voice.

'No, it's not that. Gamar?'

'Yes.'

'I have a brother.'

2

In the atrium of the Wellcome Collection, I saw Rita looking at her watch. A flock of birds hung suspended, above her head, from the high domed ceiling. She was looking at her watch because I was, at most, three minutes late. Which meant she would have been waiting there for eighteen minutes. One of Rita's favourite ways to boost her cortisol is to arrive to appointments at least a quarter of an hour early and then start asking how long you're going to be. Knowing that, I stood outside, holding my bike keys for a few extra seconds, just to wind her up.

'Hello, Reetabix,' I said, feeling her padded coat sigh against my shoulder as we hugged.

'I'm just going for a wee,' she replied.

My sister will make a point of going to the toilet at the least convenient time possible. The moment a waiter arrives, for example. Or just as your train platform is announced. During a family holiday, Rita managed to get locked in Warwick Castle because she ran off to use the toilet as they were ushering people out of the main gates. I think it's a power move. She says it's a small bladder.

If that's the case, then she must have inherited it from her mum – I regularly go for eight hours without a loo break if we're short-staffed. As I waited, I looked up to admire the flock of birds. I needed distraction. With my neck bent back like a bottle of Toilet Duck I realized that the flock of birds was, in fact, a huge collection of speculum. Speculums? Speculi? Rita would know. Maybe I'd give her a treat and ask. Squeezing my hands into fists, I looked at them: metal, plastic, ceramic. Long-beaked, tubular, crank-handled. I swallowed.

'You're looking sweaty, Nantucket,' Rita said, emerging from the toilet still rubbing at the sanitizer gel on her hands. Rita has been using hand sanitizer since dial-up internet. For years, she was the only person I knew who carried it in her rucksack. Until we all did, of course.

'Oh, just my moustache,' I said, smiling a touch unconvincingly. 'Maybe these are giving me an attack of the tremors.' I nodded up towards the fiesta of gynaecology above our heads.

'Don't. Apparently the artist is researching fertility trauma.' Rita gave the frown she always gives when talking about art – like she's about to step on to a high bridge. 'I thought they were shelving brackets.'

We made our way up the stairs in lock step, our arms crossed at the elbow. This was hard to do, as Rita is about a foot taller than me, and it also meant we were blocking the stairway to anyone wanting to pass in either direction. But Rita is a woman willing to take up space.

'You know, I've started going to a weightlifting gym,' she said, giving my forearm a vicious little squeeze under her bicep.

'Are you going to start pulling London buses while wearing vests advertising margarine?' It was exhausting to talk like this, to make jokes, while knowing I carried a secret. But it was utterly beyond me to fight against the pull of Rita's momentum. Perhaps I even wanted to stay upbeat, stay on the surface, stay in my sister's good books, just for a few minutes longer.

'I've been doing that since the Tube strike,' Rita smiled. 'But in the meantime, I've discovered that the weights room is where all the cool queer women in West Ham hang out.'

'All four of them?'

'Oh, look, everybody' – Rita threw her arm out wide and shouted down the hallway – 'Dorothy Parker's come to Euston Road!' I cringed as a man in white trainers and rimless glasses glowered at us.

'No, but seriously, are you sure they're interesting queer women and not just, you know, muscle trucks?'

'That is a Venn diagram I would very much like to climb inside,' said Rita, doing her music-hall voice.

'Well, in that case, I'm thrilled for you.' I swallowed the panic rising from my guts. 'When you start advertising whey protein on the side of the 104 bus, I'll tell all my friends that I knew you as a wafer-thin mint.'

As we entered the exhibition, Rita unhooked her giant arm from under mine and started walking purposefully towards one of the vitrine cases in the centre of the room. I followed, slowly, looking at a piece of silver tubing by the window that might have been part of the show or might just have been an exposed ventilation duct. My back felt heavy. Compressed. Apparently this is called Museum Walk: a real condition. Well, a real condition if you believe in the Alexander Technique. Which I'm not sure I do.

'Chunks, look at this.' Rita was gesturing excitedly. In front of her, in one of the cases, was a small leather notebook. I went over and rested my chin on her shoulder. The book was covered in slanted, scratchy writing broken up by little drawings of what, to me, looked like honeycomb.

'What is it?' I asked, lifting my head reluctantly.

'This?' Rita's eyes were shining. 'This is Franklin's lab log!'

'Oh, wow!' I said, blowing the words out as if I were standing over a birthday cake, rather than an incomprehensible maroon book. 'That must be where she wrote . . .' I trailed off, knowing that Rita – as always – would fill in the gap.

'Yes, the working theory of DNA and how she'd expanded it.' The words tumbled out of my sister's mouth like bees; 'DNA' felt dangerous, irresistible. I could have told her. I could have told her right then. But she was so excited. 'This is what proves that Rosalind Franklin was analysing the data, rather than simply processing it!'

I stared again at the book, to avoid showing Rita my face.

At times like this, I felt the differences between me and my sister so sharply they could almost cut my skin. She is tall, strong, rational. She plots her life like a graph. She reads instruction manuals and buys spare toothbrushes and knows the names of birds. She bought her god-daughter shares in a barrel of Scottish whisky because it would accrue in value. She books holiday months in advance and signs up to newsletters and knows the long code of her BT Wi-Fi password off by heart. Her lips are full and her ears are small. She is top heavy with a sandbag arse. Her hair is black and curly and the skin on her nose is dark with freckles. She has a dentist and thyroid checks and plays board games that last weeks at a time.

I am the runner-up. I am out of step. I am the agent of chaos.

After an hour or so of looking around the gallery, Rita suggested that we have some lunch. I can't afford museum lunches but also knew that admitting so would invite in a lot of unwelcome questions about bill providers and mortgage rates that I had neither the energy nor insight to answer. So, I followed Rita into the cafe and scanned the cold marble counter for something that cost less than seven pounds.

'I'll get these,' Rita offered, after I'd chosen a cheese roll that looked like something you'd use to staunch a wound. It was too late to swap it for the spinach and feta pie I really wanted but I was very grateful anyway.

'Are you sure?'

'Call it a surprise bat mitzvah present.'

'But we're not Jewish,' I replied.

'That's the surprise.'

Standing in the queue, I felt my panic start to rise. The secret was crawling up my throat, ready to burst out. I wanted to talk to Rita, to empty out my guilt, but I was also scared because saying it would make it exist.

'You know that DNA test you did on Buster?' My voice sounded fake. The aim had been light-hearted but the effect was shrill.

'Seventy-five per cent Highland terrier; not a Chihuahua mix after all.' Perhaps Rita was too distracted by her spinach and feta pie to notice. 'I was so pissed off.'

'Egg-beater, that dog couldn't be any more Scottish if it played the bagpipes and baked its own shortbread,' I said. Rita started to laugh, thank God, and we went to find a table. 'You're the only person who thought he was a Chihuahua.'

'He has a very Latin American temperament,' said Rita, sitting down.

'So does Richard Madeley but I don't think anyone is taking him to Crufts in the miniature category.' I swallowed. Rita looked at me.

'What?' Rita asked, her eyebrow flickering with something like concern, something like scorn. 'What is it?'

'Well.' My hunger had evaporated. I wiped the palms of my hands down my thighs and felt the shakiness in my legs.

'Hmmmm?'

'Well, I decided to do one on myself.' I watched my sister's face shift into something closer to exasperation. 'You basically spit into a test tube and then send it off to some processing plant in Milton Keynes or whatever.'

'And you're also fifty per cent Chihuahua?' asked Rita, carving out a forkful, her knife unused on the table.

'With these thighs? I don't think so.' I sighed. 'No, I just thought it would be interesting to see what Dad had passed on to us. He was always so vague about his parents, wasn't he? Like, this nose must have come from somewhere.' I touched my face. 'We could actually be a bit Welsh.' I thought of the way I'd sent off the test, imagining a pulse of something exotic in my blood. A Sephardic drop of pickled lemons, some salt-blown piece of Viking flesh, a curl of Indian saffron. 'I just thought it would be interesting.'

'So? What did you find?'

Looking into Rita's so-familiar face, I felt the ocean at the back of my throat. I wanted to be sick. But instead I swallowed.

'It said I have a brother.'

Rita said nothing.

'Well, actually, we have a brother. You and me.'

The noise as the fork hit the ground echoed through that chamber like a cannon ball. Cutlery overboard.

'No, we don't,' Rita said, in a hard, chilly voice.

'I'm sorry, Rita.'

'No.'

'It was really, really weird but Dad was on there too?'

Rita hissed in a lungful of air like a cat being scorched by flames. 'Don't you dare bring Dad into this.'

'But, Rita – the test website. There was a photo.'

'I have to go.'

I grabbed her arm. It was a hopeless gesture; if she wanted, Rita could probably snap my radius like a toothpick, and we both knew it. But she stayed sitting.

'Look, I can show you.' But as I pulled my phone from my pocket, Rita grabbed my hand and slammed it palm-first into the table. I was shocked – Rita and I might argue sometimes but we didn't break each other's stuff. Not since we were children. There was a painful silence. When I realized that Rita wasn't going to speak, I launched in again. 'Dad was on there too. In a red fleece, in the garden. I think he . . . He must have . . . Or he . . .' I couldn't say it. I couldn't narrow down all my galloping doubts into one single accusation. Before he died, Dad had taken a DNA test and never told us. Or never told me. I flicked my eyes up at Rita but her face was like a breeze block. She hadn't known either. Neither of us had known. 'Which is how they found the sibling match.'

Rita had still been holding my hand, but suddenly thrust it away so hard that I hit my wrist against the hard white marble.

'No!'

People around us were starting to look. They probably thought we were a couple; that this was a lovers' tiff or a break-up or some weird piece of role play. Rita and I have never looked enough alike for people to assume we're sisters.

'Rita, this isn't my fault—' I'd known Rita would be surprised – upset, of course. But I hadn't expected her to turn on me like this. This physical violence, in public, was unsettling.

'Our family is complicated enough,' she said, her jaw hard with anger. 'We are still grieving.' There was no catch in her voice, just cold fury. 'Anne is grieving, my mother is in the middle of fucking nowhere and you have just invited a stranger into our lives. What for? He's not our brother. Dad didn't have a son. He was a good man, Nancy.'

'I know.'

'So this person' – she spat the word – 'is a fraud.'

'Rita—'

'It's a scam, Nancy. Either that or there's been a mistake. You should complain. In fact, you should write to the company and tell them you're going to take legal action because this isn't right.'

A tiredness crept across my body as though it were dissolving into clay.

'Nancy? Are you listening?' Rita was looking at me with something like concern beneath her fury.

'Yes, yes, I—' The rest of the word was swallowed in a croak. I was retching. The lights, Rita's anger, the smell of other people's bodies were all stuffing themselves down my throat, and all I could do was push back. Eject. Heave.

'Don't you dare throw up on my trousers!' Rita was saying, standing up quickly from the table. I closed my eyes and pulled my chin into my chest. Perhaps if I could just fold myself in tight enough, this feeling would pass. I breathed in. I heard a man behind me ask to use a plug. I felt the scraping of someone else's chair vibrate through my own.

'I don't know what's going on with you,' Rita said. I chanced opening my eyes; she was still standing up. Looming over me. 'But I think you're lonely. And I think you feel rejected. So you're looking for a man to make you feel better.' Her words felt like someone pissing through my letter box. 'Dad is a good man.' I didn't correct her tense. Dad is a good man. Dad was a good man. 'And I'm not going to let some liar with nothing better to do pretend to be his son.' I swallowed. 'Look what he did when my mum left. Do you think there were many single dads back in the 1980s? Can you imagine having to explain to a load of middle-class mums and suspicious nursery workers that your wife has gone to live in a commune in the South of France and you are now the sole parent of a toddler?' I nodded. I knew the story but this was Rita's rosary; her Hail Marys, to be repeated again and again. 'Until he got together with Anne The Barrister, it must have been hell: working, childcare, heartbreak. All while my so-called mother was chasing enlightenment or self-actualization or inner peace or whatever meaningless phrase they were using that particular week.'

I knew Marie-Louise, Rita's mum, had been a press officer before she went back to France. After Dad's funeral, she and I had sat up in her small Airbnb flat and the whole story had slowly slid out. How she had felt trapped in England; how she had always been a seeker; how the racism and class system and politics of the 1980s had felt unbearable; how motherhood had temporarily washed her away. She had also explained that when she went to live in Aynac, she had done so on the understanding that Rita would live between the two places – until Rita had got to school and suddenly learned to be ashamed of her own mother. It had been the longest conversation I'd ever had with Marie-Louise: my non-mother, my father's first wife. A woman with whom I shared no blood and yet who so easily could have been my mother, under different circumstances. A woman who had loved my dad but had also left him. I had felt sorry for her but also not entirely convinced. More, I'd had the uneasy sense that hearing Marie-Louise's side of the story was somehow a betrayal of both Dad and Rita, so I had never repeated any of what she'd said.

'Some random internet scammer on the other side of the world tells you that he's your brother and suddenly everything you know about your own father just disappears?' Rita was leaning over the table now, blocking out the white spotlights in the high ceiling. 'Just ... explodes? Dies?' This last word hit me full in the face. Even Rita looked a little shaky. 'If you want to speak to him then that's your problem. But when he starts asking you for money, or about the house, or wants to come to England, just remember this: he is a liar and you—' I heard the breath in her nostrils. 'You . . .'

While I waited for the final blow to land, I stared at Rita's T-shirt. With me sitting down and her standing up, the visible hem of her bra was at my eyeline. I could see how she had tugged at the neck of her T-shirt to make it stretch, until it looked like all her T-shirts. I could see the small bulge above the waistband of her trousers. I could see the single dark mole on the inside of her arm.

'You're a wretch.'

3

'What did Rita say?'

'She said it was a scam.' I was on the sofa, still wearing my coat.

'Well, it might be.' I could hear something in the tone between each of Gamar's words. Annoyance. He was pissed off with me and making a big show of being kind. Which was somehow even crueller.

'But Dad was on there. I saw his profile. And this man shares Dad's DNA.'

'Those calculations are notoriously inaccurate.' Gamar was using his patient voice. 'He might just be a nephew or cousin or something.'

'He looked like us.'

'Like who?'

'Me and Dad.'

'OK. Well, what do you want to do?'

I stared at a patch of white paint on the floorboard in front of me. I couldn't answer the question. I didn't make those kinds of decisions. For three years, I had held on to Gamar with an entirely open hand. Like trying to catch a butterfly. I loved him and had waited for him to love me back. No pressure. No expectations. When my dad died, I collapsed but I did not cling on. I let him breathe. Three weeks after the funeral, Gamar had flown to Damascus, to save other people's lives. Because there are always people dying somewhere.

'Maybe I should wait to see if he contacts me,' I said.

'I think the first thing you need to do is talk to your mum. She might know more than you realize. And Rita will definitely tell her, anyway.'

'I'm not sure. She seemed very angry that I'd even brought it up with her.'

I waited for a reply but there was just a thick, blank silence. Like the sound of a rubber wall.

'Gamar?'

Still nothing. I looked at my phone. The seconds were still ticking but there was no sound, not even breathing. Gamar must have lost reception. Just at the moment when he was going to tell me what to do. I pulled at my zip in frustration.

'—not sure if you can hear me?'

The thump in my heart was instant, beyond control. And wasn't there a beauty in that? What other couples could say that after three years they still felt electrified by the sound of the other's voice?

'Yes, yes, I can! Sorry, what were you saying?'

'No, you were talking.' I could hear a door closing somewhere in the background as he spoke. 'But actually I did have something I needed to tell you. Nancy?'

'Yes.'

'Oh, good, OK, you're still there. Listen, I'm sorry but we're going into lockdown here.' The pain was as instant as the pleasure had been. My body actually winced. 'It's a security thing; they think it's just too dangerous to be coming in and out of the country while there's fighting at the airport like this.' Gamar left a pause and I made a noise into it. Not an assent or a word; just a noise. 'That means I won't be able to come back for longer than expected. Maybe two months.'

Of course it had not been three years. We had not been a couple for three years. It had been ten, perhaps twelve slivers of individual weeks. A month once or twice before he was pulled away by all the other people who needed him more than me.

'I'm sorry. Especially when you've got all this going on. But, well . . .'

And there in the silence hung all the things he never said; all the ways in which he was generous and I was selfish; all the reasons he couldn't commit. He was always elsewhere, saving lives. I loved him. I wanted to feel his weight against my side as I slept. I wanted to choose a bedside light together. I wanted to move his saucepans into my kitchen. But he wanted to stand on the threshold of living and dying.

'Will you be in Khartoum?' I asked, at last.

'Not for long. Next week we're going south, further inland, towards Darfur. I have no idea what the internet will be like down there. I might not be able to call very much.'

Fury burst inside me. I was being put aside. I was his collateral damage. Because anyone can be heroic if they are alone, far from home and have nothing to lose.

'OK, love,' I said, my voice as flat as milk. 'I hope it's OK down there.'

Because what else could I do? I couldn't beg him to come home. I couldn't shout at him for making me feel unimportant. I couldn't ask him to put me first. I just had to wait; to be supportive and kind and hold on until it changed. Because one day, I knew, things would change. He would move department, international policy would change, his mother would become ill: something. And then he would come home. He would take up a practice in London, move into somewhere with a garden, spend Sundays fixing things in my mum's house. One day we would go for a walk in the country and have a pub lunch with our friends. One day we would buy a mattress together. One day he would meet me from work and know the names of all my colleagues. Gamar was the man I loved and he was my future. He just needed time.

'Thanks, Nanook.' He sounded quiet.

'How are you feeling?'

'Ah, you know. It's hard. These people, they're not soldiers, they're men. Angry men. They looted the hospital; one of the doctors got killed. Not one of us, a local doctor.'

My breath caught in my chest. Killing doctors. I had tried to avoid the news but I had still seen the pictures:

streets reduced to rubble; children hiding in doorways; blood on blankets scattering the ground. And now they were killing doctors. Gamar was British, he was Eritrean; he was working for a non-government agency delivering humanitarian medical aid. But would they care? Would they even know that, as they walked through the corridors, wielding their guns? A cold fear crept down my neck. Long ago, I had stopped telling him to stay safe because I now understood that staying safe was not a choice he could make.

'I'm sorry,' I said.

'We haven't been able to bury him.'

I looked at my knee. It was perfectly still. The light at the window was as smooth and pale as an aspirin.

'That's awful.'

'Yeah. Well . . .' I heard something like a chair being scraped across the floor. 'Anyway, have you contacted him?'

'Who?'

'This guy. The one from the website who you found.'

'Oh. No.'

'Are you going to?'

'No,' I replied. Meaning perhaps. Meaning yes. Meaning I don't know; tell me what to do; how can I decide; why is this happening; I love you; come home; I'm scared.

'OK, good. At least, maybe don't make contact until you've spoken to Anne.'

'Yes.'

'I still think she might know more about this than you think.'

'You think Mum knew about him all along? And Dad?' I heard no reply. 'So you think that he really is my brother.' I waited. 'Do you think they lied to us?'

The silence that came back was as solid as concrete. Hopelessly, I pulled the phone away from my ear. *Call ended.* He had disappeared.

4

I rang Rita for four days without her picking up. On the fifth day, she answered, asked if my mum had died, then ended the call. As more time passed, I began to feel as though a part of my heart was closing over, like an oyster shell. The pain, the grit, the salty wound was growing, and the only way I could cope was to either shut it completely or tear it open with a knife.

Rita, please. I need to talk to you. And Mum. She always knows when something has happened. Can't we just discuss this like adults?

I felt nothing like an adult, of course. Adults do not spend their days eating squeezed-out cheese on Ritz crackers because it's one of the snacks they remember their father making. They do not sit on bollards outside their front door, smoking roll-up cigarettes. They do not shudder in the disabled toilet of a primary school during morning break, ruining purple sugar paper with their own tears. Rita had read the message immediately – two blue ticks giving it away – but it had taken her forty minutes to reply.

I've told Mum we're coming over tomorrow night

for dinner. She doesn't know anything about this yet. I'm not doing your dirty work for you. You'll have to tell her.

London, of course, is not a city. It is a collection of Gail's bakeries with sewers. The area where my mother lives was once a Saxon village, surrounded by meadows and streams; now it is a busy, bus-trammelled suburb, full of delicatessens, bakeries and pound-a-bowl fruit stalls. It was possible to walk from London Bridge to her front door without once leaving an A road. Put it anywhere else in the country and it would look like a town centre but here, in London, it was little more than a glance out of a car window. She and Dad had bought the house back in 1983. A three-bedroom, red-brick terrace, it had come with an expectation of more children. Rita had just turned three; already furiously strong and a dedicated eater of plums. She had smacked her way along the tiles and timbers, open-palmed, for less than a year before I was born. Had my parents explained to her what little sisters were? Had Rita felt jealous? Usurped? Or relieved to no longer be the sole demolisher of broccoli and soft furnishings in the house? The story goes that on the day I was born, Rita arrived in the hospital with a yellow metal dumper truck and insisted on putting it in my plastic see-through cot for the night. The hospital has now, of course, been pulled down to make way for a development of luxury flats.

The door to number 145 hasn't changed colour in over thirty years: goose-shit green. Set off with a black knocker in the shape of a fox and a brass letter box that slams in the wind. Everybody in the house had always hated the colour of the door but nobody had ever been willing to repaint it; an approach to interior decoration that also explains the white plastic blinds in the master bedroom, the pale grey bathroom suite and the cork tiles on the kitchen floor. As Anne likes to put it to dinner guests and visiting family: after the first eight years in a house, you just stop noticing everything you hate.

I lifted the knocker and felt a dull ache in my chest: homesickness, loss, but also something shooting down my armpit and into my breasts. At thirty-eight, my body was a kaleidoscope of unwelcome changes. The hairs exploding from my neck, the watery nausea on waking up, thickening toenails and pale yellow bruises. They added up to nothing more than age, I knew, but sometimes they felt like an omen: preparation for events unseen.

'Hello, darling.' Anne's wide face, shoulder-length grey hair and short, blunt fringe gave her the look of a cinema curtain halfway through opening. I stepped into her arms and smelled Elizabeth Arden and cheese sauce. A wiry, brown-haired Cairn terrier skidded past her feet, nearly propelled on to the pavement by its own momentum.

'Hello, Shadwell,' I murmured as the dog leapt against my knee. 'Sorry, Mum, are you in the middle of cooking?'

Anne smiled. 'No, no, I was looking through the

upstairs window.' I glanced back over my shoulder, wondering what I'd missed. 'I was watching to see if Malcolm has moved his stupid great van.'

Malcolm at number 138 has a taste for large, supposedly muscular cars. Malcolm at number 138 is a restaurant owner and dyes his hair the colour of Coca-Cola. Malcolm at number 138 asked my mother out 'for a drive' four weeks to the day after Dad died. 'Come in, come in. Would you like a drink? I have red or white.'

'Red, please.' I nosed my trainer off with each toe. 'Is Rita here?'

'Not yet, no. She texted about twenty minutes ago to say she had to do some errands on the way.'

I frowned into the coats. Rita, who was always early, was making a point. I was on my own. We walked down the hallway, which was covered with collages: real, cut-up photographs in frames. My grandfather hovering above a beach scene; a golden retriever dwarfing the ferry glued down beside it; me, aged two, propped up in a wheelbarrow. And there was Dad, in his second wedding suit, a mess of curly brown hair; Dad standing topless in swimming trunks holding a girl under each arm, his chest already flecked with grey; Dad crossing the finishing line of the London Marathon in a pale blue vest. I hardly stopped to look at these photos any more; at the man who made me and whom I loved. I've seen them so many times they had become invisible. But today they were jarring. Even as I kept walking, my eyes flicked across the construction. Who was this man? This family man? Had he known? Had he lied to us?

In the kitchen, a programme about potholing blared out from the paint-splattered radio that, like the chopping boards and jars of dried beans, had been there longer than I could remember.

'I've made a lasagne,' said Anne, turning off the radio at the wall. 'Please tell me you haven't decided to be lasagne-intolerant.'

'Mum—'

'Donna's daughter has just decided that she's vegan but can't eat pulses,' Anne butted in. 'I ask you.'

'I'm still eating everything,' I replied. Was this true? Yes and no. On bad days – on grief and heartbreak and lonely days – food sat in my mouth like sand. After Gamar had last called, I hadn't been able to eat anything all night. 'Apart from eggs, actually, Mum. They . . . they make me windy.'

'Being alive makes you windy, Nantucket. You've always been the same.' Anne reached over and stroked a line down my cheek from eyebrow to chin. 'You look worried.'

Looking into my mother's face, I felt that pull in my stomach again. A deeper, sinister gravity. Did she know? Had she always expected this moment? Or was I about to break her heart?

'I just wish I knew what you'd been up to,' Anne continued. 'It's been such a long time . . .'

'Mum, we went to IKEA. I phoned you two days ago.'

'Oh,' she puffed, 'sales shopping doesn't count. You can't catch up by a discounted bath mat.'

'OK, fine.' This old habit of hers: always wanting more of me. The more time we spent together, the more she complained that we were never together. The more affection I showed her, the more reassurance she demanded. 'Well, Gamar is still in Sudan but I'm not sure where. He may not be home for two months and they are murdering doctors at the hospital.' The momentum allowed me to say words that I'd not yet dared to put together in my mind. 'Work is fine but a bit quiet. I am thinking of getting a new kettle and have stopped listening to the *Today* programme because I cannot stand to even hear the Prime Minister's voice any more.' As I reeled off this list, Mum's face had gone through a kaleidoscope of responses: concern, pity, confusion and, last, the eye-roll of a parent who feels they are being pushed away. She stood up and walked over to the oven. I said nothing, a little awkward after my outburst. We both breathed in and out, just once. Then Mum came back to her chair and sat down with a flump.

'I'm very sorry to hear that about Gamar. No wonder you're worried. Does he sound OK?'

I knew that Mum didn't quite understand my relationship. Which wasn't a surprise as I didn't either, and I was the one in it. So it was kind of her to take care like this; to ask; to be gentle. I'd always suspected that Dad actively hoped Gamar and I would break up, although of course he was always far too loving to have ever said anything.

'He was being very pragmatic on the phone,' I answered. 'But I don't know.' I slid my hands between the fold of my legs, palms pressed together, as if in prayer. 'But, Mum, I'm actually worrying—'

Shadwell started barking as the loud crack of the door knocker boomed down the hall.

'For God's sake,' Mum muttered, getting up and heading to the door. 'All right, all right, Shadwell, that's enough. Just coming, Rita.' I heard the metallic click of the deadlock.

'How did you know it was me?' Rita asked, pushing into the hallway.

'Because nobody else knocks on a door like a lumberjack trying to fell a redwood.' I heard a rustle of material. Perhaps they were hugging. Perhaps Rita was just taking off her coat. 'Anyway, Rita. How are you?'

'Well, Anne, I'm all right.'

'All right? What does that mean?' I could hear the clop-clop as each of Rita's boots hit the floor. I'd forgotten to take my shoes off. Another mark against me.

'Oh, you know. Single, solvent and largely sane.'

'Single?'

'Yep.' Rita's response didn't invite further questions and, for once, Anne respected her stepdaughter's subtext.

'And how is your mother?'

'Well, last I heard, she was thinking of getting some bees.' They were walking down the hall towards me. I turned in my chair, strangely nervous of seeing my own sister.

'Oh, lovely. And when was that?'

'I got a card at Christmas.'

'That's nice. Honey can be expensive these days.' Anne uncrossed her hands as she came back into the kitchen, which was warm and felt ever so slightly oily.

Rita looked at me and it felt like being hit with gravel. She was so stern. So angry. If I had been a snail, I would have tucked my eyes into my shell.

'I take it you haven't told her,' said Rita. It was the first thing she'd said to me in nearly two weeks.

'I was trying.'

'Tell me what?' Anne looked at me and then at Rita, from table to door frame. A game of tennis. I pulled my hands out from my lap and ran them across my forehead, as though parting my brain.

'Nancy wants to tell you about a test she's done,' Rita said. How like her, I thought. She might as well have answered for me. She had all but revealed the secret. Except she wanted to leave the final blow to my axe.

'What sort of test?' Anne was facing me. Just me. No more volleys from the baseline.

'Well, you know that DNA test I bought for Buster—' I began, but Rita interrupted me.

'Which was probably wrong, too.'

'Well . . .' I swallowed. 'I did it because – Mum, can you please just sit down.'

Anne was hovering behind her chair, one hand on the

back. Her hesitation had needled me. If this were a war between Rita and me, she was staying neutral. She was Switzerland. Anne remained standing.

'Fine. Well, we don't really know anything about that whole side of our family, do we?' Now it was my turn to swivel my focus from sister to mother, mother to sister. 'I don't even know where Dad's parents were born, or who their parents were.'

'Well ... Your father was always very private about his family and origins.'

'He didn't have secrets,' I said, willing it to be true.

'Oh, do you want to talk about secrets, Nancy?' Rita's voice was hard-edged.

'What?' Anne was still looking at me. I was cornered. Perhaps surrender was my only form of defence.

I cleared my throat. 'I bought a proper one of those DNA tests I got Buster. And did it on myself.'

Mum frowned. 'I'm not sure that you should—' she began. But I couldn't let her derail me again.

'And I must have accidentally ticked some box that said I wanted to learn about other DNA relatives.' This was true. I didn't remember it and yet I must have. 'I hadn't meant to but I was doing it late at night, after Gamar had gone away and, well, anyway, I did.' I didn't dare look at Rita. 'Dad was on there.' At the top of a long set of stone steps, a bowl began to wobble. 'He must have done the same test as me, about three years ago.' The bowl tipped. 'And because he was on there and I am now on there, the site, the people at the DNA site' – the bowl rolled over the lip of the step – 'well, they found a sibling match.' I could almost hear the smash as bowl hit stone, ceramic on rock. Breaking, breaking, breaking. 'It says I have a brother.' Finally, I raised my eyes to meet my mother. 'In New Zealand.'

5

'I want to see.' Mum's voice was flat and hard. This, I thought, was how she spoke at work. This was how she held authority in rooms full of men.

'I don't,' said Rita petulantly.

'Bring up the photo,' said Mum, tapping lightly on the table. Calling us to order. Anne The Barrister. As I reached into my back pocket, Mum finally came round the chair to sit down. 'Hold on, I need my glasses.' They were, as always, strung around her neck on a small gold chain. Rita ostentatiously walked out of the room. I wondered for a moment if she was going to leave completely, but there was no bang from the front door, no clunking of her boots.

My hands felt like trotters as I tapped nervously at the screen. I could hear Mum breathing beside me. A daughter can read her mother's breath like fishermen read the sea.

Open Profile.

DNA Relatives.

There was Dad, beetle-browed, in his fleece. And the other man. The cuckoo. My echo. Oliver Coburg.

'Let me see.' Mum took the phone from my hands. 'Can you make it bigger?'

Since that first email, informing me of the sibling match, I had felt too guilty, perhaps too scared, to open this page. I hadn't looked at the picture or read the profile. Somehow, finding out about a man I'd never known felt like a betrayal of the one I had; to learn about a so-called brother was to disgrace my father.

'Jesus,' Anne said, almost in a whisper.

'I know. We look . . .' It was the game that all families play: who looks like whom. Who has Auntie Joyce's nose; who inherited Uncle Piotr's eyebrows, Tom's strength, Mohammad's love of poetry. It's a ritual. It is a net, woven from the bodies, the behaviour and the beliefs of its participants. It is a chant, a lesson, a liturgy that reminds us we are part of something collective; something called a family. To say that this man, on the other side of the world, had my eyes, or Dad's hair, that his shoulders seemed to sit like mine was to disrupt the rules of the game; it frayed the knots; it broke the net.

Mum's breathing had changed. Turning my head, I saw that she was crying. Not so much from her eyes but her whole face had been pulled down, pinched in, turned hard. She was shaking. Oh God, what had I done? What had I done?

'Mum, I'm so sorry.' I tried to put my arm around her but she had turned away. I felt tears falling on to my face. I had done this. I was the plough horse, kicking up mud and pain and fear as I pushed through my own stupid life.

'Rita!' Like so many times before, I needed my sister. 'Rita, you need to come in here.' Rita would know what to do. Rita would take Mum in her big, unyielding arms and say the right thing.

'What is it?' Rita caught sight of Anne before she'd even got through the door frame. 'Oh, Anne, Anne, I'm sorry.' Stepping right past me, Rita knelt at my mother's feet and grabbed her hands. She began to rub them, as if Mum had just been pulled from a hole in the ice. 'Anne, look at me.' Rita rose up to meet my mother's eyeline. 'It's a mistake. I tried to tell Nancy. This man is just—'

'I don't think it is a mistake, Rita,' I said, sounding more forceful than I felt. 'I mean, look at him. Look what it says. A fifty per cent match.'

Anne was whispering something. Not to Rita or to me, but we both craned our heads to catch it.

'He couldn't have.'

I felt a stab between my ribs. A shooting pain like the snapping of a wire.

'I was pregnant.'

Pregnant?

'Anne, what do you mean? Pregnant?' Rita was still holding Mum's hands, circling her palms with her thumbs.

Mum shivered. A long, juddering intake of breath, like a toddler who's cut open their knee. 'Look.' She nodded at the phone, lifting her head ever so slightly. 'Read it.'

Rita picked up the phone and started to scroll. First up, then down.

'I don't believe . . .' She looked first at Anne, then at me. 'Nancy, did you read the rest of the information about this man?'

'Yes. He lives in Auckland.'

'No, here, after the section about the number of DNA segments you share.' Rita's face contorted. '"DNA segments", God, what a horrible phrase.' I looked down at the screen. I hadn't read this far before. The little black scratchings were almost incomprehensible. The blood was pulsing through my neck so fast I couldn't concentrate on these dots, these tiny lines. 'His date of birth, Nancy. Look at his date of birth.'

12 June 1984.

'I don't understand.'

Mum turned towards me. 'Nancy, don't be stupid.' The viciousness caught me like a fingernail. 'If this man were your brother, then he would have had to be conceived, on the other side of the world, when I was six months pregnant. With you.'

6

I could smell charcoal. And blood. I could taste metal. Salt was gathering at the corners of my mouth and tears stung my eyes.

'I knew this was stupid,' Rita was saying. 'Just how much attention do you fucking need, Nancy?'

'What?'

'This whole thing, this whole ...' Words seemed to fail her but only for a second. '... *pantomime* is all because you wanted to feel special. Again.' I blinked, feeling exposed. 'Is that what you want, Nancy? Is that why you're so desperate for drama? Having two loving parents is too boring for you? You feel dull, with your happy childhood and own home?'

The sound that came out of my mouth was more a bark than a retort. 'My own home!' I managed at last, focusing on Rita's hypocrisy rather than considering that she might be right. 'What, that I bought with the inheritance from our dad!' I could feel sweat pricking at my chest. 'After he died. Exactly like you did?'

'Well, except I actually had most of my deposit, because I'd bothered to get a real job.'

The path through this particular wood was all mud, from having walked it so many times. Rita had a real job; I was a barely qualified teaching assistant. Rita had savings; I just wanted people to think I was altruistic. Rita was responsible; I was idealistic. On and on.

'Oh, please! And what, your childhood was so terrible, was it? With two parents who loved you and a mum who tried desperately to be in your life, except you were too brittle to ever let her in!'

'Nancy!' Mum was gripping the sides of the table so hard her knuckles had gone the colour of grape juice. 'Rita! That's enough.'

'No, I'm sorry, Anne, but it isn't.' Rita was standing now, almost blocking out the entire window behind her. 'I'm not going to listen to this bullshit any more. There was no way – no way – Dad had a child in New Zealand. Tell her. I was there, I know.'

'You were only three!' I didn't care if shouting undermined what I was saying; I was shouting.

'Oh, and what? You think that Dad secretly flew to New Zealand, when Anne was six months pregnant, and had a son he never mentioned? Thirty-nine years and none of us ever suspected it? Do you genuinely think he could have kept a secret like that?'

'Of course I don't—'

'He never left the country! He was scared of planes!'

'Oh, thank you so much for explaining my own father to me, Rita,' I spat back. 'Thank God I have you here, otherwise I'd never have known him at all.'

'This isn't—' Mum tried and failed to insert herself between us.

'Well, did you? I mean, you obviously have a pretty fucked-up relationship with men these days.' Rita was stepping back and forward on the spot. She probably wanted to pace the room but was hemmed in by the back of Anne's chair. 'Maybe you never really did get over having to share Dad. Maybe that's why you've spent the last three years chasing a man who clearly doesn't want to commit.'

It was like vinegar in my lungs. How dare she bring Gamar into this? How dare she say that about Dad?

'Rita, I think that was uncalled for,' said Mum. But I was beyond mediation.

'Oh, and your relationship with Dad was so healthy, was it?' The muscles around my jaw had turned hard. 'That's why you basically worshipped him while acting like your own mother was some kind of stranger. A witch.'

'My mother—'

'Your mother loves you, Rita. She has tried over and over again to reach out to you and every time you just attack her.'

'You have no idea.'

'Oh, I know much more than you realize.' I felt like an eagle: swollen with a dangerous power before swooping down on my prey. 'After the funeral, Marie-Louise told me everything. About your birth, all the racist shit she had to put up with here, the break-up. How she invited you to live with her in Aynac. The phone calls you ignore. She's grieving too, you know, Rita. But not just Dad. She's grieving a daughter who doesn't even want to know.'

I could feel Mum looking at me and felt a sting of regret. This was a betrayal on top of betrayal. To take the side of the woman who came before her; to argue in favour of another mother's mothering; this was cruel. But it also needed to come out. I was lancing the wound.

'You have never dealt with your anger at your mum. You've never asked yourself why none of your relationships last; why you doted on Dad; why you never wanted children.'

'Nancy, you've gone too far.' Mum's grip on my wrist was hard. I had mentioned Rita's lack of children. I had pierced the sound barrier. I had punctured the fabric of the universe. I had taken a dive down to Hades. Mum was right; I had gone too far. But also, I was right. Surely they both knew that?

'Never wanted children?' Rita was screaming now. 'How dare you! You have no idea what I want. You have no idea what it's like!'

'Well, I know you,' I shot back. My hands were shaking with adrenaline and the floor seemed very far away.

Rita lifted her chin; the bow was taut, the arrow quivered. 'And I know you, Nancy,' she began. 'I know that you are needy, immature, lazy; that you expect everyone else to make decisions for you, that you are desperate for male approval and that you have wasted so much time on non-relationships and non-jobs that very soon you'll be forty, living alone, with no kids, no career and nobody to blame. Not me or Anne, not Gamar, and definitely not Dad.'

My field of vision narrowed to a slit. There was no scream loud enough, no words sharp enough, nothing, nothing, nothing. Turning to my mother's cluttered worktop, I picked up a clay elephant I'd made in Year Two. It was heavy, lumpy and glazed so thickly it looked wet. I threw the elephant at Rita. I threw it like a bee stings a slapping hand; like a dog bites the foot that kicks it. I threw it without thinking. She was barely further than arm's reach and yet, with the inevitability of failure, I saw the elephant pass her shoulder and hit the tomato-red wall behind her. It didn't smash. The thudding sound as it hit the floor was somehow more humiliating than if it had splintered. It was a final sound; a heartbreak sound. And suddenly, as we all stared at the indentation on that hot red wall, my stomach clenched. I hunched over and watched a long, pale string of bile slide out of my mouth and on to the floor between my feet.

'Oh, for God's sake!' Anne shouted. 'What are you doing, Nancy?'

I convulsed. Something acidic lurched out of me.

'She's being sick,' said Rita, and from the sound I knew she was walking out of the room. Tears stung my eyes.

'Get to the sink!' Mum grabbed my elbow. It felt like a claw. She pushed me away from the table and round the counter into the kitchen proper. 'Rita! Rita, don't go.' I could hear her calling down the hallway but Mum didn't let go of my arm until I was at the sink. 'Rita, please.' Anne's feet slapped urgently towards the door. 'I know you're upset but we need to—' The door slammed. The letter box tapped a pathetic coda. Standing over the washing-up bowl, I began to cry.

7

Past the Compeed plasters and multivitamins, the shelves turned sober: blue, lilac, white. This was feminine hygiene. A name that told us what we already knew: women were dirty. Women leaked and smelled and bled. Women's bodies were festering places that spored life, yeast, babies, bacteria. We needed to be stripped clean, tucked away, soaked up. And we needed to pay for it. The blue price labels clocked up from £18.00, to £21.00, to £28.99. The boxes became bigger, the promises more grave. Only when I crouched down did the numbers start to shrink: £12.00, £8.00, £6.99. I picked up a pack of five strips, two plastic tests and pulled out my phone.

Contacts.
Gamar.
Call.

'Hello.' I knew by the tiny intake of breath before he started speaking that it was his voicemail. 'This is Gamar Araya. Sorry I can't answer your call but please leave a message and I'll get back to you.' He sounded formal and remote.

'Gamar, it's me. I'm sorry to keep ringing like this but I really want to speak to you. Something's happened and I just really . . .' I came to the end of the aisle, beside silver razor blades and monochrome deodorant. I tried to keep my voice steady. To sound calm. 'Well, I just need to talk to you.'

At the till, the woman serving me had two strands of hair gelled poker straight down each side of her face. They looked like fangs. She held each box in front of the scanner, saying nothing. I tapped my card against the reader, saying nothing. She put my two packages in a small white paper bag, which I hadn't asked for, and handed them across the counter.

'Thank you,' I said, not meaning it.

As I walked into my flat, I could hear the thock of a ball being hit against the wall outside and the quick, urgent instructions of a seven-year-old. I went into the kitchen and took a glass off the draining board. The water was milky with bubbles as it came out of the tap. I had been reassured by neighbours that this was safe; fine, in fact. That you could drink water that looked like chalk, in London, in the twenty-first century, and not worry. And so I drank it, the taste of chemicals only just noticeable.

Somebody had once told me never to do pregnancy tests at home because, whatever the outcome, you would be stuck with its association for as long as you lived there. Better, they said, to go to an out-of-the-way supermarket or garage; somewhere you might never need to revisit.

I knew that the future was poised at the corners of this test. Like everyone, I had become familiar with the weight of a single or double blue line on a small white piece of plastic. I chose a cup: a chipped purple Smarties mug that a Year Three student had given to me a few years ago. It had been years since I'd done a pregnancy test. Not since the heady, sour years of my mid-twenties. Back then, I'd taken pregnancy tests all the time. If I was sleepless or nauseous, if my breasts had ached or my stomach had bloated. Just in case. I had also been having more of the kind of sex that felt as if it might disappear any minute. The kind of sex that cannot withstand the interruption of contraception. The sort of sex that happens on coastal defences or rented beds.

Because it had been so long, I forced myself to look at the instructions for the test. English, Spanish, Dutch, Mandarin. So many people, all over the world, deciding their fate by the acidity of urine. I hesitated. I put the box down and got my phone out.

Recent.

Reets Manuva.

Calling.

It rang. And rang. I looked at the leaflet. I caught a glimpse of myself in the reflection of the tap, bulbous and distorted.

The phone kept ringing. I could imagine Rita at her

kitchen table, looking at the ringing phone, waiting for it to stop. I cancelled the call and typed out a message.

Please call me back. I think I might be pregnant, I can't reach Gamar and I don't know what to do.

The ticks stayed on grey. I had been abandoned by everyone I wanted to talk to. I'd lost Dad; and now Gamar and Rita were unreachable too. I felt rejected and, in that feeling, ashamed. My breathing turned jagged.

The glass of water had been purely academic; I had so much adrenaline running through my system that producing 25ml of urine was an inevitability, not a task. A few seconds in, I pushed the mug beneath me, and heard the change in pitch as it filled. The cup was warm as I placed it on the edge of the bath. It smelled of meat. My whole body smelled vaguely of meat. Meat and onions and, beneath it, something as sweet as mould. The test came in a foil-wrapped packet. I opened it and, worrying that the chemical landscape of my fingertips might somehow tip the balance, shook the contents out on to a towel. The arrows were obvious; the absorbent tip was square and printed beneath the word MAX.

I briefly considered ringing Mum. At least she might answer. But no. I couldn't. I couldn't put this on her too.

Holding the test in my hand, I felt my blood run very slow. Did it feel as if I already knew the answer? Was I moving around the room like a woman who already knew the answer? In trying to second-guess my feelings, I'd actually managed to lose sight of them altogether. Was this dread? Or hope? It didn't feel like the other times I had done pregnancy tests but neither did it feel new.

I watched the paper thicken and the line of absorbency creep up the strip like a snake. I was holding the blue end; holding it like a ticket. Ready to be stamped. Ready to read my destination.

8

Had I wilfully ignored the signs?

That would be too kind.

The truth was that the signs were unreadable.

I was thirty-eight. My period moved around the calendar like a fox and always had. My breasts were sore. I was thickening. I sweated in the night. Sadness would clench my stomach. I had always vomited. I smelled too strongly. I was tired. I felt like an unshelled egg. All this could have meant that I was pregnant. But it might also have meant that I was premenstrual. It could even have meant that I was perimenopausal.

I looked again at the towel, hanging over the side of the bath. At the strip of paper on top of it. At the two blue lines. I picked up the leaflet and read it again. *Positiva. Positief.* 積極的. For the first time in my life I was, for now, pregnant. I'd been feeding this foetus on salted crackers, roll-up cigarettes, tears and cortisol. I had ignored the truth. How old had Dad been when he became a dad? Had he ignored the existence of his son or just never known? I was nearly forty. I had drunk wine and cycled fast and slept badly. I had treated pregnancy like an ant beneath my boot. Did I even want to be pregnant? The question arrived in my brain as lightly as ash. Did I? I had seen so many women turn to ghosts under the force of motherhood. They walked at night, black-eyed, lank-haired, crying out for who they had been. They shuffled through parks, sat like fat seals on stained blankets, wore their fertility like a crown of thorns. For years, they disappeared into a world of raisins, rhyme time, rashes. They were locked into servitude and self-pity and were obsessed with laundry. Did I really want to join their ranks?

But perhaps I did. Perhaps I always had.

When I was just five and Rita eight, we would sit in the bath together and pretend to breastfeed the sponge. I would hold it up to the tiny raspberry of my nipple and make sucking noises. Rita would then hold the sponge across her shoulder and squeeze, making burping noises as the water poured down her shoulder until I howled with laughter. I would stroke my belly and imagine being pregnant. Holding babies on my parents' friends' sofas, my mouth would water. Had my sister and I been taught to view ourselves as future mothers? Or had I just always wanted a baby? Thinking of Rita and her sponge baby made me wince again at what I'd said in Mum's kitchen.

The backs of my legs were going numb against the toilet seat. I picked up another test. This one came in a single box. The litmus paper came in a hard white plastic shell. It looked like a thermometer. This time, I didn't bother to read the instructions; I just pulled off the lid and dipped it into the same mug that had been cooling by a bar of Imperial Leather. The lines took a little longer to appear. They were red. One dark, thick and strong. The other paler, a little thinner, but absolutely there. It reminded me of the game my family always played. The categorization of the sisters over and over and over again. On a beach, Dad would pick up a large black pebble and a small white shell and say, 'There you are. Rita and Nancy.' In a supermarket, he would pick up an aubergine and an egg and do the same: 'Which one's Nancy and which one's Rita?' and laugh at his own observation. Dogs, leaves, cars, bins, glasses, biscuits, lamp posts: if one was large and dark and one was small and pale, it was us. Rita was big; I was small. Rita was dark; I was fair. Rita was strong; I was weak. Rita was tough; I was fragile. Over and over again our identity was forged by a game of contrast. I was not made in my sister's image but against it.

Holding the second pregnancy test in both hands, like a wet harmonica, my mouth crumpled. I couldn't call Rita. I couldn't call Mum. I had hurt them both too much. I had accused Dad of an affair, I had undermined our family, and I had brought a stranger into the roost. I wasn't sure what family even meant any more.

Nor could I call Gamar. He was out of contact. In the field. On commission. All those phrases that elevated him beyond reproach and beyond me.

Dad. I wanted Dad. I wanted his smell: turpentine and

Dunhill cigars and mushroom Cup a Soup. I wanted the deep lawnmower growl of his laugh. I wanted the curly black hairs that snaked out from beneath his cuffs and the way his nose poked me in the eye when he kissed me on the cheek goodnight. I wanted a man to take care of me. There. Rita was right. I didn't want to be picked over by the lobster claws of other women. I didn't want to have to answer questions and give an account of myself and feed their disappointment. I wanted Dad. I wanted Dad to lift me off the floor and tell me it was all going to be OK. But Dad was dead. I had seen his body. I had touched his too-cold, blue-cold, drowned-cold hand.

I opened my phone.

DNA Relatives.

I clicked the letter-shaped icon. I started writing before fear could stop me.

Hello Oliver,

I'm not sure if you've already seen this, but apparently we share a sibling DNA match. I'm sorry to say that my dad passed away two years ago, so I can't really explain it. Perhaps you know more?

I'm sorry if this message is a shock. I'm not sure how accurate these things are but I wanted to reach out.

Yours sincerely

Delete.

Love

Delete.

Best wishes,
Nancy

The reply vibrated before I'd decided which bin to put the test wrappers in.

Hey Nancy,

Great to hear from you. Weird news, eh? I'm sorry to hear about your dad.

I was struck by the 'your dad' but kept reading.

My mum is ill so isn't able to give much insight. Maybe, like you say, it's just a blip in the system.
I'm actually coming to London next month to do a run of shows at the Soho Theatre. I can ping you a guest ticket if you want to meet? I'm not sure where I'll be staying – London's not cheap, is it? – but you can reach me here or on my cell at 021 104 3547.

Oliver

P.S. Thanks for writing. I didn't want to be the one to make the first move but it's cool to hear from you.

I clenched the phone. An ill mum? A visit to London? Looking for somewhere to stay? Rita was right. He wasn't a relative. This wasn't a coincidence. It was fraud. Someone had clearly got hold of my details and was trying to scam me. Sure, he looked like Dad in the photos, but who was to say the photos were of him? He could have stolen them from anywhere. I had been so desperate for male affection that I'd reached out to a stranger, a liar, and all because – what? He had my eyebrows?

Except. I hesitated. Except Dad was on there too. And he had matched with us both. And when I'd looked this man up, there were videos of him doing stand-up. It was a lot of effort to go to just to try and scam me: a 38-year-old teaching assistant on eighty-five pounds a day. Still standing in the doorway, I started writing another message.

Hello Oliver

I'm sorry if this seems rude but can I just ask: why did you do the DNA test in the first place? Were you hoping to find people?

You know, you read about these things and I just wanted to ask a few more questions before we talked about meeting up.

I chewed the inside of my lip.

Thanks,
Nancy

Send.

I turned on the tap and washed my hands in cold water. My phone was sitting, face up, on the top of the toilet. Oliver didn't reply straight away this time. Was that a bad sign? A good sign? What time would it be in New Zealand anyway, if that's really where he was? I looked at the time on my phone: noon on a Saturday. That made it, what? Maths collided with geography in my head. I typed Auckland into an international time website. One in the morning on a Sunday. Was that likely? If he was a stand-up comedian it might be. Or this liar might just as easily be sitting in his bedroom in Braintree, typing messages to seven different people at once. As I put a hand on the door handle, my phone vibrated.

Hey Nancy,

Fair enough. You need to be pretty sharp about all that stuff, especially as a woman.
    I actually took the test because my mum – her name is Anahera Coburg if you want to look her up – has got dementia and I thought maybe one of these DNA tests could tell me whether I might have inherited it. The doc said not to but, well, I didn't think it could do any harm. I wasn't expecting to find anyone on there, to be honest! I've already got a brother, Brendhan, and thought that was pretty much it.

If you want to talk on the phone or whatever before I come to London just shout. I'm a pretty open guy (kind of goes with the job). But no pressure if you'd rather not. I'm still trying to get my head around it all myself.

Cheers,
Oliver

9

A few days later, I woke up to Hebrew pop music. The noise was so distorted by amplification that it was like listening through tin foil. Raising myself on to one hand, I pushed aside the curtain and saw a man in a clown wig and dressing gown leaning out of the sun roof of a Renault Espace. The driver of another car was honking in time to the bass line. An astronaut with a long black beard was carrying a mermaid in a puffa jacket on his shoulders across the pedestrian crossing.

Purim. The Jewish festival of fancy dress and feasting. The day when this corner of London became charged with the petrol of misrule. Flammable, sweet, shiny, ancient. I had considered getting the bus to work today; I'd imagined that afternoon's midwife appointment would mean an examination, and I was embarrassed to turn up with sweat in my knickers. But getting the bus during Purim would be a nightmare. I'd have to cycle. Pulling back the duvet I looked briefly at the sheet for blood. Not today. Was I pleased? Disappointed? With nobody there to witness it, I struggled to know how I felt. My interior monologue was reduced to observation.

There are my legs. There is the sheet. I am still pregnant. It is seven o'clock.

Like a trick, the moment I had learned I was pregnant, I had begun to be pregnant. Symptoms rushed in like rats through a gap. The smell of toast, soap, my own fingernails filled my mouth with bile. My breasts were like two great blisters. As I reached for my phone, the brief touch of wrist against nipple shot through me like a pin. I sucked in a breath. There was a message from Oliver; our first since exchanging phone numbers. It was a picture of him on a verandah, sitting on a sofa made from timber crates. The bush behind him was acid green and spiky, the sky shamelessly blue. I scanned his face, my tongue touching the roof of my mouth. His curly hair rose straight up from his forehead, his smile showed no teeth. I thought of my father, lying in a hammock in Suffolk, smoking after dinner. I studied the stubble on Oliver's chin and clenched my teeth. Were we? Did I? The shadows in the background were so hard, almost monochrome, that it looked as though the garden had been screen-printed. White light. Black leaves. Brown eyes. Could I say he was good-looking? This man whose DNA said he was my brother? Perhaps it was narcissistic to describe someone who was genetically your kin as attractive. But something in me felt restored just looking at the lines of his face. An inexplicable sense of seeing something I already liked. With the phone still in my hand, I walked to the kitchen and put on the kettle.

Evening Nancy. Dinner on the verandah here in God

Zone. *I've got my dates for April, should be landing on the 7th. Shows start on 9th. Kia ora.*

I licked the corner of my lip. In three weeks' time, the cuckoo would land in England. Rita wasn't speaking to me, apart from a weird and stilted conversation after I'd texted her a photo of my pregnancy test, when she told me – rather coldly – how to book my first midwife appointment. Mum seemed tense; she had done ever since I told her about Oliver's visit. But I also wondered if she had suspicions about me. I had heard nothing from Gamar. Every time I checked my phone, the silence hollowed me out.

I googled Oliver's name and, for the first time, followed one of the links. It was a video of him on stage. In the white circle of light he looked even taller. He was leaning down into the audience, talking to a woman in the front row.

'Hey, what's your name?'

'Tina.' Her voice came out of the dark.

'Look at that, ladies and gentlemen, all the way from Geneva. Proud Mary herself.' The crowd gave a polite laugh. 'Sorry, Tina, you must be pretty sick of Tina Turner jokes, eh? But seriously, I have a bit in my show where I need someone to shout out after ten minutes. Can I give you that responsibility, Tina?'

The camera stayed locked on the stage so I watched this man. I watched him give a big, flirtatious grin. I watched him let a curl of hair fall across his eyes as he bent down beneath the lights.

'Here's my watch, so you don't get tempted to look at your phone halfway through. I don't want you leaving me, Tina, because you get a better offer.' He fiddled at his wrist and handed over what looked, at a distance, like a black Casio watch with a white face. I gave a start. I had that watch. I wore it in class. Obviously, it's a pretty standard watch but even just this coincidence was enough to make me feel strange. What was I going to discover about myself by watching this man? I flicked the tab closed on my phone. Too much. It was too strange to watch him walking and moving and wearing my watch before I'd even met him. I opened up the message and read it again. *Verandah. God Zone. Kia ora.* It was like he was giving me a firework display of Kiwi masculinity and I wasn't sure what to send in reply.

The pregnancy that had secreted itself in my body like a spore was growing, even though I hadn't decided if I wanted to keep it. My options were open and unknowable. The kettle boiled and I poured hot water on to a Barry's decaf teabag. I was drinking decaffeinated tea out of anxiety, rather than maternal concern. Since finding out I was pregnant, real tea – or, God forbid, coffee – made me feel as though I'd just set my house on fire. I opened the fridge for milk. All I had in there was mayonnaise, a courgette, orange nail varnish and a jar of cornichons.

I took a photo of my mug – it was green and had been my grandmother's – and sent the picture to Oliver in response. What could be more British? What didn't involve my own face?

Great. I'm in London all that week. Maybe we could meet up?

As I watched the ticks turn blue, I felt an uneasy echo. Texting a stranger. Second-guessing the words I used. Studying his photo. Waiting for a reply. Was this too close to dating? Shuddering slightly, I put the phone down on the worktop.

10

'Good morning, dear. This your first time? Midwife will need a urine sample.' The woman's voice came through a large plate-glass screen. 'The toilet is just back out through the door and on the right.'

They didn't believe I was pregnant. They were trying to catch me out. She thought I was asking for attention.

'I've got my pregnancy tests. I can show you.' I started to open my bag to show the receptionist the white plastic tests I'd been carrying around like key rings for the last week, but the look of horror on her face stopped my hand.

'No, dear, I do not want to see those.' She pursed her lips. She looked at me over the top of her glasses and pinched her mouth until all I could see was a sea urchin squatting on her face. 'The urine sample is for the midwife. Please.'

My scarf had stuck to my neck. The cubicle was too small to turn around in when I was wearing my rucksack. I had to reverse out, still holding the jar in one hand, and shake off my bag. I accidentally passed a sleeve beneath the hand drier, which sprang to life like a lion, roaring heat down my leg. I filled the jar, dampening the paper label, aware that I had left my rucksack, laptop and coat scattered on the floor outside like the aftermath of an attack. Someone had stuck a tiny advert for an all-female removals company on the back of the door, beside a poster about domestic assault. Why was I here? Or, more to the point, why was Gamar not? It was unfair. He should be there to hold my coat, chat to the receptionist, ask the midwife all those medical questions that I would never think of. Instead, I was screwing a yellow plastic lid on to a beaker full of wee, having already marked myself out to the staff as a maniac.

A few minutes later, I walked slowly into the waiting room, holding the urine sample like a flick-knife, halfway up my sleeve. A woman in a navy skirt suit, thick tan tights and a brown hat was lowering her tiny son on to one of the sets of weighing scales at the side of the room. Another woman, heavily pregnant, sat with a toddler on her knee. The toddler was playing with a set of keys and kicking her legs into the air. In the corner, a woman in a white jumper trimmed with ostrich feathers sat beside a man with wet-look hair. Her face was the colour of clay.

'Nancy?'

A midwife with big flicks of eyeliner leant out of the doorway. I moved towards her, feeling like a child being taken to the teacher's office.

'Hi, Nancy. I'm Alwen; it's a Welsh name,' she added

quickly, as though predicting small talk. I stayed silent. It had never occurred to me that the midwife might be younger than me. But this woman must have been, what, twenty-four? She wore Reebok Classics. She probably ate Frazzles. How could I possibly explain to her that I might not want to have a baby; that I didn't know what a family was any more? She was a midwife; someone who had dedicated their life to the production of babies. And what's more she was a child; she'd know nothing about the agony of love.

'I see you've brought me a pot of wee. Very kind.' As her hand reached across the table, I saw a thin line of writing tattooed up the midwife's wrist. The surface of the urine sample was rippled as I held it out to her. I was shaking. 'I'm just going to check it for protein and things, see what's going on in there.' I nodded, aware that I still hadn't spoken. 'Now, this is your booking-in appointment. So today I'm going to ask you a lot of questions. Some of them might seem a little strange and some might sound a bit repetitive but I assure you they're all necessary.'

The papers on Alwen's clipboard looked like a DVLA form: numbers and tick boxes and columns of writing. 'We'll check your weight and blood pressure too and, depending on how far you are along, we might even have a listen. OK?'

It was as though I was on a train, pulling out of a station, but without either a ticket or a suitcase. This woman thought I was here to discuss the health of the baby. My baby. The phrase still sounded out of tune in my own head. She saw a 38-year-old woman embarking on motherhood. But I was no such thing.

'Errrr, actually ...' I reached under my hair to touch my neck. 'You see. I'm not actually sure ...' The midwife's face didn't move. 'It was an accident.'

'We usually get to that around section four.' She wasn't smiling. My face turned hard in response. 'Shall we start with the easy bit first? Can you confirm for me your name and address?'

'Nancy Albany. Flat Six, Theydon House, Hertwold Road.'

'And is that your permanent address?'

'Yes.'

'Are you married, cohabiting, single, divorced, civil partnership or widowed ...' I almost laughed. How could you have so many options and yet not a single one that fits?

'Well, I'm not quite single but we don't live together.' I slid my hand around the front of my neck until I was clutching my throat. 'Actually, he's abroad at the moment. In Sudan.'

'All right, well, let's just leave that section for now.'

I looked out of the small, rectangular window above the midwife's desk and saw a brick wall. About a metre up from the ground, a plant sprouted from the mortar. How? What soil nourishes a plant scraped into life on the surface of a brick wall? How can a life start with so little attention or, in my case, intention?

'Is this your first pregnancy?' I nodded. 'Right. And do you know the first date of your last period?'

I dragged my eyes back to the midwife's face but she was still looking at the form. 'I think it was early in November – around Remembrance Day – but I might have actually had one since then,' I replied. 'I'm not sure.' For me, periods were something that came, hollowed you out and went. They were not orderly, or predictable or wanted.

'OK. Well, let's just say the eleventh of November and take it from there,' the midwife said, writing something on to her paper. 'That would make you' – she turned to an A3 planner on the wall beside her desk and started counting little squares – 'eighteen weeks.'

The toad squatting in my stomach grew heavier.

'Are you taking folic acid?' This time I did laugh. A spluttering, mirthless laugh as I pictured my dinner of toast and Rolos. 'I'm sorry. I just don't think you understand.' I spread my hands across my thighs. 'I didn't realize I was even pregnant until last weekend.' Behind me, a clock ticked. 'So I came here today to sort of, ah, see what my options were.' I resisted the urge to chew at the ragged flesh on the inside of my lip. 'I'm thirty-eight and my family . . .' The toad in my stomach flicked out its tongue, across the bottom of my ribs. 'I've just found out that I have a brother in New Zealand, which must mean that my dad had an affair when Mum was pregnant with me. My sister isn't speaking to me. My partner isn't due back for a few weeks, maybe longer. I haven't told my mum or any of my friends, I keep being sick and I'm just, very ... scared.' The lanyard around Alwen's neck was fuchsia pink with the word 'MIDWIFE' printed in capitals. The lanyard had slipped under her collar so only the word 'WIFE' was visible.

My mouth was dry. I waited. Then, in a low voice, Alwen said: 'One in ten men cheat on their partners when they're pregnant.' In that sentence alone, I heard the rhythm of her Welsh accent. For the first time, she was talking to me, actually *to* me. 'My husband cheated on me with our second.'

'You have children?' The words broke out before I could stop them.

'Yes. Two daughters.'

'But ...' I looked at her hands. 'You're so young.'

'I'm twenty-nine.'

I remembered my dad. Not really him, but a photo of him, standing against the tomato-red wall in the kitchen. He is holding me, wrapped in a wool blanket. I look like some underground creature: hairless, black eyes bulging from a wrinkled pink face. His jeans are high around his waist and tight on his hips. His hair is dark and thick. He must have been just twenty-five in that photo. He was handsome. He was young. I thought of Gamar, in a field thousands of miles away. Electrified by sleepless nights, the power of death beneath his hands, surrounded by the smell of earth. There would be other doctors there. Foreign staff. There would be women – women so close he could feel their breath against his arm. Without saying a word, Alwen reached out her hand and ripped off a square of the blue paper spread across the examination bed beside her desk, and handed it to me. I must have been crying. Or at least, I must have looked like I was crying.

'Right, Nancy. I understand.' Alwen's voice had returned to its professional, near-English pronunciation. 'For now, I'll just say that at eighteen weeks, you'll no longer qualify for telemedicine – that's a termination at home. You'd have to go in for a surgical abortion – a dilation and evacuation. You'd be under general anaesthetic but would have to come in the day before just to open up your cervix.' She wasn't looking at her notes at all. She must have given this speech before, many times. 'You can have a D and E up to twenty-four weeks into a pregnancy so you do qualify but you'll have to decide' – she looked into my eyes and a shower of needles passed across my scalp – 'very soon.'

I looked at the leaflets on her desk.

'Now . . .' As Alwen breathed in, she kept her teeth together, like the rattling of a snare drum. 'As you're unsure about the date of conception and eighteen weeks might not be right, you will need to go for a scan. Just so we can check everything.'

'A scan?' The word was like a slab of marble on my tongue.

'You'd have one anyway, prior to termination. But as you're undecided, it's a good idea to go ahead so we can check the progress of the pregnancy.' She turned to her computer and started typing. 'I can book you in at Homerton but you'll also need to make an appointment with your GP to discuss a possible termination. OK?'

I folded the piece of blue paper, now wet, in half. 'The scan.' I folded it again. 'A termination.' I pushed it against my chest. 'Right.'

11

Since coming out of the midwife appointment, I had wanted my mother. I had felt shaky and unmoored by the decision ahead of me. While I would normally have called Rita, I suspected that she might unleash her fury on me if I tried. Also, Rita didn't know about pregnancy. She'd never felt this queasy emptiness, or the shooting pain between her ribs, or slid through this kind of tiredness. My God, I was tired. I was tired all the way from my eyes to my ankles. It was as though I was swimming against a tide of unconsciousness all the time. I could sleep between blinks. I also felt covered in a thin film of oil, like the inside of an empty crisp packet. If I said this to Rita, what would I get? Blame? Disinterest? Condescension?

But Mum would know. The thought that I had eked out this very punishment on her while squatting in her womb had filled me with a kind of guilty adoration. At first, I'd wanted the big, charcoal-smelling arms of Dad to quell my panic. But I'd been wrong. The real sacrifice, the real comfort, should have come from my mother.

She had done all this for me. She had made me. I owed her everything.

What I really wanted, of course, was to sit on the sofa in a pair of red polyester pyjamas and watch *Ballykissangel*, while Mum ironed her shirts for the week and Dad cleaned his brushes in the kitchen sink. I wanted to retreat and regress. So, next best thing, I'd called Mum from the bike stand outside the midwife appointment. I had suggested we meet at the South Bank the next day, after school. Had I sounded like I'd been crying? Perhaps. She'd agreed quickly. We would meet outside the Royal Festival Hall at four thirty, a time when you could drink tea or wine without necessarily needing to explain either.

That day at school, I had been struck by a vision of the baby having its soft head crushed against the waistband of my trousers. I'd seen the skull, fractured in two by the pressure. When had I started to expand like this? When had my clothes become tight? Before taking the test, my body had been untouched by pregnancy, I was sure. And yet now I was sick and sweaty, and my stomach was a roiling sea. I had undone my flies during Year Three phonics and spent the rest of the day pulling at the hem of my shirt.

'Hello, darling.' Mum was sitting at a table, holding a Kindle in a brown leather case. 'I got here a bit early to stock up on birthday cards.' She was wearing a pair of clear-framed glasses, while two other pairs sat on the table beside her. The rotation of eyewear involved in being middle-aged was something I still couldn't fathom. Even though, I suppose, I was nearly middle-aged myself.

'Hello, Mum.'

'How was school?'

'Oh, a bit tiring.' I stayed standing. 'Jonah Frinton threw Ruksana Begum's pencil case out of the window and Mr O'Leary left it all to me to sort out.'

'Oh, that man.' Anne frowned. 'I don't know why you don't just get your PGCE and become a real teacher so you can—'

'I know, Mum, I know,' I interrupted. 'Please can we not have this argument again.'

'Fine, but—'

'What would you like to drink?'

Mum knew she was being fobbed off but had the good grace to let it happen.

'Perhaps a gin and tonic, I think.' My nose quivered at the thought of such a bitter drink. 'But don't worry about food. I brought us each one of these.' Out of her bag, Mum pulled two cardboard tubs. She popped the lids and there were a pair of golden pasties, smooth and faintly shiny. 'One chicken, one veg.' The smell of pastry, of turmeric, ginger, Scotch bonnet – of all the takeaways I grew up round the corner from – enveloped me. My mum had carried comfort across London.

'Perfect. I'll just be a minute.'

Turning to the queue for the bar, I could feel tears needling at my eyes. I'd already caused so much drama for this woman. Was I really about to present her with an unborn, illegitimate, unplanned baby too?

'Oh, are you not drinking?' Mum asked when I came back carrying a cardboard cup in my other hand.

'No.' I had meant to add more but the sentence ran aground in front of me.

'Well, I wish you'd said. I could easily have had a cup of tea.'

'Sorry. I just . . .' Wet sand gripped my words.

'Never mind. Lovely to see you.' I winced. Was it? Could it really be? The last time I'd been face to face with Mum, I'd cut open the major artery of her marriage. I had turned the easy square of our family into a teetering, lopsided star.

'I'm so sorry about the test.'

'I know.' As she rubbed the back of my hand, I felt Mum's wedding ring grind against my veins. 'I am too. This week has been, well . . .' She breathed slowly out of her nose. 'I hadn't realized you could lose a husband twice.'

'Oh, Mum.' I dug my heels into the floor.

'Sorry. Perhaps that sounds a bit dramatic. I am just so cross that Clive isn't here to explain himself.' She pushed a piece of hair off the arm of her glasses and looked at me. 'But, darling, I don't blame you. I'm not sure I'm even ready to blame Clive. I just feel, well, confused. As do you, I imagine. Is that what you wanted to talk about?'

'Well.' I tilted my head back, trying to stem the unshed tears. I wasn't making this easy for either of us by delaying.

'Or has something happened with you and Gamar?' Mum was still holding my hand, which, I now realized, was damp with sweat.

'Sort of.'

'Sort of?' If Rita had been there, she would have jumped in, provoked me into a confession. But with Mum, it was the painful uncoiling of a spring.

'Well, I still haven't spoken to him but . . .' I looked down. Surely I looked different? And surely my own mother had noticed?

'Nancy.' I must have stopped speaking for longer than I realized. Mum was staring at me with an unwavering focus. Was this, I wondered, how she looked at her clients? How she scored through their denial and their bravado as a barrister? All those years in employment law, she must have come across so many people trying to cover their backs, cover up the details, giving only one side. 'Just say the words.'

And then I realized. She knew. Of course she knew. You might be able to keep sex and smoking and shoplifting a secret from your mother for a while, but not this.

'I'm pregnant.'

'How pregnant?'

'A bit.'

'How many weeks?'

'About eighteen.'

'Right.' Anne picked up her glass and took a sip. 'And is it Gamar's?'

This surprised me. Somehow, of all the questions, I had not expected my fidelity to be scrutinized.

'Yes, of course it's Gamar's!' Then I thought of Oliver. And DNA. And the fact that there was no 'of course' about sex or loyalty in this family. 'I haven't been with anyone else. For years.'

'Right.'

'Mum . . .'

'As I understand it, you can only have a termination up to twenty-four weeks, unless there are exceptional circumstances.' Of course Mum knew the law. 'Are you . . . ?'

I looked out at the Thames. The filthy grey water slapped against its concrete banks. The rusty chains and plastic bottles. The great, sucking tide that pushed its silty water out into the sea and back every day.

'I have a scan on Monday. And I can ask about a termination then.'

Mum nodded. 'Would you like me to come with you?' she asked.

Had I mentioned the termination to my mother precisely in the hope that she would take pity on me? Perhaps. When Rita accuses me of being passive, I think this is what she means: my total inability to admit to the things I want, in case I don't get them. But the point was, it had worked. I wouldn't have to go to the appointment alone.

'Oh, yes please, Mum. If you can. It's at five fifteen. That was the latest appointment I could get.'

'At which hospital?'

'Homerton.'

'Of course.'

As I took a sip of my too-sweet, too-milky drink, Mum took a deep breath. It wasn't a sigh but an inhalation. As though she were expanding herself for what she was about to say. 'Perhaps an abortion is the right thing to do.'

My heart quickened. Maybe it *was* the right thing to do. Maybe I had just needed the permission of my mother to admit what I had always known: that I was not ready to have a baby. That I didn't want a baby. That I had no money, no stability, no real experience of babies. That I was old and the risks of disability or illness or miscarriage were too high. That this was just an accident that I could now, for a few more weeks, undo.

'Hmm.' I raised the cup and held it against my forehead, feeling the warmth against my bone. There was a pause.

'But' – I saw Mum's nostrils flare – 'if you did want to have the baby, you could move in with me. Not for ever but for the first six months at least. I could move to the attic and you could use the second floor as a sort of flat. Well, you'd have a bathroom.'

As I watched her talk, I realized how stupid I had been to think that Mum didn't already know. Clearly, she had been planning this conversation ever since I vomited on her kitchen tiles. She'd probably spoken to her whole book group about it: working out the logistics and drawing up her boundaries. I was being presented not just with a choice but a contract.

'I'm not going to push you for an answer, but time isn't on our side.' I moved the cup down to my chest as she spoke. 'I can help you until the baby starts nursery. Being a single parent is extremely hard and I don't want you to think that you don't have help.'

I frowned. 'I might not be a single parent.'

'I'm sorry?'

'I'm not a single parent yet.' Mum was being generous but at the heart of that generosity was the grit of doubt. Or, perhaps, disapproval. She had no faith in my relationship and never had. 'Gamar is in the field, so I haven't been able to tell him. That doesn't mean he doesn't exist.'

'I see.' Mum rotated her glass a quarter-turn to the right but didn't lift it off the table.

'I don't know. Maybe this will change things,' I said, as much to myself as her.

'What things?'

'Well, with Gamar.' I swallowed. 'I've always sort of thought that if I just held on and gave him time, he would probably do what all men do in the end. Settle down. Commit.' Mum was clearly trying very hard not to wince. 'He just has so much going on with his work and all the travel and everything at the moment. But when he finds out about this, I don't know. He might . . .' I trailed off.

'He might ride in on a big white horse and marry you?'

Something flared in me. 'I don't think he can ride a horse.'

'Well, neither can you.' Mum reached across and picked up my other hand. 'Nancy, this is your decision. You can't leave it to Gamar to make. For one thing, you don't have time. But also, darling, you will be the one who has the baby. Not him.' Now it was my turn to frown. 'Oh, I know everyone talks about co-parenting and equal parenting these days,' said Anne, sounding every inch her age. 'But the truth is, with babies, you're the one doing all the work. You are the primary parent. You'll be doing the feeding, the nappies, the appointments, the nights. You're the one they'll want. Your voice and your smell. And that goes on for years. Yes, men can be involved, but really, darling, it's your decision. After all' – she lifted her glass from the table – 'you're the one who has to be pregnant and give birth. That makes it your choice.'

My mother had always had the capacity to make the unreasonable sound reasonable. I knew that what she was saying was outdated and wrong. I knew the load could be shared. But I also couldn't think how to challenge her. She was a parent and I was not. She had given birth and raised two daughters. In the world of babies, she had been an active participant, while I was just a passive observer.

So I said, 'I know' and turned my hand over to hold hers.

'You're probably hungry.' Mum opened one of the cardboard tubs. 'Shall I cut these in half and we can share? Unless you want them both yourself?' She smiled. 'I remember when I was pregnant with you, all I wanted to eat was ham and parsley sauce. Anything sweet turned my stomach.'

My throat lurched in response to the smell of the pasties. I was ravenous. I also wanted to be cosseted.

'Let's share them,' I said, reaching for my half before Mum had even pulled the knife away. I could feel a little sheen of oil coat my thumb as I picked it up. I took a bite and the golden glow of baking filled my face. I chewed, tasting spices and butter and potato. For a few seconds, it was perfect. The constant, gnawing hunger that felt like seasickness had gone. I looked at Mum. Light from the window was caught in her grey hair, turning it gold. Could I really live with her again? Become Bertha in her attic, with a howling baby, overheard in every step? Hang my knickers on her radiators? Have her listen to me on the phone? Watch me change nappies? Criticize my choices? I would turn thirty-nine sleeping in the room where I had once read Garfield comics and practised rolling joints with dried oregano. When I thought of an adult future, it didn't involve hiding in my childhood bedroom, breastfeeding a baby while my mother and her friends played canasta downstairs in the kitchen.

Suddenly, the saliva in my mouth started to turn watery. What had been warm and savoury was now earthen and bitter. I felt as though I'd just swallowed a mouthful of soil. So quickly, the high of not feeling sick had been replaced with active disgust. Onion and cumin were coating my tongue. My stomach shuddered. I looked at the second pasty on the table and nearly retched.

'Mum, I can't eat any more, I'm sorry,' I said, trying to hit just the right note of bravery and self-pity to induce her sympathy.

'Maybe you should try ham and parsley sauce,' she said. 'Your dad used to buy me these bags of it. You'd put them in a pan of boiling water for ten minutes. He was delighted – he ate mashed potato and boiled ham every night for about a month.'

I swallowed, closing the lid of the other pasty so I didn't have to look at it any more.

'Was he pleased when you got pregnant?' I asked, struck that this conversation hadn't happened before. But then I'd never been pregnant before.

Anne looked briefly down into her glass before answering. 'He was delighted. He loved babies and fussing about. He got so excited about building a cot and going to all those antenatal classes.' She smiled sadly. 'Marie-Louise always said that if she'd been forever pregnant but never actually had a baby, they would still be together now.'

This was more than I could process. The idea of Dad impregnating someone else; of lusting after some other woman's pregnant body; of Rita being wanted before me. It opened up so many questions I couldn't bear to think about. Was he a letch? Had he known about Oliver? Did he prefer Rita? Had he wanted more children? If all men, deep down, want to pass on their genes, at whatever cost, what did that say about Gamar?

I wasn't ready to start unpicking the men in my life like this, so instead I thought of Marie-Louise, in France, learning that Mum was pregnant. Had it dragged through her heart like a bread knife? Or had her spiritual life at Aynac insulated her from that kind of thing?

'Do you think she was jealous when you and Dad got together?'

'I don't know.' Mum held her left thumb in her right fist. 'Marie-Louise and I were never close. Although she did send me some beautiful linen cot sheets when you were born. I always took that as a sort of blessing.'

I looked down at my front. I was wearing a pale green shirt that I had bought nearly ten years ago from a charity shop in Whitby. The material was loose enough that you couldn't see the mound of my belly. I didn't know if I was hiding the fact that I was pregnant or just didn't quite believe it. The whole notion of something living inside my body felt too unlikely, even as I looked and felt more and more pregnant by the day. I thought again about what Mum had said about Clive and his love of babies.

'Mum, do you think most men do want to have children?'

Anne looked up at me. 'Once they have them, I think most men are happy. But I also think most men are scared.'

'Of what?'

'Well, I think they are scared of growing up.' She tapped the bottom of her glass against the table. 'They are scared of failing. And, ultimately, they are scared of their own mortality.' Mum said all this without a wobble in her voice but I could see the shimmer of tears in her eyes. 'Having a baby reminds them that they are no longer children themselves. At least, some men.' She sniffed. 'Other men, of course, get people pregnant like they're collecting stamps.'

I blinked.

'Are we going to talk about this man? Oliver?' Mum asked. 'I presume you've been in touch with him?' I felt a rush of shame and guilt and panic as she said his name. 'I would rather you told me, Nancy.' Was this how she cross-examined people, I wondered? How she whittled down their defences to get to a public truth?

'Actually, I have. I'm sorry, Mum. I was just feeling weird and lonely, with Gamar out of contact and Rita not speaking to me.'

'I see.' Her cool, professional tone was like oil, as I slid further into my confession.

'He's actually coming to London in April to do some shows at the Soho Theatre.'

'He's an actor?'

'A comedian.'

Mum nodded slowly. 'And are you going to see him?'

I heard a chair scrape behind me. I felt the hard edge of the table against my elbows. I considered lying: telling Mum that I wanted nothing to do with Oliver. That it had all been a mistake. I could have pretended that I wasn't curious, or lonely. I could have said that I felt no draw to this man at all. But the truth was, even just looking at the photo of him, I had felt the return of a part of me that had disappeared when Dad had died. I had felt the tug of likeness. I had looked across his nose and shoulders and neck and realized that I was seeing part of something that lived in me too. Something that linked me. Somehow, just looking at him, I became more sure that I existed. Was this what they called kinship? Kith? To look around and see yourself reflected back to you in the wonky mirrors of your family?

'Nancy?'

I pushed my finger into the edge of the table until the knuckle clicked.

'I think I'll meet him.' I didn't dare look at Mum as I spoke. 'He's only going to be here for a few weeks and I'd . . .' I trailed off. Cups were pulled from a dishwasher in a cloud of steam. A woman in cream heels clipped past the window. The revolving doors made their slow circles.

'Well, I would like to meet him too.' I jerked my head up to see Mum staring right at me. 'Whether he is your brother or not, I want to meet this man.' Her eyes shone. 'I have some questions.'

12

By five o'clock, the whole of Kingsland Road was blue with smoke: from cars, buses, cigarettes, kebab shops, vapes and motorbikes. Instead of taking the quickest route to the hospital, I decided to cycle along the canal. There would be joggers running down the towpath like rats – there would be actual rats – but at least I wouldn't be sucking on the exhaust pipe of three hundred unleaded engines.

I'll meet you at the Costa Coffee in Reception at 5.

Mum had texted at 4 p.m., meaning she was probably already at the hospital, over an hour early. Rita would have done the same. It was what I'd hoped for. Gamar hated waiting and so always tried to time things to arrive at the last minute. Which meant I was always in a sour state of panic by the time we set off. Dad had always been late too, but more out of chaos than by design. As Mum loaded the car, he would be fluttering up and down the hallway shouting things like 'Do I need wellies?' or 'I can't turn off the heating' or 'I just need to finish this varnish layer' while Rita and I sat like conscientious objectors in the back seat.

'I just think it's obnoxious to ask to see a physical receipt...' As I turned off Whitmore Road and headed down to the water, I overtook a woman talking into her phone. She was wearing bootcut leggings the colour of digestive biscuits. I could trace the contours of her buttocks like a gravestone. Had she ever been pregnant? I wondered. It was hard to tell from behind but I thought she probably hadn't. She was too compact to have been overwhelmed this way. I had heard friends describe their joints softening during pregnancy: elbows suddenly bending backwards and old knee strains disappearing. Their whole bodies had been changed by the double life they temporarily sustained. But I felt neither soft nor taut. If anything, I felt like a preheating oven, humming with an effort that so far had produced nothing.

The trees were still mostly bare as I cycled past the low-rise housing blocks and former industrial buildings that lined the canal. I was wearing a denim jacket with a sheepskin lining that was almost too hot to cycle in but was short enough not to get caught in the chain. Leaving at 4.20 p.m. meant I had half an hour to make what should have been a fifteen-minute journey; so when a woman with a double-width buggy came out from under a bridge and towards me, I stopped and waited for her to pass. I didn't want to look into the buggy. Cheeks, blankets, chewed toys, toes, dummies, sheepskins. So, instead, I pulled out my phone and reflexively checked if Gamar had texted me. Every time I looked at the screen, at the blank stare of unlit glass, it still pinched my heart. Where was he? How much longer? Why? There had been blackouts before, of course. In the first year we were dating, he'd gone to Damascus and was out of contact for thirty-six consecutive days. But back then, our relationship had felt feathery. It had been soft, ticklish, likely to blow away under too much force. Today, I was heavy with the weight of Gamar's absence. In my body and heart, I felt laden with the emptiness where he should have been. As the woman with the buggy edged around my right pedal, I quickly typed out a message.

Hey love, when you get this, can you please ring me as soon as you can? Nobody has died, I just need to speak to you.

How many ways could you spell out H-E-L-P?

Another person came round the bridge in front of me. This time, it was a man in a French workman's jacket and desert boots. He smiled sheepishly but didn't speed up to get out of my way. I held on to the metal railing at the edge of the towpath and, instead of meeting his eye, looked down into the green, sun-sucking water. Right below me was a coot. It was sitting on a nest made from an empty Strongbow bottle and the algae-covered flotsam of the canal. Water reeds, sticks, the kind of clear plastic tray that once held a sausage roll, red leaves, the shiny corner of a crisp packet and feathers. There was a white stripe down the centre of the bird's head that became its beak. Perhaps sensing my lowering gaze above her, the bird rose up and shook out her wings. In that second, as she stood, I caught sight of five pale speckled eggs beneath her black chest. There they were. Five tiny, unhatched lives, millimetres away from all the filth and cold of London. How would she survive the bitter nights of spring, out here alone on her dirty nest? Where was the father? What was she eating? When the eggs – if the eggs – began to hatch, how would she stop each chick from sinking into certain death beside that nest? Teetering on my unmoving bike, I held on to the black metal at my side and stared.

'Could you get them to just upload it on to the server now so I can sign it off before we go in?'

The woman with the bootcut leggings had somehow caught up with me and was still spitting into her phone. Glancing round, I saw her lips, like two wine-stained slugs, pulled across her face. Before she could overtake and block the underpass again, I wiped my face with the sleeve of my jacket and kicked off.

NHS Foundation Trust
Opened in July 1986
Main Entrance

I locked my bike to a grey steel arch and walked in. Four forty-seven p.m. I was thirteen minutes early.

'Nancy, I bought you a decaf flat white.' Mum kissed me on the cheek and I inhaled Green Tea by Elizabeth Arden. 'But, you know, there's actually a restaurant; you can eat macaroni cheese and apple crumble next to a thoracic surgeon while they have their lunch break. It's quite extraordinary.' She was walking around the elephant, and we both knew it. Trying to keep things light and surface level and jolly. 'Your department is just down here.' Mum took my hand and led me along a corridor decorated with black and white photographs of stone sculptures. I was used to linking arms with Rita, having her hand round my shoulder; it felt odd to be taken to the maternity unit by my own mother. She was doing her best to step into Rita's usual role but it made me feel even more childish, even less prepared somehow, to be led around by Mum. Still, I would never have found the right ward without her. Directions are not my forte. We got to a large sliding glass door and stepped into a very bright, very warm waiting room. The chairs were blue, plastic and wipe clean.

'Hello again,' said the receptionist. She had thin dreadlocks the colour of blackcurrant wine gums.

'Hello,' said Anne, squeezing my hand like a jockey pushing on a horse. 'This is my daughter.'

I smiled. Then realized I had to say something.

'I'm here for a scan.' This was vague, even for me. 'At five fifteen.'

'What's your name?'

'Nancy Albany.'

'Go straight up. There's a lift here on the left or take the stairs and walk through the double doors on your right.' She nodded at me, then smiled at my mum.

Obviously, Anne had well and truly scouted the premises before I got here. By now, this receptionist probably knew all about Gamar and Dad and the DNA test. And Mum probably knew all about her son's GCSE choices and new kitchen.

As I walked into the reception area upstairs, I noted the display of thank-you cards pinned to the wall. Nectarine-cheeked babies wrapped in yellow blankets; black and white portraits of sleeping newborns; hands so small they seemed almost translucent. I felt a small rush of disgust. I didn't want to join this world of rosy commodification. The baby that was inside me felt remote and impossible and dangerous. I was sick and bulging and uneasy. The whole experience up to now was so far away from crochet photoshoots and laminated cards that I wondered if I could really be pregnant at all. A woman behind the counter told me to take a seat and that the sonographer would call me when they were ready. There was a large screen on one wall. An episode of *Homes Under the Hammer* played out, unwatched, into the room. Mum picked up an eight-month-old copy of *Country Living* and, obviously trying to appear relaxed, read out: '"When the Levington Hewitts first walked into this 1700s cottage during a house hunt two years ago, it was love at first sight."'

I was aware of my nostrils, of my bladder; I wanted to take off my shoes and spread out my toes as far as they could reach. Mum looked at me.

'Darling, it's OK. They do this all the time.' She didn't understand. I wasn't nervous about the sonographer making a mistake or electrocuting my intestines. I just didn't belong here. I wasn't ready. If she'd been with me instead, Rita would have laughed about the cards. She would have started making up names for the other couples in the waiting room and laying bets on the size of the sonographer's eyebrows. Rita had always been able to take charge of a situation. Or, rather, Rita was always able to take charge of me in any situation. She was my shield and my conspirator. Without her, I felt nervous and exposed, like a worm waiting for the boot.

'Ms Albany?' The sonographer was tall, with red hair and a thick pelt of pale fur all down his arms. I stood up. 'Hi, I'm Laurence,' he said. 'Please, come in.' He gestured into the room like a doorman at a hotel.

'Can my mum come too?' I asked, like a four-year-old wanting to board the ghost train at a fair.

'Of course.' Laurence clasped his hands together, as if consciously trying not to touch us.

'Anne,' said Mum, introducing herself. Laurence nodded and let the door close behind him. The room was dark and cool. In the middle of the floor was a bed, already lined down the middle with a runway of paper towel.

'So, I understand this is your first scan,' said Laurence, sitting down on a swivel stool in front of a bank of screens and keyboards.

'Yes,' I answered, lowering myself tentatively on to the bed.

'Anne, you can take either of those seats.' Laurence glanced at a desktop computer and then back at me. 'I can also see from your notes that you're considering all options.' A prickle of electricity went up my neck.

'Well, I . . .'

'Don't worry – that's something to discuss with your midwife and GP.' The sonographer waded in to my floundering silence. 'I'm just going to be checking for a heartbeat and taking some measurements.' I nodded. 'Would you like me to turn off this screen?' He pointed at something the size of a television beside the head of the bed.

'No, that's OK,' I answered. Was I trying not to make a fuss? Did I actually want to see? Had I answered before the question had unravelled in my brain?

'OK. Well, just let me know if you change your mind.' I heard Mum adjust herself in the seat behind me. 'Now, if you could just lie back here and lift up your shirt so your abdomen is exposed.' As I lay back, Mum clasped my hand. 'Now, this might be a bit cold.' And with that, he squirted a dollop of blue gel on to my stomach. 'Are you all right . . .' There was a slight pause. '. . . Nancy?'

'Yes,' I answered.

'OK, let's have a look.' Laurence pulled out something that looked like a white 1990s computer mouse and pressed it into my stomach. A fuzzy greyness crackled across the screen. 'That's just your bladder,' he explained, moving to the right and pushing in a little harder. And then, suddenly, there it was: a snoutless river dolphin, lying along the bottom of my womb. It was both the most beautiful and most unsettling thing I had ever seen. The pale bulbous forehead, the rounded belly tapering to a smooth, indistinguishable tail. I could see no arms or legs, no comprehensible bones. And yet, as I looked again at that great, shining orb of a head, the profile made me gasp. It was Dad. It was Rita. It was me. It was even, I realized, Oliver. The indentation between eyebrow and nose was as familiar as the smell of my own skin; as the sound of my sister's laugh; as my father's walk. There I was and there it was. Something in my blood had gathered together into a face and that face was Albany.

'All four chambers of the heart are fine,' said Laurence. 'And I can see the blood flow to the brain and kidneys is just as it should be.' Kidneys. This tiny translucent unperson in my body had kidneys. And a heart.

I looked across at Mum. Her eyes were shining like milk-bottle tops. Huge, silver circles in an otherwise darkened face. And yet she'd remained completely quiet.

'I'm just going to take some measurements here, to help get an idea of dates,' said Laurence, pressing the keyboard, moving the machine a few centimetres across my skin, pressing the keyboard again. Over and over, like an astronomer scanning the skies for life. As the image zoomed in, I became lost in a night sky: tiny white stars; the smudge of galaxies. Velvet blackness rotated as the sonographer moved his wand up and in and to the side. Then, at last, he typed something into the computer and the image panned back, wide angle. There they were again, so familiar and so alien and so small. A baby. My baby. I heard Mum breathe sharply through her nose. I didn't turn to look. I didn't check if she was crying. But I linked my fingers through hers and rubbed my thumb across the back of her hand. I was pregnant and my baby had a heart.

'OK, Nancy. I've got everything that I need now,' said Laurence. 'You can use this to wipe up,' and with a tiny flourish he pulled about a metre of blue paper towel from the roll behind me. Quickly, I sat up, blinking into the lights and screens around me.

'You're going to go and speak to the midwife now,' said Laurence, looking at me with an expression as neutral as concrete. 'I've sent everything over to her.'

'OK,' I said, not understanding at all.

'Here?' asked Mum, and even in just that word I could hear the emotion pushing at her throat. 'Or do you mean we have to make another appointment?'

'No, no, if you just go back into the waiting room, the midwife will call you in shortly.'

As I edged off the bed, Laurence offered a totally unnecessary arm to help. He must spend his days helping elephantine pregnant people on and off beds, I thought. I said thank you but didn't take his arm, although I did feel his hairs brush against mine as I stood up.

'Right,' I said, reeling from what I'd seen on the screen.

'Thank you,' Mum added as we blinked our way out of the room. 'Thank you very much.'

'Not at all.'

In the waiting room, I hunched over my phone. I was scouring my emails: *Médecins Sans Frontières, Gamar, Khartoum, contact, Sudan, in case of emergency*. Finally, I found it: the phone number for the hospital where he had been based. With an urgent sense of hope, I rang the number.

'Marḥabā.'

Immediately I faltered. This had been a mistake.

'Hello?'

'Hādhā al-mustashfā al-turkī?'

I could feel Mum's eyes on me.

'Is that the Turkish Hospital?'

'Marḥabā.'

This wasn't working – I couldn't understand what they were saying.

'I need to speak to Dr Gamar Araya.'

'Ṭabīb? Doctor? Ṭabīb?'

'Yes, doctor. Dr Gamar Araya, please. Médecins Sans Frontières.'

'Anā āsif. Hal tataḥaddath al-'arabiyya? Hādhā al-mustashfā al-turkī.'

Where was he? How could I find him?

'I'm sorry.' My voice was quavering. 'I need to speak to one of the English doctors. Gamar Araya.' And then, even quieter: 'He was based at this hospital.'

'Hādhā mustashfā. Hal hādhihi ḥālat ṭāri'a?'

Hopeless, hopeless, hopeless.

I hung up and nearly threw my phone on to the floor. I felt Mum's arm around my shoulder but she didn't say anything. In fact, we hadn't spoken to each other since going in for the scan.

'Ms Albany?' A woman in blue scrubs was standing by the reception desk. One of her enormous hips rested against the wood-veneer counter. Mum and I stood up together and shuffled towards her like a broken crab.

'Hello, Nancy, I'm Christine, one of the midwives based here in the hospital.' She had two small gold hoop earrings and no make-up.

'Hi,' I said.

'Hello,' answered Mum at the same time.

'This is my mum,' I explained again.

'Nice to meet you.' Christine smiled. 'Let's go into my office.' She led us behind the desk to a small corridor. I tried to clear my face of signs of crying.

'Come in and take a seat,' said Christine.

The room was small and spartan. There was a Charlton Athletic mug next to Christine's keyboard and a tiny Eiffel Tower snow globe attached to her keys. Mum and I sat down in the padded plastic chairs.

'How are you doing, Nancy?' Christine asked. She

looked at me: a long, quiet, open look, and in that moment I knew this was a woman who had seen everything. She had lifted blue babies out from people's opened bodies and rubbed breathless infants back to life. She had touched foreheads and sewn up flayed skin and been bitten. She had told people their babies would not survive and she had been told that the baby was a mistake. There was probably nothing I could do or say that would push her off her axis. She was an NHS midwife; she weighed life and death in her arms. And me? Who was I? A 38-year-old woman with her own flat, a mother who loved her and a body that had created a baby. I was pregnant. After years of waiting and observing and evading, it had happened. I didn't look at Mum but carried on facing Christine. I thought of Dad's cold, pale hand in the funeral director's. I thought of Rita and me stroking our pretend bumps in the bath. I thought of Gamar's eyelashes and Oliver's forehead and those tiny kidneys. I thought of pills and forceps and suction. I thought of breasts and milk and heartbeats. I thought of standing on the beach at Weymouth, screaming Dad's name into the grey, wet air. I thought of the coots in the nest in the canal. I thought of blood and love and distance and secrets. I thought about my ribs. I pushed my lips together, breathed in and said:

'I don't want a termination.'

13

'Rita?'

'Yes.'

'Hi, Root. Can you hear me OK?'

'Yes.'

'Oh, OK.'

'What is it?'

'Right, sorry. Yes. Well, it's just that, um, Oliver is in London now. He got here on Thursday, I think.'

'...'

'Rita?'

'Yes?'

'Ah. Well, I told Mum that he was here and she wants to meet him.'

'What?'

'Mum said she wants to meet Oliver. Actually, she said she had some questions for him.'

'Oh, for God's sake.'

'I'm sorry, Rita.'

'So you keep saying.'

'Rita, please.'

'Please, what?'

'Fine, nothing. OK, fine. But, um, well, Mum and me are meeting Oliver next Saturday at Coal Drops Yard. He's staying in Kilburn and Mum will be down south so it seemed like somewhere everyone could get to.'

'It's somewhere you can get to.'

'What?'

'Well, it's pretty close to you.'

'It's actually closer to you, Rita.'

'Maybe geographically.'

'I see. And you've started measuring distances metaphysically, have you?'

'I'm not going to—'

'Rita, I didn't mean that. I'm sorry.'

'What time on Saturday?'

'About eleven, I think.'

'I think somebody should be there to look after Anne.'

'Look after her?'

'Yes.'

'But—'

'We still don't really know anything about this man. I still think it could be fraud, Nancy. I mean, if he really is Dad's son then how was he born on the other side of the world? And none of us ever knew?'

'I don't—'

'And what does he want from us now? Money? Was he abused as a child and he wants compensation? Maybe his mum's dead too and he thinks—'

'His mum isn't dead. He's talked to me about her.'

'You've talked to him?'

'A bit. Not on the phone. Just messages.'

'Well, still. I'm just saying, he might be dangerous. And if you and Mum are meeting him in person, then I think I should be there in case anything kicks off.'

'OK. Well, thank you.'

'Anne told me about the hospital.'

'What did she say?'

'That the sonographer had really hairy arms.'

'Ah.'

'And that the baby was twenty weeks old. And healthy.'

'Yes.'

'I'm glad.'

'Rita?'

'And that you're not going to – you know.'

'Hmmm.'

'Have you told Gamar?'

'I've tried. I've messaged and emailed. I even phoned the hospital in Khartoum but he's still completely out of touch.'

'God, that's been weeks. I don't remember him ever being out of contact for this long before.'

'It's the war.'

'Yes, I suppose.'

'I . . .'

'Do you worry that he's—'

'Rita!'

'What?'

'Don't say it.'

'But do you?'

'No. Well. I mean, sometimes.'

'He won't be.'

'Thanks.'

'I'm still really not sure about you meeting this Oliver man, Nancy.'

'But, Rita—'

'Even if what he says is true, what does that mean for us? Do you think Dad could have kept a secret – or lied to us – our whole lives?'

'I think he might not have known.'

'What? Not known that—'

'Rita.'

'No, Nancy. I'm sorry but that's what we're talking about there. And this is all your fault. I don't know why you did that test. Maybe your hormones made yo—'

'Hormones? Rita! You sound like an actual misogynist.

'Rita?

'Rita?

'Oh, so you've hung up on me. Fine.'

14

I knew who he was as soon as I walked into the cafe.

He was sitting with his back against the wall, so the first thing I saw was his profile. The nose was mine. The lips were mine. The hands that held his coffee cup were Dad's – blunt, almost square fingertips. This was Oliver. I had the inexplicable feeling that I already knew him.

As I came through the doorway, he looked up at me. Perhaps he had looked at everyone who walked in, but in that moment I believe he knew me too. I smiled. He started to stand up. I found myself waving, a little awkwardly, as the distance between us quickly closed. I put my arm down. There was a book on the table beside him: Steve Martin in a white suit and rabbit ears. And an empty espresso cup.

'Hello, Oliver.' My eyes flickered across his face, as though I couldn't take him all in. As if I were looking at a skyline.

'Hey, Nancy.' He stepped out from behind the table, as though he might hug me. Then he seemed to change his mind. He reached out and squeezed my shoulder instead. Something shot up my arm. This wasn't like being touched by Gamar or one of my friends. The weight and shape of his hand had been electric.

'Hello.' A sharp voice came over my shoulder.

'Oh, and this is my sister, Rita,' I said quickly.

'Your sister?' Oliver frowned. 'But she's black.'

The choking silence that followed was unbearable.

'A detective and a comedian.' Rita stepped in front of me and pulled out a chair from beneath the table.

'Sorry, sorry.' Oliver took a step back. 'I shouldn't have said that. I just didn't realize. Here.' He put his hand on the back of Rita's chair as though to help. Error after error.

'I know how to sit down.' Rita's voice was ice sharp. 'And I'm not black. My mother is black, and French. I am mixed race.'

'I'm sorry, Reen—Rita. I just didn't realize Nancy's sister was . . .'

'Black?'

I felt as if someone had forced me to bite down on tin foil.

'God, sorry. Can I start this again?' Oliver dropped into his seat, grabbed a fistful of hair against his forehead and closed his eyes.

'Go on.' I suspected that Rita was thrilled by this misunderstanding. She had wanted a reason to dislike this man and, straight out of the gate, he had given it to her.

'OK.' Oliver unclenched his fist. He looked at Rita,

then at me. Then back to Rita. 'Right. Nancy, Rita, hello. I'm Oliver. It's good to meet you.' Rita stared at him, as though at a smear of roadkill. 'And, Rita, I apologize. Nancy did mention she had a sister but I just assumed ...' I felt Oliver's foot tap the floor. 'I don't know what I thought. I suppose I just thought she'd be, like, white as well.'

'Like you?' Rita almost snarled.

'I guess.'

I shifted my weight a little in my chair. I needed to intervene. I needed to smooth this out. But it seemed beyond me. As beyond me as if someone had asked me to climb air.

'I'm sorry,' I said into the burnt-plastic silence. 'Maybe I should have said something. I just never think about it.' Rita exhaled through her nose. Oliver tilted his head to the side a little. 'What would you both like? I'll go up and order.' Oliver looked like he was about to say something else, but then changed course.

'Well, hey, let me get them,' said Oliver. 'I'd like to.'

I turned to Rita.

'I don't think I want anything.' This was a sulk and we both knew it. She was doing the dance but I knew the steps.

'Thanks, Oliver,' I said, hanging my bag off the arm of my seat. 'I'd love a decaf cappuccino.' And then, as he came past me, I added in a low voice: 'Rita will have a tea.' Did they drink tea in New Zealand? I didn't know.

Never mind. He only had to order it – he wasn't the one with the kettle. I sat down next to Rita. Our knees touched briefly and I felt her pull away.

'You do look different,' she said.

'Do I?'

'Yes. Sort of ...' She paused. '... waxier.' It was the perfect word and we both acknowledged it.

'I am a church candle.'

The door behind us banged against its frame. We turned and there was Mum, unhooking her bag from the door handle. There were two little pink circles on her cheeks and her hands were moving a little too quickly. I stood up but Rita was already halfway across the floor. I watched them hug politely. Rita said something I couldn't make out; Mum nodded quickly and then swept her eyes across the cafe. Instinctively, I looked across to Oliver. He was standing at the counter with his arms folded. The shape of his neck, the way he leant back slightly on his heels, how his hair curled behind his ears was all nearly but not quite the match of Dad. Like the printout of a digital photograph: recognizable but imperfect. I looked back at Mum. She was staring at Oliver, holding her bag in front of her. Suddenly she looked like one of those women who stand at bus stops in tights the colour of PG Tips and pale blue raincoats. She looked fleetingly, shockingly, old. Oliver, who had no idea what my mum looked like, made his way through the tables back towards me with an unreadable smile on his face.

'I got you chocolate on top,' he said, putting down my cup. 'And Rita an English Breakfast.' He looked up, obviously wondering where Rita was, and saw the two women staring at him. Something pulled tight in Mum; she straightened, dropped the arm carrying her bag and hardened her face from shock into something more neutral.

'Oliver, this is . . .' I tried to stand up but my stomach nudged the edge of the table, spilling tea into Rita's saucer. 'Ah, this is my mum, Anne.'

'Hello, Anne,' said Oliver. He held out a hand. I had warned him that Mum and Rita wanted to meet him. But I was worried that this had been a bad idea. Maybe I should have met him first, alone, before launching our unhappy trinity at him. Mum offered him her hand, a little hesitantly. But instead of shaking it, Oliver brought up his other hand to cup it. The politician's hand sandwich. The businessman's palm squeeze over a freshly signed contract. It was one step away from that chest bump that football managers give players as they're brought off the pitch for a substitution. Was that really the kind of man he was? Mum gave a very tight smile and extricated her hand.

'I'll get Anne a drink,' said Rita, pointedly looking at the small yellow cup in front of Oliver's seat.

'Oh, no, I can—'

'Do you want a tea or coffee?' Rita spoke over him, as if he weren't there.

'An Earl Grey, please,' Mum answered and I heard the

beating of wings in her voice. She was doing everything to keep it together.

'How's your jet lag?' I ventured. But I'd only got halfway through the question before Mum had started her own.

'Oliver, have you seen a photograph of Clive, my late husband?' Oliver looked surprised, and a little abashed, but I knew that this was how Mum dealt with conflict – straight to the point.

'Ah, yes. There was a profile photo on the website.'

'And had you seen that before you contacted Nancy?' This was Anne in court. This was Anne pulling gently on the line before reeling in the hook.

'Well, yeah. When I got the match, the photo came up straight away.' Oliver dipped the very tip of his finger into the foam on top of his coffee. 'And then Nancy contacted me.'

'I see.' Mum looked at me, then at Oliver. 'I hope you don't mind me asking . . .' Mum's voice was still a little shaky but I knew she'd carry on. I almost envied her steeliness. 'Do you think you're Clive's son?'

'Ah.' Oliver frowned. 'I mean, I'm still not sure . . .'

'Not sure?' Rita pounced. I hadn't realized she was standing behind me.

'Well, I mean, I guess the DNA evidence would say that.' Oliver hesitated. I watched something happen to his jaw that I knew from my own face. 'But, you see, I grew up thinking my dad lived down South, with my brother.'

'Brendhan?' I asked.

'You didn't grow up with your brother?' Anne's eyes had barely moved from Oliver's face. What did she see? I wondered. Was she staring into the past? Into the face of a man she fell in love with forty years ago? Or into a mirage? A mask? A stranger?

'Brendhan – that's my brother – well, he left when I was eleven.' We had met for barely ten minutes and we were already here: unearthing our childhoods; digging into the mess; holding up knots that could not be untied.

'And what about your stepdad?' I looked at Mum. This was a pre-planned interrogation.

'Stepdad? Oh, right.' Oliver put his hand on the back of his neck. 'Guy. I mean, I called him Dad. I thought he was my dad.' I wanted to rescue Oliver but I was also hungry for the story myself. 'Nah. He left too.'

'How come?' asked Rita.

'I don't know.' It was the closing of a curtain. This was not our story to look at. Oliver turned to me and, in that second, I wanted to touch his face. I just wanted to feel the texture of his stubble and the weight of his bones. 'So, like, on the DNA website, your dad—'

'Our dad, according to you,' said Rita. I noticed she was holding the cup of tea to her cheek.

'Hmmmm.' Oliver bit his top lip, then dragged his teeth slowly down the skin. 'Anyway, you said in your email . . . I mean, did you . . . ?'

'Know he had a son in New Zealand?' Anne interrupted.

'Yeah,' said Oliver. I felt a twist in my stomach. 'Sorry, this is kind of heavy shit, straight off, eh?'

'We had no idea.' What I'd meant to sound gentle came out almost pleading. Don't blame us. We didn't know.

'It's not the sort of thing you think about,' said Mum, and I could tell a little of her armour had slipped.

'I'm sorry,' Oliver said.

'Thank you,' I replied.

'So, how did your dad die?'

Rita's chair scraped back against the floor. 'Right. That's it,' she said, her hands whipping across her body like someone waving away an unwanted taxi. 'I don't need this.' She spat the words. 'I don't need any more fucking family.'

The tables around us fell silent. Anne made to stand up but Rita was already slamming her way out of the door.

'I'm sorry,' I whispered. To Oliver, to Mum, to myself.

'I think . . .' But Mum left the rest of the sentence hanging. Gradually the cafe resumed its previous volume.

'Listen, I think me and Rita got off to a real bad start,' said Oliver. 'I respect her.' Something in his voice changed. 'You know, growing up with Mum, I've always admired strong women; women who speak their minds.' The unpleasant thought struck me that this sentence sounded rehearsed; like something Oliver said fairly regularly. 'Maybe I shouldn't have asked about your dad.'

'Perhaps it was the way you asked,' said Mum a little

tightly. 'It was rather ...' Again, she left the statement hanging.

'Yeah.' Oliver quietly took a sip of his coffee. I cleared my throat to speak.

'Oliver?' Mum had clearly decided to stay and see this thing out. 'Did you really have no idea that you might have an English father – a biological father, I mean?'

Oliver shook his head. 'No.'

'Your mother never said anything? Even after your stepfather left?'

'Mum's always been kind of a free spirit, in a way.' Oliver looked out towards the window in what, again, felt like a slightly studied gesture. What was he saying? That his mother had slept around? That she'd lied? What kind of woman was she, who had buckled the frame of my family so entirely and got away with it? But then again, who was I to criticize another woman for getting accidentally pregnant? 'And then recently – well, like in the last ten years or so, she's started to lose some of her memory and language capabilities.'

'I'm sorry,' said Mum.

'Thanks,' Oliver replied.

'It's just that ... well, Oliver, I'm sure you can see this from my position.' There it was again: the lawyer's voice. 'This man gets in touch with my daughter, from the other side of the world, saying that he is her half-brother—'

'I emailed him, Mum,' I tried to clarify. 'And it was the website that showed the DNA match.'

'OK. But what you're saying – sorry, what the DNA

test is saying – means that you were actually conceived when I was already pregnant. With Nancy. It would mean my girls confronting the fact that their father was unfaithful to his pregnant wife.'

Oliver let out a low whistle. It was the kind of reaction I'd only ever seen before in cowboy films. Perhaps, I thought, if you spend your life on stage, performing a version of yourself, you start to behave like an actor all the time. I was about to say something, when, unexpectedly, Oliver reached across the table and took my mother's hand.

'Anne – I hope I can call you Anne?' He paused but Mum didn't reply. 'When I did that test, I honestly had no idea any of this would happen. If I had, maybe I would have taken the doctor's advice and left the whole thing alone.' He pushed a curl off his forehead. 'At the time, I just knew Mum was sick; I wanted to know whether I might have inherited some dementia gene; and, like' – he smiled a little sadly – 'I thought my dad was a guy who worked on the boats in Invercargill and sent me my birthday card on a different date every year.' Mum raised her head. It wasn't quite a nod but she hadn't taken away her hand. 'I don't want to bring you guys any trouble. I'm not after money. I'm not expecting to be treated like a member of your family. I guess this thing has just kind of shaken up my whole belief in who I am and where I came from.' Oliver swallowed. Was this genuine sentiment? It felt real. But it was also so close to a script. 'I can't ask Mum, because she can't remember anything. I can't ask Guy because, well, I don't know where he is and we haven't, like, spoken in over twenty years. And so I thought, while I was over here anyway, doing these gigs, I might be able to find some stuff out.'

I realized that my eyes were watering, which Rita would have absolutely put down to pregnancy hormones.

Oliver let go of Mum's hand and sat back on his chair. I waited for her to respond. Partly because I didn't know what to say and partly because I didn't want to draw attention to the fact that I was nearly crying. We were quiet for about three seconds. Then Mum shifted in her chair.

'You do look rather a lot like him,' she said at last. 'Rather more than either Nancy or Rita do.'

My phone, which I had put on the table, started vibrating. Rushing to silence it, I saw the name on the screen.

Gamar calling.

15

At Terminal 2, the smell of croissants mingled with cleaning fluid and polyester. I was wearing a loose blue dress with gold buttons down the front and white trainers. The dress was cut so you couldn't see my swollen abdomen or the way my breasts spilled out of my bra. Even side on, I looked normal. By which I mean not pregnant. I stood at the arrivals gate, leaning on the metal railing, my bag on the floor at my feet.

Gamar had been ringing to say that he was being flown back the next day for the regular rest and recuperation leave he got when working in a war zone. He'd be spending eight hours in Khartoum and then a plane straight to Heathrow. Taking the call had brought the date with Mum and Oliver to a bit of a halt but I'd had to take it. When I'd come back to the table, Mum had been asking Oliver polite questions about the Soho Theatre dressing rooms. I was disappointed but also too tired to dig in to anything more substantial again. After a few minutes, the waitress had come to collect our cups and soon after that we'd left, saying that we'd make a plan to meet again.

The glass doors rolled open and a tall woman in a

long red wool coat walked out. She didn't hesitate at the gate but glided on, past a display tower of SpongeBob SquarePants key rings, towards the sign for the Underground. Where was she coming from? I wondered. The arrivals board said Edinburgh. Who flies from Edinburgh to London? It's a five-hour train journey. The earth is on fire.

By 8.37 p.m. I was convinced that Gamar wasn't coming back. There had been arrivals from Los Angeles, Düsseldorf, Oslo and Mumbai. I had watched women cry, couples kiss, businessmen shake hands with their drivers. Then, picking up my phone to check for messages, I saw a pair of legs. They were walking like a policeman: toes slightly turned out, heel hitting the ground first. I knew, by the sudden liquid feeling behind my knees, that this was Gamar.

I shouted his name, too loudly, too throatily. As he turned to look at me, I felt air rush into my lungs and a galloping between my thighs. He was so handsome. He smiled, and I rushed down to the end of the railing, desperate just to touch him.

'Nancy,' he murmured on to the top of my head as I leant in to his chest. He was here. At last he was here. Solid and breathing and within my grasp. 'Nancy?' I smelled sweat and dirt and sandalwood. I felt his collarbone against my forehead. I tried to kiss his neck but he pulled away and looked down at me. 'Nancy?' A little more sharply this time. He was looking across my body. Neck, hips, chest, back up to my face. 'Nancy, tell me.'

Every word I knew dribbled out of my head. Under his gaze, I became blank and stuttering. I wanted to put my hand on my front but knew I couldn't. And so I just stood there. Gamar didn't move. People with suitcases jostled past us. Travel pillows attached to rucksacks. Trolleys. I still said nothing. 'Nancy, I phoned you.' There was time. There was still time for him to break into a smile. To pull me close. For his eyes to shine with affection and delight. This could still be as I had scripted it in my mind. Shock, delight, affection, commitment. 'You didn't say . . .' He hadn't stepped back but the gap between our bodies had started to grow. 'Why didn't you tell me?'

'I did try, Gamar,' I said. 'I phoned *you*.' I licked my lips. 'Sent you messages, emails. I even called the Turkish Hospital.'

'What?'

'I was trying everything to get through to you. I didn't know where you were and your phone always went straight through to voicemail.'

'You told the people at the hospital?' His face was closing down.

'No, no.' I rushed to placate him. 'They were speaking Arabic and I couldn't understand. So in the end I just hung up.'

'Hung up?'

'Yes, on the hospital.' Suddenly, I pictured us standing on two ice floes in the middle of a cold black sea. We were drifting away from each other while huge chunks of ice crashed around us into the water. Gamar rubbed a fist across his forehead.

'But you are . . .' I waited. 'You're pregnant?'

'Yes.'

By the time we reached the front door of my flat, tears were cascading down my face. I'd held it together on the Tube and mostly on the bus, but now I could see my own letter box, my curtains, it was pouring out of me. Gamar hadn't said another word the whole journey home. I'd wanted to stop to buy milk but had somehow been too afraid to say. And so, with the grinding momentum of two unhappy people who know an argument is coming, we'd pushed all the way home in a grey silence.

As we came into the flat, Gamar didn't take off his shoes. He didn't take out his phone or wallet. Didn't stretch or open the fridge or put his hand on the back of my neck. He just sat on the sofa and stared at the floor. He hadn't touched me since the arrivals gate. Not once.

'Would you like a . . .' Maybe, I thought, I could pull this around. I could put on the radio, make a drink, break the claggy silence between us. But as I walked into the front room, all momentum ebbed away. Gamar stared at the floor. I cleared my throat. 'A cup of tea?'

'Not really.'

'Coffee?'

'No.'

I felt a twitch in my stomach. 'Do you want anything?'

'No.' Gamar didn't look up. 'I'm very tired.'

Something in me snapped. 'You're always tired.' The air crackled. 'Whenever I want to talk about something important, or the future, or our relationship, you're suddenly exhausted.' The taste in my mouth changed. Lemon rind. Black pepper. Bitter and sharp and slightly of earth. 'Did you sleep on the plane?'

'What do you—?'

I interrupted him: 'I'm tired.' I was standing just inside the doorway. 'My body is doubling my volume of blood and I am tired.'

'Fifty per cent,' said Gamar quietly. 'Not doubling.'

'What?'

'You produce fifty per cent more blood during the first trimester of pregnancy.' He finally looked at me. 'That's half, not double.'

Petty, I thought to myself. The greatest obstacle to affection is the petty man.

'Gamar, can we just talk about this, please?'

'Fine.' Because, of course, what the petty man wants, perhaps even more than to be right, is to be rational. He can talk about this. He's not being emotional. He's not like you. 'How many weeks?'

'Twenty-four.'

'Have you been to the doctor?'

'I've seen a midwife.'

'And did you ask about a termination?' The question didn't shock me, but it hurt.

'Yes. Well, I did. But I've decided.' Come on, Nancy. Come on. 'I don't want a termination.'

His eyelids fell shut. As though in prayer. Sleep. Surrender. All I wanted in that moment was to go to him. To kiss his forehead, sit beside him, share his space. But I couldn't move.

'And' – his eyes were still closed – 'I get no say?'

What had I done? What was I doing?

'No, it's not like that,' I said. 'I wanted to tell you, talk to you about it. God, Gamar, don't you think I wanted you to be here? To make this decision together?'

'But you didn't.'

'What?'

'You didn't make this decision together. You made it. You.'

'Gamar.'

'I told you. I always told you.' His hands went up to his temples. 'I don't want a baby.'

Agony. It was agony.

'You said you didn't know.'

'I said I didn't think about it.'

Could he hear himself? Did he recognize the meaninglessness of what he was saying? 'How can you say that? That you just never think about it?' I was starting to move, back and forth, on the balls of my feet. 'What is it that you're thinking about, then? When your friends have babies, when your sisters are pregnant, when you treat a pregnant patient or a baby? What are you thinking if not "Would I like a baby?"'

'I'm just not thinking that.' Gamar sat back. If this were a boxing match, he would be dropping his fists. Reeling me in.

'But I just don't understand why.'

Gamar lifted his foot a little in the air, before bringing it back down on my carpet. It wasn't a stomp, but it reminded me of a toddler. Someone not getting their own way. 'I . . .' Gamar pushed his knees apart and then back together. 'I don't want to be a parent. I . . . I don't have the bandwidth.'

'Just say it.' I walked towards him, needing the height, needing to be on my feet. 'You don't think I'll make a good mother.' Into the silence rushed every terrible thought I've ever thrown at myself. Selfish, stupid, passive, incapable. Needy, childish, ugly, mad. Thoughtless, dull, pitied, broken, boring, lazy, predictable, oafish, clingy, stuck. Gamar pressed his fist into the sofa cushion.

'For once, Nancy, just for once, this isn't about you.'

Now it was my turn to hit something. I brought my fist down hard on my leg. 'How can you say this isn't about me?' He'd said I'd be a bad mother. He hadn't denied it. 'I'm the one who is pregnant. I'm the one who *you* got pregnant, Gamar. I didn't ask for this. You impregnated me, then left. Left me behind, in complete silence, for weeks. I had to make this decision on my own because you left me completely on my fucking own. I'm the one who is pregnant. I'm the one who is going to give birth, or miscarry, or have something else go wrong. So yes, actually, it is about me.' My voice was climbing the walls. 'This *is* about me.'

'You have no idea.' Gamar's voice was acrid. 'You have no idea what having a baby is like. You're a baby yourself.' Childish, selfish, clingy, thoughtless, lazy, broken. 'When you see the things I see, the way kids are living. When you realize how dangerous it can be.' He had his hands on his knees. 'Having kids. The future. The climate . . .'

I didn't believe him. I knew what he was saying was true but I didn't believe him. This wasn't about the end of the world. This wasn't about the world at all.

'What is this really about, Gamar?' I had my hands in my hair. I could feel the ripping pain between my ribs. 'What is it you're really scared of?'

'I'm not scared,' he shouted. He was scared.

'Just tell me.'

'OK, fine.' And then his face broke open. He was looking at his hands but his expression was one I had never seen before. 'When I was young, my mum, she . . .' He stopped again. I found I was biting my lip. 'She had a breakdown. I mean, that's what we'd call it now. That's not what people said at the time.' I waited. 'My dad left when I was about ten and after that, well, she couldn't cope.'

Another woman abandoned. Another child left to cope. Here it all was again. But unlike Oliver, there was no mystery to Gamar's situation. No DNA test, no foreign phone numbers, no dramatic revelation. Except this one, right now: that he had carried around an agony all his life and never once shown me. That he had hidden his pain. I had never met Gamar's mum. How? How in all this time had I never met his mother? Every time I'd suggested it, she had been busy or ill or visiting her sister. Or so he'd said. Why had I never questioned it? Demanded? Invited myself over? Why had I let him slip away from anything that made us feel like a couple?

'So then I . . . well, I had to bring up my brother and sisters.' The look on his face was still unfamiliar. Despair, shame, pain. This was not the rational face of a doctor, or the confident face of a lover. This was someone I had never seen before. 'I had just started secondary school but suddenly I had to look after my four younger siblings.' He swallowed. 'And my mother. I have already been a parent. I do not want to have a baby.'

And so there it was. Without thinking, I touched my belly. 'You should have told me this.' There was still a layer of soft flesh over the bump. I was not yet a drum.

'I couldn't.'

'No,' I said. 'You could. You just didn't.'

Gamar looked up at me. 'Well, it doesn't matter any more. You've decided.'

I was still trying to process what Gamar had just told me but something in this tone pulled me up. I had decided. I had decided?

'Gamar, I'm thirty-eight.' My eyes were dry. 'Family is important to me. You knew that.' I put my hands on my hips. 'You knew that when you ejaculated in me, with no condom, over and over again.' I smelled blood. 'You never told me about your siblings, about your parents, about all that. But you knew about me.' The adrenaline was making everything in the room feel smooth. Slightly unreal. 'And when I went to the hospital and saw that body on the screen . . .' I paused to run my tongue across my dry lips. 'I saw something.'

Gamar frowned.

'Not like that. Not the . . . baby. I mean, I realized something.' I had not said any of this out loud before. Not to Mum; certainly not to Rita. 'There is a future here, in my body.' I pointed at my stomach. 'It could be . . .' The right words were edging away from me like scared animals. I looked at Gamar. At his shoulders, his fist, the curve of his mouth. Why couldn't he just want me? All of me? Why couldn't he just love me enough to want a child with me? 'So many people, Gamar – my friends – have found people who want a baby with them. People who love them enough for that.' Saying it out loud was almost unbearable. 'Through IVF and everything, they have pursued the same thing. Together. Because they love each other.' I let my hand fall. 'But you . . .' I was starting to shake. 'You shut it down. You shut me off. Gamar, I've never met a single member of your family.'

'Urgh.' Gamar really did slam his hand down then. 'What are you even saying, Nancy? That you want a baby because all your friends have one? Can you even hear yourself?'

That wasn't what I was saying. That wasn't true. Was it? I was starting to lose my grip – on what was real and what was fair. 'I don't know if I'm ready to be a mother yet.' My heart was thundering. 'But this might be my only chance.' Gamar made a noise in his nose that sounded like pure spite. 'But if you don't think I can do it, then I don't need you to do it with me.'

'Need me?' Gamar shot back.

'I want this baby to have a father.' I did. 'But only one that actually loves them, actually wants them.' I was speaking faster than I could think. 'You don't want a baby. You don't want this baby.' I was shocked to find myself pointing at my stomach. 'And you don't want a baby with me. Fine. Fine! Then you can own that. *You* can explain that to people when they ask. When people we know see me looking pregnant in the street, you can tell them that you walked away. Because you were tired. Because you didn't have the bandwidth. That you got me pregnant but didn't want it. That's fine. That's your choice. But it is a choice. And it's one you've made, not me.'

Gamar stood up and walked quickly to the window. For a second, I honestly wondered if he was about to jump out of it. 'A choice?' He punched the back of the sofa. Really punched it this time. 'A choice! Are you actually calling this a choice?' His lip had curled into a snarl. 'I have been back in this country for, what, two hours? And you've just told me that you're going to have a baby, whatever I say or think or do? You're doing it. Unilateral. Already decided. And what? You'll raise it with your lesbian sister and some grieving widow on the other side of London? You're naive, Nancy. You have no fucking idea what you're talking about. You haven't ever looked after anyone but yourself.'

'I—' But he shouted over me. Actually shouted.

'Have you been at a birth? Seen what happens? Women die, Nancy. They die all the time. And babies die. When was the last time you held a baby?'

'I—' My mind went blank. I had held babies. Of course I had.

'Have you ever, in your life, stayed up an entire night, and then the whole next day, while a baby screams and screams and screams? Watched their limbs go floppy, listened to their breath, watched their chests stop moving?' Gamar was looking at the ceiling as he spoke. 'If you have a baby you won't be able to work, to sleep, to see anyone. You'll be at home, feeding and cleaning and scared. You'll be numb, Nancy. You'll be desperate. You'll want to walk away. You'll imagine killing it. You'll want to run away but you can't. Because without you, they die.' Spit was flying out of Gamar's mouth. His eyes were almost black. 'I know, Nancy, because, unlike you, I've actually done it. I've done it, OK? I've done it. I've raised babies. My brothers and sisters. I had to cook for them and get them dressed and take them to the doctor if they got sick. I had to make up their bottles and wash their nappies and clean their teeth. I took my mother's papers to the bank and got out the money to pay our rent. I potty-trained them, Nancy. I taught them everything. So don't say I'm closing something down because I'm telling you: having a baby is the closing down. It's the end of everything. And I don't want to do it again.'

I started to cry. 'Gamar.' I wanted to hold him. 'Gamar . . .'

'I've seen it, Nancy.' He spat out the words. 'At work. I've been to orphanages, to hospitals. I've seen the burials, the wards. And . . .' He covered his head with his hands and pulled it down to his chest. 'I can't.' I wondered if he was crying. 'I won't.'

After all these years, he had finally opened up. And it was just a wall. A block. Fear and pain and his power to say no. And me? What had I fallen in love with? The power of my own hope? My own imagination? In the blankness where Gamar had hidden everything from me, I had painted a future of love and commitment and affection. I had ignored who he was.

Because what Gamar had really been was an absent man. The man who left. The man who never promised to stay with me for ever. I'd believed that my father loved me utterly and then disappeared into death. But Gamar had been absent. He *had* stayed peripheral. Come and gone. I was right about that. Perhaps I had eventually fallen in love with Gamar precisely because I'd thought, in that way, he would never be able to hurt me the way my father had. After all, how can you grieve for someone who was never there?

'I'm so sorry,' I whispered, coming to kneel on the sofa in front of him. 'I'm sorry.'

Gamar took a long breath and I could almost see him packing himself away again. Loading the stones on top of each other until he had almost disappeared. 'Nancy, I don't want a baby and I cannot stop you having one.' I felt a tear hit one of the buttons on my dress. 'I will support you – with money. I will do that. But you cannot make me want it. I don't want to be a dad. I don't want to have a baby with you.'

'Why do you keep saying it like that?' The old wound had ripped apart so easily. Ugly, boring, oafish, dull. 'With me? Having a baby *with me*?' Clingy, selfish, broken, mad.

'Because you're pregnant.'

Before I could stop myself, the question blazed from my mouth. 'What do you actually want from me?' I shouldn't. I should never. And yet I had.

'I don't want anything from you.' He looked as close to crying as I'd ever seen him.

'Are we breaking up?' I asked, watching myself disappear under the surface.

'You've given me no choice.'

16

After the door to the flat closed, an underwater quiet swallowed me. No talking, no ticking, not even a car outside. I walked across to the dining table – even my footsteps seemed silenced – and picked up my phone. A message from an old work colleague. An email from a spa I had once gone to for a hen do.

I searched Rita's number and listened to it ring. It was late, but I needed her. I needed the proximity of someone close. Someone who would hold me, let me rest my head on them, shield me from the world.

Rita, I know things are a bit tense at the moment but Gamar just broke up with me. He says he doesn't want to be a father. Can you please ring me?

I pulled up Mum's number. It rang seven times and then went to voicemail. I didn't leave a message. I couldn't bear to admit, in a sentence, how far I had fallen from her hopes.

Opening WhatsApp, I saw Oliver's face. Just the thumbnail of him, behind a microphone, on stage. I remembered the feeling as he'd touched my arm in the cafe: the electric jolt. He'd sent me a message earlier this evening – the same time that Gamar had been shredding my heart into fibres.

Hey Nancy. I don't suppose you know anyone who Airbnbs a room or anything? Staying with Marcus and Lizzie has been great but I think it might be time to give them some space.

I had been impressed when Oliver said he was staying with Marcus – a stand-up comedian who regularly turned up on TV panel shows and voice-overs. His girlfriend Lizzie was a model; I walked past her seven-foot-tall face every time I went to Superdrug. I wondered what their house was like. And it probably was a house; someone in London must be able to afford a house. Did they throw dinner parties full of ad executives and TV producers? Did she have a cupboard just for shoes? Did he practise his jokes in the bath? It was soothing to lift my brain from the roaring furnace of my own unhappiness for just a moment and to rest it on *Sunday Brunch, Live at the Apollo*; to imagine their shiny, easy life. To skim along the surface.

How long would you be looking for? I wrote. Then added: *Is everything all right?*

I hadn't drunk anything for more than five hours and was suddenly thirsty. My throat felt raw. I went into the kitchen, drank a glass of water and then pulled out a non-alcoholic beer. I had started drinking these in front of the window, ever since my bump had become more visible. For some reason, the idea of someone looking up and seeing a pregnant woman drinking beer entertained me. In the same way I had enjoyed walking home from school holding those chalky cigarette sweets, hoping someone would think I was smoking. My phone buzzed in my back pocket.

Two weeks, tops. I've got an open ticket back but I reckon I'll go home after my show's finished. And yeah, I'm fine. Marcus got a bit jealous (huge misunderstanding) but nothing major.

I thought back to the way Oliver had flirted with the woman in the video who took his watch. I thought of the way he'd held Mum's hand and had looked at her from under his thick eyelashes. I thought of the way two women had turned to look at him when we'd left the cafe. It was hard to believe that all of this was unintentional – or a misunderstanding. And yet, wasn't there a bit of me that wanted to take his side? That enjoyed the glow of his charisma? Had I not hoped, secretly, that he might awaken some untapped magnetism in me?

I was also a bit disappointed that Oliver was going back to New Zealand so soon. The very fact that he was so detached from my usual life meant I liked talking to him. This man knew almost nothing about my relationship, my past, my friends. He didn't know my patterns or my failures. He probably hadn't even guessed I was pregnant and so, in this small corner of my life, I could be a different version of myself. I could be new.

You can always stay on my sofa if you can't find anything.

My fingers wrote out the message while I watched the words appear. And he could. I had rolled out the sofa bed for less: friends of friends, people in London for job interviews, women at parties who had missed their last train. Summer term started next week and I would be at work during the day; he'd be gigging in the evening. It was only a couple of weeks. Also, in some hidden corner of my heart, I liked the idea of having a man in my house. Not to plug my bitter loneliness. But not *not* that either. Oliver would be there to help me carry shopping up the stairs and to open the door at night. He might even fix the kitchen door where it stuck. Was this the desperate thinking of a single, pregnant, rejected woman? Perhaps. But what choice did I have?

For real? That would be great. If your housemates didn't mind.

I took a step towards my bedroom. I was exhausted. My body was sliding off my bones.

It's just a one-bedroom flat – no housemates. If you get a better offer, take it. But I can be back-up.

I crawled beneath my duvet. The front of my dress was damp with tears, my throat raw, my phone warm in my hand. Within seconds, I was asleep.

Oliver had two pieces of luggage: a brown suede holdall and a black courier-type rucksack. He had travelled across the world with less stuff than I took to sleepover in South London. When I'd opened the door to him, the following Sunday, there had been a tricky moment on the doorstep. Did we hug, shake hands, kiss like Europeans or high-five like Americans? In the end, I'd shuffled backwards and he'd stepped in, stooping in the doorway slightly. He wasn't actually so tall that he'd needed to stoop. The stooping was either some show of humility or a response to the jumble of coats, shoes and tote bags that he'd had to slide past just to get into the flat.

That night, I had made up the front room, moving my grey sweatshirt and an unread copy of the *New Yorker* on to the dining table so I could pull out the sofa bed. I had put a lamp on the coffee table in case he wanted to read and given him a clean towel that I'd owned since I was eighteen. Oliver had brought wine, which I opened but didn't drink, and baklava, which I ate every single piece of. A few times, I had caught sight of Oliver in the reflection of a mirror or as I shook out the duvet, and been hit like a spade by how much he looked like Dad. The way he leant in the doorway with his arms folded and his flat feet (unlike me, he had taken his shoes off in the hallway). Without Mum and Rita there, we talked easily about minutiae: the price of crisps at the Soho Theatre; the difference between English newsagents and New Zealand dairies; a podcast we'd both been listening to about a big fraud case. We didn't touch physically at all but I showed him how to turn on the extractor fan, where I kept the teabags and the fact that the kitchen tap turned the wrong way. At about 9 p.m. I apologized for being tired, said something about waking up early and slunk off to my room. Although it was only April the flat felt warmer. I left my door slightly ajar. I put on the audiobook of Malcolm X's diaries, read by Laurence Fishburne, to fall asleep to. Eventually, tired and heartsore, I lost consciousness.

The next morning, I woke up to find all the washing-up done and put away. The counters were clear, the sink empty. My hob was silver, rather than smeared with brown. With a rush of shame and pleasure, I realized that, as I slept, Oliver had cleaned my kitchen. Even Rita had given up cleaning my kitchen, and last time Mum had come over she'd very quickly suggested going out to eat. I heard the creak of the sofa bed's metal frame and Oliver came out into the hall.

'Oh my God, Oliver, I'm so sorry. Was it revolting? I'm afraid that, living on my own, I just don't see the mess any more.'

'Morning,' he replied. His face was creased and puffy but somehow it came across as roguish. I became aware I wasn't wearing a bra. Most of my bras hardly fitted any more; every morning I piled my body into clothes that felt like being bitten. Waistbands, shoulder straps, arm holes, seams – everything was tight.

'How did you sleep?' I asked. There was a smell coming off my skin.

'Oh, the bed was great.' He smiled. 'It took me a while to nod off, though.' Nod off, I thought. When non-English people spoke English they could sound so old-fashioned. 'I think my brain's so used to that hit of adrenaline from being on stage every night that even on my nights off I struggle to switch off.'

'Was that what prompted you to fish sweetcorn out of my plughole?' I asked.

'Ah, I thought that was just a snack you'd left out for me.' Oliver rubbed the back of his neck. 'Along with the lone tomato down the back of the bin.'

A small voice said, 'Look at you, standing in the kitchen, joking with your brother.' But I wasn't. He wasn't. Was he? Sharing a sense of humour doesn't make someone your brother. I also felt ashamed that this handsome stranger with famous friends had seen how I live. How the beastly, unwashed corners of my life had been splayed open.

'You really didn't have to—'

'My mama taught me well,' said Oliver, and I didn't know if he was putting on a character or if this was his character. We both went quiet, him not quite in the kitchen and me not quite sure how to stand.

'Do you want a bath?' I asked. It was seven o'clock in the morning. It was a deranged time of day to have a bath.

'Aaaah, sure,' Oliver replied.

'I have a shower as well,' I said, a little stilted. Somehow, all the ease of a few minutes ago had drained out of us. Had he heard me crying last night? Could he see my stomach? Had I left mouldy yoghurt in the sink?

'You're going to work soon, though, ay?' Oliver rested a hand on the top of the door frame and I saw a tiny strip of pale skin and dark hair beneath his T-shirt.

'Ummm, yes.' I performatively looked at the clock on the wall, even though I knew the time.

'Well, you should get first dibs on the shower then. I can always have mine tonight.' Housework, jokes, sharing a bathroom, pyjamas: weren't these the things that families were made of? 'I'll leave when you do.'

'You don't have to,' I replied. 'Honestly, you really don't have to. I mean, even if you're a kleptomaniac or something, I have nothing worth stealing.' This time the laugh was a little less convincing but we both did it anyway.

'Are you sure?' Oliver ran his bottom teeth across his top lip. I felt a spasm in my jaw.

'Honestly. I have a spare key Mum cut for me.' I opened the kitchen drawer, as though looking for it. It wasn't in there; I just didn't want to squeeze past him to get it.

'Cool. Thanks.' Oliver dropped his arm. 'And while you're out I can work out how I'm going to get the chandeliers and gold bullion away without a van.'

I looked at his teeth when he smiled. They were very even. Not English teeth at all. Would half-siblings have similar teeth? Rita had a gap between her front teeth, just like Marie-Louise. When we were little, she would put blades of grass in the gap and tickle my cheek. So perhaps not. God, I missed Rita. We had never fallen out for this long before.

'I'll put the bed away,' said Oliver, turning to the front room.

'Oh, there's no rush,' I said. 'I'll be out all day so you can Hugh Hefner it if you want.'

Oliver looked at me a little oddly. 'Don't worry – I'm not going to start pissing in jars.'

I frowned. Where did that come from? 'Well ... I'm glad to hear it,' I said, a little awkwardly. 'British plumbing isn't that bad.'

'Yeah, and I can't fly a plane either,' he added over his shoulder.

I was confused. 'Did you ... bring a silk dressing gown?' I asked, absolutely milking this miserable joke for all it was worth.

'No ... ?' Oliver looked at me oddly now. I peeped in at the room behind him. My sweatshirt was neatly folded on top of a pile on one of the dining chairs, along with newspapers, socks, headphones, a pair of scissors. Even the bookshelf looked tidier.

I went into the bathroom. The windowsill had been cleared. The half-empty tubes of lip balm and bottles of Rescue Remedy had been put away. I nudged the bin open with my foot. It had been emptied. God knows what sedimentary layers of horror had been in there. As I turned on the shower, I thought of the first night Gamar had ever stayed. I didn't have a bathmat because I'd always dried my feet before stepping out of the shower. Gamar had left a puddle you could sail boats on in the middle of my bathroom floor. I hadn't said anything, of course. How could I have? Instead, I'd pushed my dress from the night before across the pool with my foot; yellow, cotton. If Gamar had wondered what I was doing, he hadn't said so. But we hadn't been that kind of couple. We'd never questioned each other; I'd learned not to. Despite a painful urge to call Gamar, I still hadn't. Nor had I heard anything from him. In the week before Oliver had arrived, I'd heard every noise in the flat as a knock at the door; Gamar asking to be forgiven, telling me he loved me.

It was Dad who had taught me to dry my feet in the bath. Just as he'd taught me how to wash my own back. And how to roll in shallow water to rinse my hair. What would he say if he were to walk back into his life now? Would he confront Gamar? Would he tell me how to apologize to Rita? Would Rita forgive me, if Dad were here to make her? And what about Oliver? That flinching, unanswerable question: what did Dad really know about Oliver? A choking sound echoed off the bathroom tiles. Oh God, Oliver could hear me. Oh God. I started to rinse the soap from my armpits. Hunger was bubbling around my stomach: a feeling of trapped air. Or could this be the baby? I stood absolutely still but nothing more happened. I heard the metallic clang of the sofa bed in the other room, even over the noise of the shower. I should get out. Oliver would want to get ready. As I turned off the water, I felt the bubbling again. My body was becoming a science experiment.

'Would you like a cup of tea?' Oliver shouted from the kitchen. Wasn't all this just a bit overfamiliar? He had been here for one night and was already tidying my shelves and offering me my own tea.

'Ah, I'm fine, thanks,' I called back. I absolutely didn't want to stand next to Oliver in a towel. Oliver was dark-haired, broad-shouldered, his mouth a tantalizing curve. He was friends with television presenters and probably dated models. The contrast between him and my pale, lumpen body would be like comparing carved rock and soft cheese. My self-esteem couldn't handle it.

I wanted to speak to Rita. I wanted to talk to her about grass in teeth and keeping potatoes under the stairs and Dad's three-inch baths. She was the co-author in the story of my childhood; our memories were a shared repository of stories we told and retold to each other. Still in my towel, I pulled up her number. A text would go unanswered so I called her. It was half past seven but I knew she'd be up. I could picture her in her kitchen, stirring yoghurt through her porridge – a tepid, milky slop that turned my stomach.

'Hello?'

'Hi, Rodney, it's me.'

'I know. What's happened?'

'How are you?'

'Normal. Fine.' I heard Rita's kitchen door clunk in the background. 'Why are you calling?'

'I just missed you.'

'Missed me?'

'Yes. I missed you like a misty morning.' We both knew I was trying too hard.

'OK.'

I took a deep breath. I was wading out into a cold

river and couldn't see the bottom. 'I was just thinking . . .' I stalled. '. . . about how you used to tickle me with grass between your teeth.' There was a pause. Was Rita softening? Had I managed to reach her at last?

'OK if I jump in the shower now?' Oliver's voice roared through from the hallway.

'Who was that?' Rita asked quickly.

'Oh, umm.'

'Is there a man in your flat, Nancy?' She said the words 'a man' like a nun.

'Yes,' I half shouted, to them both.

'Gamar?' Rita sounded unconvinced.

'No. I haven't heard from—'

'Then who was that?'

The question hung in the air. Seconds ago I had felt on the edge of reconciliation. We had been going to laugh about teeth and exchange kind words.

'Umm, it was Oliver.' I was speaking quietly, almost whispering.

'Oliver!' Rita's voice cracked like a whip. 'What is he doing in your flat?'

'He stayed here last night,' I said. 'He needed somewhere to stay and I was feeling so shit with everything.' I dropped my voice even lower. 'The pregnancy, Gamar, and I was missing you, Rita. It's been so—'

She cut over me: 'Oh, don't put this on me, Nancy.'

'I'm not. I was just so . . .' The word formed in my mouth like a slug. 'Lonely.'

'Nancy, he's a misogynist and a liar and a fucking

gold digger.' Rita was shouting so loud I thought Oliver might hear her through the cardboard walls. 'He's only been in the country for a few weeks and he's already moved in with you. For free. You can't trust him, Nancy. You don't know him. He'll go through your flat and humiliate you.'

'Humiliate?' I tried to cut in. 'What are you talking about?'

'Haven't you watched any of his stand-up?'

She had caught me. Because, since watching that first video, I had started to tell myself it was just a stage persona. As he and I had written to each other, learned each other's style and habits, I had turned further and further away from the version of Oliver woven across the internet. He was a comedian, I'd told myself, but he was also kind of an actor. He was playing a role in his comedy. The Oliver on stage wasn't my brother – he was a job.

'He talks about women like they're just accessories to his penis,' said Rita. 'Like his joke about all lesbians dressing like magicians – it's just the kind of lazy homophobia you get from men who see women as sexual objects.' I closed my eyes. 'And when he's not doing that, he's moaning on about how hard he finds it to talk to men; how he's an outsider; how only women can really understand him. I watched him on some panel show talking about how he can't go to the gym in case one of the guys in the changing room asks him about his car, so now he does yoga. As if that makes him John Stuart Mill.' I stopped myself from asking who that was.

'He cleaned my flat,' I said, my voice as small as a walnut.

'Of course he did,' Rita hissed. 'God, Nancy, you're so naive.'

The shower started to run and I could hear Oliver humming. Not loudly. His voice was high, gentle. I dropped the phone to my lap. He was humming Joan Baez. For the first time since Dad had died, I was listening to a man hum in the shower. Of course, Dad didn't hum Joan Baez. He sang Bob Dylan. Or more likely Leonard Cohen. As the water fell over his face, he'd rumble out 'The Partisan' or 'Suzanne' while the rest of us fidgeted and stomped around on the landing, waiting for our turn. He'd had a terrible voice. I would have pulled out my collarbone just to hear it again.

I had spent the last two years straining to hear my Dad everywhere. I had waited for him in the dark and listened out in doorways. Now there was a man, a man with curly black hair, humming in my shower. Rita might think I was naive but, in that moment, I didn't care. If this was fraud, then I'd take it. If Oliver was a con man, I would be conned. After all, what was my alternative?

I didn't notice Rita hang up. I ignored the time on my phone. I didn't feel the towel on my back go cold.

17

'So there I was, naked, bleeding, slamming around my kitchen, bits of fly paper stuck to my face and roach powder all over my feet...'

In the dark of the theatre, I stared at Oliver. Really stared. I looked at the way his feet pointed at twelve and three, like a dancer; I watched him pull his hand through the dark brown curls that gathered above his ears; I looked at the hems of his trousers. Why does a man climb on to a stage? Because he's lonely? Because he's angry? Because he feels naked off it?

'And I thought, maybe she's right...'

It had been four days since Oliver had come to stay and, although we were sharing a flat, I had hardly seen him. Yesterday, he had been asleep when I left for school and I had been asleep by the time he came home from his gig. He had left me a note, explaining that he'd made a stew with lamb and pearl barley for me; that he could get me guest list for Thursday and that he had bought me a better chopping board. In turn, I had bought him a copy of *Private Eye*, I'd washed up my plate after breakfast and I'd brought home one of the plants from school to try and make his room more cheerful.

'Maybe the totality of the human worth cannot simply be measured...'

I tried to concentrate on what Oliver was saying but my mind went back to Gamar, like a rat nosing down a pipe. I had heard nothing from him in over a week. I assumed he was still in England. He would surely tell me if he was going back into the field – but then perhaps not? He had agreed to financial support but nothing more. He was not going to be a father. Even though he had made someone a mother. Even though he had made a child.

'... by whether you put lime in your Coke.'

I had told the deputy head at work that I was pregnant. She had hugged me, with tears in her eyes, and said that it was wonderful news. She had told me that when she was pregnant with her daughter, she had once crawled under her desk at 3 p.m. and fallen asleep until six, when the cleaners came in.

'Any other single mumma's boys in tonight?'

I sucked in a breath. I did not want to hear Oliver talk about his parents on stage. I was not ready for my dad to become part of a routine.

'Yeah, you can tell us by the way we sit down to pee.'

With relief, I took a sip of my lime and soda. It was almost all ice. A man behind me at the bar had pushed against my back until my bump was squeezed against the hard metal edge of the counter. He had been talking over his shoulder to another man. I had felt his chest and the sharp buckle of his belt push into me. I had braced myself against the bar and pushed back into him. He hadn't noticed.

'Or when we sing the Bodyform song.'

Rita had not been in touch since our phone call. Mum had rung yesterday evening and mentioned that Rita had started dating a woman who made soap using plants foraged along the banks of the New River. I thought of the grass between her teeth. Did she tickle her new lover with elderflowers and cherry blossom, picked behind Green Lanes? Mum had started knitting a blanket, she said, but it was coming up very big.

'And the way we cry when we don't get our own way.'

Suddenly, the air bubble feeling was back, but this time, something slipped against the wall of my abdomen. It wasn't like the fluttering of a butterfly but the quick twist of a lizard. A slither. I put my hand on the side of my stomach, just above the line of my knickers. The movement came again. Slight, unnerving. As much air as bone but it was there. I had felt it flicker inside me and, so lightly, the pressure against my hand had changed. As though something were lumping out at me.

'I was the only other person on the whole row, right?'

I was pregnant. Although I'd known it rationally, I was now starting to believe it, emotionally. I was a pregnant person. A life-giving vessel. A co-creator. Inside my womb something had flickered into life from just sex. Sex. Such an unbelievable thing. But I had sustained it. I had poured my blood into it and breathed my air into it and fed it with my cells. I was making something. My baby was inside my body. I was pregnant.

'You ever see guys doing this?'

And if I was pregnant then I had agency. Yes, the pregnancy had happened to me but I was also doing it. Right now. I was being pregnant. I was growing and swelling and beating and moving. I was a person making a person. That was what Gamar hadn't understood; maybe even I hadn't understood until now. I didn't need him because I was already needed. I was already the entirety of something's – someone's – universe. I was the sea and the land and the sky. I was the big bang. I was gravity. I was oxygen. Without me, they didn't exist.

'Like, give it a fucking rest, mate. We've all had pockets. Ya know?'

18

I felt awkward waiting in the bar for Oliver to come out. I didn't fit the bill for a groupie. I was wearing a mustard-coloured man's shirt, flat boots, chewed-off lipstick and a rucksack full of mixed nuts. I smelled of Olbas Oil; I had dabbed it on my collar to mask the scent of other people's bodies. There was no space in any of the booths, so I sat on a stool in the corner, under a poster of a man wearing a snorkel. I hadn't brought a book and so I googled 'twenty-five weeks pregnant size vegetable'. My baby was the size of a spaghetti squash. I then googled spaghetti squash and saw a picture of a female hand scraping out the insides of a large yellow vegetable with a fork. I tried not to think of the baby, scraping the flesh off its bones with a fork. This baby was the length of a banana. I had felt it, pushing around my body. My boss knew. I was pregnant now.

It was late to ring Mum. Gone ten. But I wanted to share this extraordinary experience with someone. I started to type.

Hello Mum. I've just been to see Oliver's show at the Soho Theatre. It was actually quite funny.

My hand hovered over the screen. How could I fit so much in this small message?

I felt the baby tonight. It wasn't what I expected at all. Not a kick, more of a wriggle, but I felt it. I thought it was just wind.

I had told Mum about Gamar but not all of it. I was too ashamed to admit, even to my mother, that I was having the spaghetti squash of a man who didn't love me. Who offered me nothing but money.

Anyway, I just wanted to tell someone x x x x

A group of women in their twenties were sitting at a table in the middle of the room. One of them, with hair the colour of apricots, was sitting up very straight. She was wearing a crumpled white shirt and no bra. I could see shadows under her clavicle and the dark circles of her nipples. I remembered lying in Rita's bed on a Saturday morning as a child. We were pointing at my nipples and saying, in our slow-motion voices, 'straaawberrrrry' and then at hers, saying 'chooocolaaaate'. We were ice creams. We were fresh scoops. We were little.

The woman at the table kept looking at the door with her high, straight neck. I was looking too, waiting for Oliver. I knew he wouldn't want to come home with me but I didn't want to scuttle off without saying something. It had been kind of him to put me on the list. He'd even offered me a plus one but I had declined. Who would I have taken?

I sucked a mint that had gone soft in my bag. If I stayed much longer, I would have to buy another drink.

I tried to think of some of the jokes Oliver had told. He'd talked about the flight here. He'd talked about pigeons and how they look like a *kererū* with an office job. He had talked about his mum: how she had taught him to roll her cigarettes; how she looked like Keith Richards; how many 'uncles' he'd had. He didn't talk about her now, the softening of her memory, but kept her as a character: hard leather and smoke. That was what performers did, of course. They created people out of stories. They created themselves on stage.

I heard boots on the stairs. I looked up and saw Oliver coming towards the bar. He had changed into a white T-shirt with the sleeves rolled up. He looked tanned, flushed, twinkling. As he came into the bar, the girl in the white shirt stood up and started to walk towards him, her hips jutting. I watched him slide an arm around her waist and he kissed her on the soft point where her cheek, ear and neck met. I busied myself with the strip of paper around my old mints. The people on the table had all turned to watch Oliver and the girl in the shirt, who were now talking, their faces just a little closer than normal. The girl was grinning. Oliver's mouth, curled up in a half-smile, had something of the wolf about it. As he turned his head, to speak closer to the girl's ear, he caught sight of me and the smile broadened. Releasing the girl, he held his hand up at me in a static wave. I saw him say something into her ear, then to her group of friends. They all turned to look at me. Feeling like a ball of mozzarella on a bar stool, I pulled the rucksack further into my lap and tried to set my face into a neutral smile. The girl nodded, slightly, then pointed back at her chair with a thumb. Oliver squeezed her shoulder and started to walk towards me. Others in the bar were looking at him. Whether they had just seen him on stage or whether this tanned man with his damp hair, no coat and no luggage just attracted people's gaze, I couldn't tell. I felt the crackle of being with someone at the centre of attention. I felt his reflected heat.

'Oliver!'

'Hey, Nancy, thanks for coming.' He smelled of eucalyptus.

'Well done!' Well done was probably not what you were supposed to say. 'It was brilliant.'

'Ah, that's—' He slapped his broad, hard stomach with a flat hand.

'I loved all the stuff about you and Anahera,' I said. Had I used her name on purpose? To prove that I was more than just another fan? Was her name my flag in the ground?

'Really? Which bit?' It wasn't an idle question. He wanted details. He needed this.

'Umm . . .' I scrabbled. 'That story about her turning up to school in a Wu-Tang T-shirt. I can really picture her.'

'Yeah.' Oliver smiled but looked at the floor.

'And all that stuff about the parties and learning slide guitar. And her mussel fritters. And the eel.'

'Ah, I'm glad you liked that,' said Oliver. 'I wasn't sure how well it would translate.'

'No, it was great.' How reassuring, I thought, to meet someone who needed as much reassurance as me. I knew that hunger. I could understand it. And, unlike Gamar or Rita, Oliver didn't close down, or curl in when he felt it. 'You've got a real presence on stage.' I flicked a piece of hair out of my face. 'And . . . I loved the music at the beginning.'

'Right.' Oliver looked a bit crestfallen but only for a second.

'Anyway, I'll leave you to your public.' As I eased myself off the stool, Oliver took my hand. It was an almost courtly gesture. Then he kissed me on the cheek and said, 'See you at home.' And despite myself, I felt special. Here, in front of this bar full of people, this man had come straight off stage to talk to me. He wanted my opinion. He valued my company. I liked the idea that people in the bar might be wondering who I was. It gave me social status, prestige, importance: all the things I could never feel on my own.

I didn't see Oliver again until Friday afternoon. He hadn't slept at the flat and, because he was always so meticulously tidy, I couldn't tell if he'd even been back to change his clothes. When I stepped through the door after work, he was in the kitchen, making coffee. The smell hit my fatigue like a slap. Saliva rushed into my mouth and I half ran, half collapsed into the bathroom. I retched but wasn't sick. I spat into the bowl, feeling the weight of my stomach as I leant over.

'Hey, Nancy, is it too late for you to have a coffee?'

Choking back the acid waves pushing at my throat, I called out, 'No, I'm fine, thanks.'

When I stepped out of the bathroom, a minute later, my face washed and my teeth stinging with mint, Oliver was sitting at the dining table, holding *Private Eye*. For some reason, I didn't believe that he was actually reading it. It looked like a prop.

'You OK?'

'Umm, yes, thanks. I'm just ...' Walking across the room, I felt like a hen.

'Hungover?' I could see Oliver's bicep beneath his close-cut black T-shirt.

'No, a comedown,' I said, and smiled. Lowering myself on to the chair, my stomach nudged the edge of the table. Had Oliver guessed I was pregnant? Or, having never seen me otherwise, did he just think of me like this? The word 'bulbous' came into my mind. I was a bulb. A turnip, or tulip; my growth was now pushing up above ground where everyone could see. 'How have you been?' I asked, taking a sip of the water he'd put on the table for me. The rules of this domestic arrangement were becoming increasingly vague. Initially, Oliver had talked about staying for a couple of weeks. A stop gap, while he found somewhere. But sitting at the table, drinking coffee, cleaning my oven, cooking me dinner: it didn't feel short-term. And, although I knew it was odd, I didn't mind. I wouldn't ever have admitted it, but having a man-shaped body in the flat shaved a few inches off my loneliness.

'Ah, pretty good, thanks. I had a meeting today with

someone from radio comedy?' Oliver's upwards inflection, which was familiar to me from after-school soaps, was less annoying than when English people affected it.

'Oh wow, that's good,' I said, although I couldn't picture what such a meeting would look like. 'And did you find somewhere to stay?'

'Ah, right.' Oliver looked uncomfortable.

'Just last night, I mean.'

'Oh, I see.' He smiled and scratched his jawline. 'Yeah, I stayed with Melissa?'

'Was that the girl with the orange hair?' I managed not to add, 'Who you had your arm around.'

'Aaah, yeah, I guess it is kinda orange.'

'Cool.' I didn't know what to add without sounding prurient.

'It was nice. She showed me around her area. Like, south? Maybe Camberwell?'

'Oh, yeah, Camberwell. That's a cool area.' I had been to Camberwell once for a private view and my only memory was of a tall white house with palms in the garden. 'Did you spend today with her too?'

'Ah, nah, she had class.' Oliver took a sip of his coffee.

'What kind of class?' One of the other teaching assistants had taken up improv classes a few years ago. She would leave early on a Thursday to go and stand in a room above a pub and pretend to be an improv comedian pretending to be a policeman.

'She's studying Criminology.'

I was baffled. 'What do you mean?'

Oliver gave me his curling smile. 'She's a student at LSE, doing Criminology.'

'A student?' I remembered the group at the table. 'Oliver, how old is Melissa?'

'Aah, maybe twenty-four?' Oliver pursed his lips like a boy trying to repress a giggle. Was he joking? Or was he proud of himself.

'Twenty-four?' It screeched out of my mouth like a seagull.

'Yeah, she's a mature student.'

'Not as mature as you, Oliver.' I couldn't stop myself. 'You're nearly forty.'

'Sorry, what?'

What was I doing? This wasn't my fight. That girl – woman – girl – had clearly been willing. And twenty-four wasn't eighteen. Then again, as a woman in my thirties, wasn't it my duty to protect other women's hearts? Defend their bodies, even against themselves? Even if I'd never managed to protect myself.

'Just – that's quite an age gap.'

'Oh, I see.' Oliver rubbed a finger along his eyebrow. The way he said it, it was as though I was being petty and conservative, rather than a strident member of the sisterhood. I didn't want to sour this. I didn't want to annoy him. 'You're right, Nancy.' I was wrongfooted again. 'I think sometimes when you're kind of lonely and in a new city, you're just drawn towards people who are open.' Lonely? Was Oliver lonely? 'And they tend to be in their twenties. By our age, people start to close in on themselves. Married, kids, mortgages, all that. They shut out the world.'

I had no idea what my face was doing. This speech was not what I'd been expecting. None of this had been what I was expecting. Ever since I'd spat in that tube, my life had unravelled into a series of unexpected events.

'Melissa and I got talking after one of my gigs and she's just a really intelligent, forceful person.' Oliver thumbed the corner of *Private Eye*. 'I've always been drawn to strong women.'

This was definitely a line he'd used before.

'Sorry, it's none of my business,' I said.

'No, you're right to pick it up. I mean, of course you are.' Oliver looked at me from under his eyelashes. 'As a feminist, you have to protect other women, right?' I blushed.

Just then, I felt something like the squirt of a perfume bottle under my skin. It was followed by a flick. Instinctively, I put my hand on the front of my stomach. Under my fingers, something moved. A tap, rather than a kick, but it was there. I breathed in sharply.

'Nancy? You OK?' Oliver moved his hand towards me, across the table.

'Yes, fine. I just ...' When our eyes met, I felt a tug, deep within me. Part physical, part sadness. 'I'm actually pregnant, Oliver.'

His eyebrows shot up, a gesture I knew from Dad's face. It was surprise, or the performance of surprise. 'For real?'

'Yeah.'

'Wow.' He puffed out his cheeks. 'Did you, like, do it on your own?'

I realized that, in all the time we had messaged or spoken, ever since Oliver had arrived in the country, I had probably never mentioned Gamar. At least, not in the present tense.

'Like, artificial insemination? No.' I smiled then. 'I got inseminated the old-fashioned way, by my ex-boyfriend.'

'Did you mean to get pregnant?' It was such a bald question I couldn't help but answer it.

'No.'

'Ah, shit, so is that why you broke up?' Oliver's hand was still in the middle of the table, but now he'd pulled his fingers into a soft fist.

'No. Well, sort of. Yes.'

Oliver nodded. 'I get it.' Did he? 'My ex, Layla, had been trying to, like, settle. Get pregnant.' This surprised me. 'You know' – he gave a little laugh – 'lock me down.'

I felt the back of my neck fan out like a cobra. 'What do you mean?'

'What?'

'What do you mean, lock you down?' I thought of the girl with the apricot hair and visible nipples. I thought of Oliver's hand on her narrow waist. I thought of Gamar walking through my front door. I was suddenly filled with an anger that I'd never been able to direct before. An anger that I didn't want to admit even to myself. 'It's not a punishment, Oliver.' I tried to smile but all I did was show my teeth.

'What?'

'For someone to love you.' I touched my collarbone, where Gamar had once kissed me. 'It's not a punishment if someone wants to have a baby with you. It's a compliment.'

'Yeah, except, you know . . .' Oliver's eyebrows were doing something strange. 'I'm not even sure I want kids.'

'OK.'

'But I kind of got the feeling that she'd just go ahead and do it anyway.'

'Do what?' I knew the answer but I wanted to make him say it.

'Get pregnant.'

I gave a short, humourless laugh. 'It's not a trick.' I could hear my breathing. 'You can't get pregnant on your own. You can't trick sperm up yourself.' Oliver didn't say anything but the words continued to roll out of me, oiled by years of disappointment and pain. 'And the stakes are quite a lot higher for the woman in that scenario, don't you think? To end up pregnant, sacrificing her life to being a mother?' I saw Oliver lick his lips. A quick, darting gesture.

'Seriously, though.' I was a fire and I was burning. 'If you don't want a baby, then isn't it just as much on you, the man, to be in charge of contraception. Isn't it?'

Oliver said nothing.

'You have to make sure you don't get someone

pregnant. It's on you to stop that happening. Maybe even more than her.' I thought of all the nights and all the mornings when Gamar had had sex with me, without using a condom, without pulling out. How I had been the one to take the pill, take the hormones, take my temperature, take precautions. How he, a doctor, had ignored the fact of his body in the pursuit of pleasure.

'Yeah, I mean—'

'If you don't want kids' – my heart was too loud – 'why don't you get a vasectomy?' Surprise swept across Oliver's face. I bit my lips together. That had been too far. I had stopped talking to Oliver and started talking to a man. All men. All the Gamar men, the Oliver men, all the men who treated women's bodies as problems and not people. All the men who expected us to swallow pills and push twists of wire into our cervixes. All the men who thought it was fine to make women live in a state of synthetic pregnancy for decades. All the men who didn't come to the appointments. All the men who didn't pay at the pharmacy. All the men who asked if we 'were using something' instead of using something themselves.

'Get the snip?' Oliver's mouth twitched.

'Yes. I mean, yeah, if you don't want kids, you could . . .' I felt something tug inside my stomach. 'Instead of worrying about it happening by accident you could actually stop it happening ever.'

'It's pretty major surgery, though, isn't it?' Oliver said.

I thought of the women I knew. I thought of the episiotomies and the coils and the caesareans. I thought of the tears and prolapses and lost threads and laparoscopies. I thought of blood and pain and swelling and bovine, sexless misery.

'Yes, I suppose it is.' I tried to smile, tried to keep this a conversation rather than an argument. 'But women go through quite major medical interventions now, don't they, whether or not they have children?' Maybe I had inherited more of Mum's debating style than I'd realized.

Oliver looked at me. 'What do you mean?'

I lifted my hand to my earlobe. 'Well, if you get a coil they do it without anaesthetic, and it might come loose and puncture your bowel. If you do accidentally get pregnant and don't want to keep it that might involve an operation. Then there's birth, obviously, which can be . . .' I drop my hand. 'It's just not like we're not getting surgery.'

Oliver nodded, then reached up and scratched his head. 'Maybe they'll finally make a male pill, though, eh?' he said. I couldn't tell if he actually agreed with me or just wanted to move on. Either way, the vibration in the room started to smooth.

'Would you take it?' I asked, surprised. 'A male pill?'

'Shit, yeah,' Oliver replied. 'I don't mind pills at all.'

'Oh, right.' I smiled. 'That's good. I don't think my ex would have taken the pill. Even though he's a doctor.'

'A doctor?'

'Yes. He's in Sudan at the moment. Emergency medicine, you know, because of the war?'

There was a pause. Oliver nodded but I wasn't convinced he really did know what I was talking about. I didn't know where he got his news or how he voted or what he read. In fact, despite just having a more honest conversation with him about sex than I'd ever had with a man before, I didn't really know much about Oliver at all.

'Jeez. I mean, good on him. That's a proper job,' Oliver said. 'But you'd think a doctor would know a little more about contraception.'

He was right. Gamar should have known better. He should have taken responsibility. I could blame the distance, war, technology, but the truth was he had just left. He'd got a woman pregnant and left the country. It had all happened again.

19

The next afternoon, I walked around Walthamstow Marshes, listening to *Astral Weeks* by Van Morrison on my headphones. I am not someone who longs for the countryside. I like trees and love the sea but I also get overwhelmed by silence and darkness and space when I'm in the middle of nowhere. Sometimes I look out from train windows and my eyes just slide across the landscape. Without a house or wall, a building or bridge, I can't read it.

But since moving to North London, Walthamstow Marshes has become etched on to my insides. The boggy orange grass in winter, the tall clumps of water reeds, the brambles, the birds, the belted cattle with their short legs and large, square faces. I like how, just metres from a London I understand, the ground here slips into something wild and messy and neglected. I like watching the mist rise off the River Lea and how the sun stains the tops of the trees pink in the evening. I like the flashes of green parakeets and the sickly smell of elderflower. I like the men in their long black coats and the whirr of generators by the narrow, painted boats. And so, slowed down by the weight of my pregnancy, too tired to jog, I walked along the flattened grass and tried not to look at the families. Oliver had a matinee that day and Mum was in Hastings, visiting her friend Reenie. I'd texted Rita, offering to buy her lunch at the Riverside Cafe. I thought that she might be ready to start talking again. I missed her and, thinking that she might be tempted by eggs and rowers, had held out the olive branch. But she'd said she was busy. She didn't say with what or who and I couldn't ask. Still hoping to open a conversation, I'd sent her a picture of my bump, straining against a T-shirt she'd brought back for me from Disneyland Paris when I was eleven. Her reply had been short and unaffectionate: *Getting bigger*. This coldness was almost as painful as her fury.

I woke up on Sunday morning to the sound of Oliver talking. This was the first time that I'd slept past him. Or perhaps, I thought, he hadn't been to bed.

'No, I'm in London.' He sounded sharp. 'If they had rung me, I would have seen it.'

There was a pause and I heard a deep, rattling voice on the other end. Even through the digital friction of FaceTime, you could tell he was talking to a man.

'So what are you saying?' the other voice rumbled.

I looked at my phone. It was 7.09 a.m. My bladder was pinching but I didn't want to interrupt Oliver.

Didn't want to interrupt him in my own flat? At seven o'clock on a Sunday morning? While a baby lay across one of my internal organs? I was being ridiculous. I got up without trying to stay quiet.

The living-room door was open when I came out of the toilet and I could see Oliver, talking into the screen of his phone. His elbow was propped on the table and he was wearing a shirt but no trousers. His legs were covered in dark, curly hair. Like Dad's. Like mine would be soon if I didn't do something soon.

'But is Ma OK?'

Ma? Had something happened to Oliver's mother? Perhaps he was on the phone to the care home. Although do care homes use FaceTime? I stood in the doorway, ready to come in, ready to help.

'Ah, yeah, she's fine now,' the deep voice rumbled. 'I got a call from the local police but they weren't heavy about it or anything.'

'Police?' I saw Oliver's calf muscle twitch.

'Yeah. One of the fishermen at Whangārei found her sleeping in his boat.' For a moment, I thought the call had turned to static. Then I realized that the crackling noise coming from the other end was somebody laughing. I took a step further into the room and saw a big man with reddish hair on Oliver's phone screen. 'Yeah, this cop, he says' – the red-headed man put on a nasal, whiny voice – '"I'm afraid to say that Mrs Coburg was wearing nothing but a sarong."'

'Sorry?' Oliver wasn't laughing.

The man was still chuckling. 'No undies, Ollie. Just a pareo. A lavalava. You know?'

Oliver's shoulders went slack. 'What, they called you

for that? Because Ma was having a nap on some boat in a lavalava?'

'They said she'd been found unconscious.'

I could now see that the man on the phone had a gold front tooth.

'What do you mean?'

Maybe I should leave, I thought. Maybe I shouldn't be listening to this.

'Yeah, well, you know. Like you said, she was just having a nap.'

'But the boat guy, he called the cops?'

'Well, see, she was probably acting pretty confused. I reckon the guy took her to be drunk.'

Oliver's neck flashed red. 'Well, I doubt it. Mum's hardly a big drinker.'

'I know, I know. But they didn't know that. Here was some old girl, probably sounding pretty slurry, bare-arsed in the bottom of his boat on a Saturday night. You can see how it happened.' Oliver sucked his teeth while the other man went on. 'Anyways, I spoke to the home and everything, and it's all sorted now.'

'Is she on her own?'

'Nah. I popped in. Although, well, I'm going to be going away for a bit. Me and Cherie, well, we're getting divorced and I need to clear out of the house while her and the girls move out. We're selling it, see.'

I watched Oliver rub his hand along the top of his thigh. 'Right. Sorry to hear that.'

'Yeah, well, I caught her fucking one of the seed sales reps on our kitchen floor.'

As I shifted the weight on to my other foot, the floorboard beneath me creaked. Oliver turned and I gave a small apologetic wave.

'Oh, hey, Nancy. Sorry, I—'

'No, no, I'm sorry.'

'Is there someone with you?' The voice on the phone crackled out.

'Nah, yeah, it's Nancy. I'm, well – like, I found her on a DNA site?' Oliver turned back to the man he'd been speaking to. 'She lives in London so I've just been crashing on her couch.'

'DNA site?' The man's voice broke into a laugh. 'I've never heard that one before.'

'Nah, for real. She's my half-sister?'

'What?'

'Yeah, I did one of those DNA tests and it came up as a sibling match.'

'Bro, are you fucking with me?'

I stepped towards Oliver. I could see now that the man he was talking to had a beard the colour of dried grass. There was a tattoo of two dice on his neck. And as he scratched his chin, there was a thick silver ring on his thumb.

'Hello,' I said. I sounded very English.

'Ah, hey.' The man was more thickset than Oliver and his colouring was different, but he had the same curl in his mouth. 'I'm Brendhan, Oliver's big brother.' His face broke open into a big, meaty smile. It was impossible not to smile back. Then I thought back on what I'd just heard. This was Oliver's brother. But he hadn't heard about me at all. Had Oliver been keeping me a secret? Was he worried his brother would be upset? He didn't look upset. Why hadn't he told him?

'He rang to let me know about Ma. Mum,' said Oliver. 'Apparently she fell asleep on the beach.'

'Oh dear,' I said, scrabbling to get a hold on the dynamic here.

'Ah, the old girl's all right.' Brendhan's voice was like a bonfire, full of cracks and spit and heat. 'I went to see her tonight and I can go again on Tuesday, on the way to my solicitor. Yeah, I have to drive to Whangārei now, to get my pocket picked and my balls clamped.' I assumed this was a reference to his divorce.

'How long do you have to be away from the house?' Oliver's leg was bouncing under the table and his voice sounded different. If he weren't talking to his brother, I'd have said he was nervous.

'Six weeks, give or take,' Brendhan replied.

'Right.'

'I just sold a couple of cattle so I've got something to tide me over while the divorce goes through. Reckon I might even go away proper; get out of God Zone.'

'Well,' I heard myself say out of politeness, 'if you want to come to London for a visit, just let me know.' I smiled. There was no way this hairy-faced, fire-voiced farmer was going to come to London.

'Ah, yeah.' Brendhan smiled. 'I can visit Abbey Road and we can all crack open those family secrets together.'

'So, are you and Brendhan close?' I asked later as we washed and dried the breakfast things in my narrow little kitchen. Oliver was washing and I was putting away, even though my bump was making bending increasingly uncomfortable.

'Not really,' Oliver answered, looking into the sink.

'How much older than you is he?'

'Five years. But he left home when I was, like, eleven.' I waited, wondering if I was pressing on a bruise. 'Yeah, I remember his car – you could drive at fifteen, then, in New Zealand,' Oliver continued. 'He'd ripped out the back seats of this old Ford Laser and replaced them with a mattress.' I watched a small smile creep across Oliver's face. 'I'd spent weeks making him a tape of all his favourite songs off the radio. You know, like, Neneh Cherry, Guns N' Roses and stuff. He drove all the way down to Bluff, to work on the boats. With his dad and uncle.'

'Why did he leave home?'

Oliver shrugged. 'I was never quite sure what happened. All I knew was that Ma didn't talk to Brendhan again for years, so I didn't either.'

'Really?'

'Yeah, nah. Like, how does an eleven-year-old stay in touch with a grown man in 1995, you know? I had no mobile, no internet. I don't think I even had an address for him. So he just kind of disappeared.' Oliver looked over at me and I nodded. I thought of my falling-out with Rita. This was probably the longest we'd ever gone without talking. And even now, we'd texted. There was no way we could go nearly thirty years without speaking. Could we? 'Anyway, pretty soon I got into comedy, and girls, and so the gap kind of got filled.'

'But you're in touch now?'

'Not really.' Oliver shook the water off his hands and I passed him a tea towel. 'Not loads. I'd heard he'd come back up North a few years ago. That Mum and him were speaking again. She gave me Brendhan's number but I never called him. After all that time, it's kind of difficult to know what to say. You know?' I nodded. 'Ma would mention him, sometimes. She probably did the same to Brendhan. But honestly, I kind of forgot I had a brother most of the time. He had a little lifestyle block up there with some kids – two maybe? – and grew a little weed.' I tried not to look shocked. 'That's where Ma gets her supply.' I can't have been doing a very good job of acting cool because as soon as Oliver looked at me, he started to laugh. 'Quite the family, eh?'

20

Oliver was still sleeping on my sofa bed a week later, when Mum came over. I felt embarrassed having Oliver there, his washing drying on my radiators and his coffee on the kitchen side. Through my mum's eyes I could see the strangeness of this domestic set-up; the way I had let this man slide into my life, just as my real sister stormed out of it and the father of my child had run away.

'It's very clean, Nancy. Are you actually nesting?' Mum looked across at the empty dining table and the neat sofa.

'It's a bit early for that.' I scratched the sore skin beneath my bra.

'Not necessarily,' she said. 'Judy Miles went into labour after just twenty-six weeks. Poor George spent the first three months of his life in hospital. Although you'd never know it now.'

Why, I wondered, did everyone want to tell me these stories? Last week, when I was buying apples, a woman in the greengrocer had started telling me about the haemorrhage that had nearly killed her daughter during labour.

'Well, I'm not preparing to have an extraordinarily premature baby by rearranging my bookshelves,' I said. 'To be honest, this is mostly Oliver.'

'Really?' Although Oliver was in the kitchen, Mum turned around to face his direction. 'So it's like that, is it?'

Before I could ask what like that was, Oliver came back in with a cafetière and three mugs. 'Do you have milk, Anne? Or sugar?' He came close to my mum. She would be able to smell his aftershave.

'Just milk, please.'

'Good on ya.'

I smiled at Mum. I wasn't sure why she had come over, although we had all talked about meeting up again, that time in the cafe. She was probably going to tell me I needed to fix things with Rita. She was right, and I wanted to, but I had no idea how. When we'd fought as children, one of us would buy a KitKat or start talking about *Neighbours* and that would be that. This cold, long-distance seething was new.

'Now, I don't really want to talk about the test, or the past today,' Mum began, looking across the table at me and Oliver. 'I know you probably both have questions and so do I but I don't think we're going to be able to answer any of them here.' She was addressing us as a barrister. We were her clients. And, I suspected, she was about to propose a deal. 'But, as you know, Nancy, after

Clive died, well . . .' She swallowed. 'I put almost everything in his studio. And, to my shame, I have left most of it there.' I could feel the effort she was making to modulate her voice. 'There was a will, of course. But there was no mention of . . .' She paused. 'Well, of any of this.' I looked at Oliver. He was biting the corner of his thumbnail. Instinctively, I ran my index finger across the hard slivers of skin that marked my own. 'I have been thinking about going through his studio for a while. And I would like you to come over and go through it with me. I've asked Rita and she's already agreed. Oliver, I very much doubt we'll find anything that references you or your mother but you may be useful in moving some of the trunks and larger furniture.'

The following Sunday, Oliver and I travelled south together on the Tube. Walking from the station, him tall and freshly shaven in a black T-shirt, me in trainers and maternity leggings, I thought how easily we could be mistaken for a couple. Just as Rita and I were. I didn't mind people making the mistake. It was nice to be read as the partner of a handsome man, rather than the pregnant ex of a scarpered commitment-phobe.

'Hello, you two.' Anne opened the door. 'Oh, sorry, Oliver. Shadwell! Leave him alone. Can I get you anything? Because Rita is on her way but we might as well make a start.'

The closer you got to Dad's studio, the taller the grass became. Thicker weeds, fallen leaves. The door was locked. I watched as Oliver stepped forward and took hold of Mum's shoulder as she tried, shakily, to fit the key. 'Here, I'll have a go.' Mum took a step back, looking small and a little nervous.

As we stepped in, I held my tongue against the roof of my mouth. Paintings leant against the walls like drunks, sometimes three deep. It smelled like damp tea towels and, in the corner, a paraffin heater the colour of Nescafé was absolutely cold. A table in the middle was covered in piles of paper. Box files. Manila envelopes. Ring binders. As well as cigar boxes, cassette tapes, film canisters and little fabric bags, each one full of Dad's life. I opened one of the ring binders at random and found about twenty quotes for double glazing. This was what Mum had been putting off sorting? This?

I picked up a matchbox and pushed it open with my big thumb. Inside was a piece of shell that looked like an oil spill.

Mum turned to Oliver. 'After Clive . . .' My phone started to vibrate. 'After Weymouth, two years ago, I was still working, so I just didn't really have the time to go through everything.' I pulled my phone out of my pocket. 'The girls didn't want to do it and nobody was using this space so I just . . .'

Callenda Medical Practice calling.

It was the midwife. I started towards the door, still holding the matchbox.

'Hello?'

'Hello, is that Ms Albany?'

'Yes, Nancy. Yes.' I slipped the matchbox into my pocket, opened the door and stepped outside.

'Hello, Nancy. This is Emily, one of the midwives here at Callenda. I'm just calling because I'm looking at the results of your latest blood test. It's nothing to worry about but you've got slightly high protein levels in your urine.'

I said nothing.

'So we'd like you to come in for another test. Would Friday week work for you?'

I blinked. 'Ah, what time?'

'Ten thirty?'

'I'll be at work but I suppose I could.'

'Good. Or I could do ten past four?'

'Fine. That's fine.'

Oliver was hunched over the table, a dark curl of hair in front of his face. It was like looking at a plaster cast of my father. If only, I thought. If only he were really here and we could just ask him.

'Great. OK, Nancy. See you then.'

Oliver was looking at some photos of Dad and one of his old dealers, Martin. It must have been taken in the early nineties. Dad was in a khaki smock, standing in front of a large canvas that looked like the bottom of a ship's hull. His abstract phase. He was looking at the camera from under thick eyelashes, his smile just a little mocking.

'That's at the Cording Gallery,' Mum said. 'It feels fairly redundant to say it but you look like him, Oliver.'

'I do, don't I?' Oliver rubbed the edge of the photo with his thumb. I heard knocking coming from the house.

'Oh, that's Rita,' said Mum, and went to answer the door.

I started looking through an accordion file that had been squatting on top of a VHS player. I'd expected paper but in fact each section held a different shadow puppet. They were hectically colourful, with thin dowel rods attached to each arm.

'I've never seen these before,' I said.

'They look like they're from Bali.'

I looked over at Oliver. 'Dad never went to Bali.'

I could hear Rita as the back door of the house slammed shut.

'What is it you actually want us to do, Anne? If it's just a case of sorting through all his papers, I'm not sure why the cuckoo has to be here.' The insult rang across the garden and I blushed.

'Rita.'

'I don't care if he hears me.'

Rita was wearing a zip-up blue boiler suit and an expression like burnt toast. Buster was twirling in circles next to her on the lawn like a drill.

'Hello, Rita,' I said. 'Or should I say Mario.'

'Hello.' I waited for the next bit. Hello, egg. Hello, lumpy. Hello, Nancelot. But it didn't come. We were still in the tundra, then.

'Hi, Rita.' Oliver was closing the latch on the shadow

puppets. 'Nice to see you. I hope you don't mind me being here.' He had heard. 'Anne asked if I could help move some of the heavier furniture.'

The air crackled.

'Yes. Well, you see, some of this' – Mum gestured at one of the bigger piles – 'like the old video player and the orange crates and things that are just taking up space. I thought, if we put the back seat down on my car and you, Oliver, helped load them in, then I could drive it all to the British Heart Foundation.'

'OK, but I really just don't see why we're doing this now.' Rita touched her nose. 'The three of us could have sorted out Dad's studio before.'

'But you didn't,' Mum replied, then she started wrenching open the shallow drawers of a plan chest. They were obviously too full and the noise as they stuck against their runners was like an animal in pain.

I went back to the table. Posters advertising exhibitions. A book on Dürer. Three rolls of masking tape. Nobody talked and Mum hadn't put on the radio. The smell of my father was held in every crease of paper and along the spine of every book. Rita was stacking tins of paint into a crate. Oliver was ferrying a nest of tables through to the front garden. I looked across at Mum. She was still standing by the plan chest, reading. Her body had gone very still.

'What's that?' I asked, taking the excuse to shift the weight of my distended stomach during the short walk to her corner.

Mum whipped round. 'Oh, nothing. Just old papers, like all this stuff.' She shut the drawer with a screech and stuffed something into her back pocket. 'All the shit your father left me to clear up.' Her voice was odd. She lifted her chin into the room. 'Anyway, maybe it's time to have a cup of tea.'

Rita had turned to look at us. Had she heard the same note in Mum's voice? Seen her face? Noticed the fire blanket of distraction being thrown over something? What was in that drawer that had startled her?

21

'I can't believe it.'

Oliver and I were sitting on a bench in Springfield Park under a copper beech tree the colour of bruises. It had been a week since that awkward afternoon, going through Dad's studio, and I was glad to be this side of the river instead. A group of small children in white shirts and cream dresses were throwing handfuls of grass at three bored-looking mallards. The sun was shining.

'What?' I could feel the baby squirming against my ribs. The midwife had said that this much movement was a good sign; that what I was feeling were kicks, meaning the baby was facing the right direction. Facing the ground. Facing the hole that was an inch too small for its head.

'I've just got a message from Brendhan. He actually is coming to London,' said Oliver.

'Really? When?'

'This week. Apparently he got some amazing deal and just booked it.' Oliver looked genuinely surprised.

'Does he have somewhere to stay?'

'Ah, nah, I said he could just share your bed.' I swung my head round but Oliver was smiling. 'He's got an Airbnb in Earl's Court.'

'Why Earl's Court?'

Oliver scratched the soft skin behind his ear. 'Kangaroo Valley? Haven't you heard? It's kind of the law. If you're Antipodean and arrive in London, you go to Earl's Court. Just like British people go to Christchurch.'

'I've never been to Earl's Court.'

'Well, exactly.' Oliver started typing again. 'Proves my point.'

The baby kicked, hard this time. The feeling, like a bolt of electricity, made me gasp.

'Hey, you OK there?' Oliver put his hand on my arm.

'Yes, just the baby going mental. I think they've got a knee under my rib.'

'Far out,' said Oliver, looking down at my side. 'Isn't it incredible what the human body can do? Well, what your human body can do?' There was another kick, but further forward this time. 'Jeez, did you see that, Nancy? Your T-shirt actually moved.'

'See it? I got the 3D version,' I replied. Oliver was still smiling and looking at my front. 'Do you want to see if it happens again? The midwife says they can feel the heat of your hand on my skin, apparently.'

Oliver flicked his eyes up to meet mine. 'You don't mind? I don't want it to hurt you.'

I pushed my denim jacket behind me and pulled up my T-shirt. It felt reckless but also strangely joyful:

having watery sunshine on my skin for the first time in what felt like months. Having my bare stomach out in front of Oliver. 'Go for it.'

Oliver put his hand right over my belly button. Nothing happened. I had an unlikely twinge of performance anxiety, not wanting to deliver an anticlimax to what had, up until then, been such an intimate moment between us.

'What's with you, kung fu?' Oliver said, lightly tapping my skin with the flat of his forefinger. Then, as if in response, there came another kick. More of a knee this time. 'Holy shit!' Oliver looked up at me, a smile so big I could see his gums. 'What a bruiser!'

I looked down at the purple, mottled skin. At Oliver's dark brown hand. The black hairs at his wrist.

'Sorry, I'll take my hand away now,' he said quickly.

'Ha, don't worry.' I pulled my T-shirt back down. For a few seconds, neither of us spoke. Then I said: 'How long's he coming for? Brendhan?'

'A couple of weeks.'

I licked my lips. I was gearing myself up. 'And how long do you think you're going to stay, Oliver?' We had talked about it before. But not for a while.

'Ah, I can clear out any time, Nancy. All you have to do is ask. Especially with the baby and everything.'

'No, I'm not saying that.' I didn't want him to go. Not now.

'Nah, seriously. I'm sure I can find a room. Or I might even be able to get one of those service apartments for a bit.'

'Oliver, I'm not saying that. I like having you in the flat.' I did. I liked coming home to my dinner already made. I liked having someone there to take in my parcels. I liked – although I would never say it to him – having a man around.

'Sure?'

'Yes. I just wondered if you'd talked to your agent or whatever; if you had an idea of how long you might be here.'

'Ah, well, I'm doing a screen test for a TV panel show thing in a couple of weeks and I'm getting gigs so my agent's happy. I was thinking I'd probably stay for June at least? I checked with Ma's home and she's fine. Not been asking about me or anything. I doubt she even remembers she has a son, to be honest.'

'Oh, Oliver, I'm sorry.'

'Yeah, thanks. It's hard. But then you know that – losing a parent.'

I nodded. 'I'm sure it's not the same, though,' I said. 'With Dad, he just went swimming one day and never came back.' I tried not to think about the pale blue sea. About the texture of his skin in the morgue. The police's tentative questions about his state of mind. 'I can't imagine losing your mum the way you are.'

'How do you picture him?' Oliver asked. 'Like, when you remember him, how old is he? I think in my head Ma is always about forty-five.' He lets out a dry half-laugh. 'Shit, I'm nearly forty-five.'

I smile and close my eyes. 'Well, to be honest, I usually

picture him doing something. Like bending over and mixing paint, or chopping carrots, sharpening his pencils. He was always, like, low-level busy.' Oliver didn't say anything. 'And I suppose I remember him from when I was about ten? When his hair was still all black and he wore DMs and smoked cigars.'

'Cigars?'

'Yeah.' I laughed. 'He'd use jam jars as ashtrays. Mum didn't like him smoking in the house so he'd either be in his studio or out in the garden. Fiddling with a plant that had fallen over, a cigar in the crook of his fingers.'

'Now I'm picturing Winston Churchill.'

'Oh God, no, he'd have hated that,' I said. 'He was a real pacifist – took us to CND rallies at the weekend and stuff. We usually ended up going to the pub on the way home for chips and lemonade and his friends would all play darts with me and Rita.'

'Sounds fun.'

'One time, Rita hit a bullseye, first throw, and Dad carried her through the Alexandra on his shoulders singing "We Are The Champions". He loved being the centre of attention like that.'

'Huh.' Oliver touched his forehead. 'Maybe that's where I get it from.'

I didn't turn to look at him properly. Suddenly, the stakes of this conversation were too high. I worried that eye contact might make me start crying.

'And when is Brendhan coming?' I changed the subject.

'End of this week.'

'But that's exciting.' I tried to sound excited. 'Having your brother over.' Since that first phone call, where I'd seen Brendhan through the glass face of Oliver's phone, I had hardly thought of the rattling, ginger man who shared the other half of my half-brother's DNA. 'Isn't it? Exciting? I mean, you can show him around. He can come to your show.'

'Jesus.' Oliver pulled his hands through his hair. 'My show.'

'What?' The little children by the pond were now throwing small sticks and pebbles at the ducks. They'd gone from feeding to taunting.

'All that stuff in my show about Ma. I can't do that in front of Brendhan.'

'Why not?'

Oliver gave a sigh. 'Before Brendhan left, it wasn't exactly the Waltons.' He pulled out a packet of cigarettes, tapped the top, then put them back in his pocket. 'Like, I have this memory.' Oliver looked at me, as though deciding whether to carry on. I considered touching his shoulder but didn't. 'I'm at the kitchen table and Brendhan's holding my hand down, slamming a butter knife into the gap between my fingers. You know? The old cowboy trick.' Oliver mimed it on his knee. 'Faster and faster? And Mum's just standing at the stove, with a ciggie in the ashtray, staring out of the window. I'm shouting and hollering and Brendhan's laughing his nut off.' Oliver was trying to tell it like a joke. 'I . . . I start crying and, well, Mum just turns up the radio and carries on frying eggs.'

I swallowed. 'But he's come here to visit you,' I said at last.

'He's come here because his wife was fucking a tomato-seller.'

'A tomato *seed*-seller,' I corrected.

Oliver laughed. 'True.'

'Aren't all older brothers a bit like that?' I looked out across the park. 'All older siblings, actually. Rita used to wrap me up in the curtains and then attack me with a p—'

Across the lawn, I saw him. Green shirt, short black hair, the turn of his feet. It was Gamar. Walking alone across the park with one hand in his pocket. He had come to find me. He knew the cafe, the marshes, the view. He was here to tell me that he loved me. That he wanted me back. That he wanted to father the child we'd made.

'Nancy?'

I stood up, ready to run. My heart crashing around my chest. The baby divebombing my abdomen.

'Nancy, are you all right?'

But then Gamar turned to his right. The shape of his head was wrong. The slope of his shoulders. The width of his neck. This was just a man. A stranger. Still staring, I sat slowly back down.

'Sorry.' I was full of adrenaline. 'I thought I saw someone I knew.'

'Must have been someone pretty intense.'

Stupid. Needy. Childish, clingy. Stuck. My mouth was dry. Incapable. Ugly. Mad.

'My ex. You know, Gamar. The ex.'

'Oh, the ex. You still not heard from him?'

'No.' I felt embarrassed.

'But he said he wants nothing to do with the baby?' Did Oliver agree with Gamar? Take his side? He was a man, after all. A man whose own father had left when he was a child. Maybe Oliver saw no need for fathers?

'He's disappeared. Again.' I touched my earthquake stomach. 'He came, threw my entire life off course and then just left. Disappeared.'

'Sounds familiar,' Oliver said. I bit my lip. 'But, just speaking as a guy – and obviously I don't know your ex,' he added quickly, 'I don't think you should spend the next few months waiting for Gamar.' He was rubbing his knuckles over each other. 'Like, maybe he just needs some time to get his head round it all. Maybe he'll change his mind. But if you want him to be involved, you're probably going to have to go to him and say it.'

'Do you really think so?' I asked, looking over at the children by the pond. Same hair, same limbs, same skin: they were like a family from a children's book.

'Worth a shot,' Oliver said.

22

Dear Gamar,

I thought I'd email, rather than message on WhatsApp. I've got an extra scan coming up because of my high Papp-A levels. I still don't know if you want to be kept up to date with this – or how often you're even able to check your emails at the moment. But I thought it was probably the right thing to do.

I bit the corner of my mouth until I tasted metal.

I'm due on August 8th and I'm going to do it at the birth unit in Homerton Hospital, unless something goes wrong. I've asked Mum to be my birth partner but you're allowed two.

It felt like begging. I deleted the final sentence.

I've asked Mum to be one of my birth partners.

Better.

I did a tour of the birth unit on my own after work one evening, and felt so lonely and so scared I cried.

Delete.

Sometimes, I wonder what would happen if I died. I picture them cutting the baby out of my dead body and giving it to Rita.

Delete. Delete. Delete.

I will be finishing work for the summer holidays on July 22nd.

You don't care.

This all could have been so different if you'd just loved me, you bastard.

Delete.

Hope you're well.

A lie.

Best wishes.

Delete.

Nancy.

23

'Nancy? Nancy, are you all right?' Oliver was in my room. 'You were crying out in your sleep. I didn't know what was wrong.'

He came over to the bed as I sat up. 'I dreamt I lost the baby,' I said. He sat on top of the duvet, pinning me to the mattress, and stroked my hair. I slipped my hand under to feel my belly. Still. Nothing. Oh God. Oh God oh God oh God oh God. 'I can't feel anything, Oliver. I can't feel anything.'

'Shit. OK. Um. Let's call the midwife.'

It was dark outside. The middle of the night.

'There must be an emergency number or something – 111? I mean, 999?' Oliver pulled out his phone.

'Wait.' I remembered something from one of the leaflets. After my last scan. 'Just wait. I need ice. A big glass of very cold water.'

Oliver rushed out and came back with a pint glass. There was a thick green line at the bottom and peas floating on the surface.

'You didn't have any ice but this is cold.'

I drank the pea water in one go, using my teeth like a barrier. Like a whale sifting for krill. I stood up and started jumping on the spot. Tears were still flowing down my face.

'Oh yer girl. That'll do it,' Oliver said, standing beside me. 'Anything yet?'

'No. I'm going to lie down on my left side.' I got back on to the bed. Oliver sat on the floor and took my hand. We waited. I tried to breathe but the juddering cries kept getting caught in my chest. I had felt the icy water travelling down my throat. I closed my eyes and tried to picture it squeezing along my intestines. Past the baby. A rush of ice as it lay, crumpled in my womb. Suddenly, I felt a flicker of electricity. A lurch. Was that it? I stayed absolutely still. A twitch. Then, at last, a definite push. Elbow, leg, shoulder; I couldn't tell. But something hard was moving against me. 'Oh, thank God.'

'You felt something?'

'Yes.' The room was orange-black. Oliver was a shadow on the ground. My eyes felt as wide as manholes. 'Do you want to feel it?' I was in my nightie, XL from Walthamstow Market. Red with a frill across the chest.

'Where?'

I put his hand on the spot. We waited. The seconds crept past like guilty men. Then, a kick. A real kick this time. A lumping against my skin that felt like frustration.

'That's it!' Oliver kept his hand against my front and stroked it, just slightly with his thumb. 'Far out.'

I let out a long, slow breath.

Oliver hadn't met Brendhan at the airport. He hadn't gone to Earl's Court. And although Oliver had finished his run at the Soho Theatre, he was still doing gigs most evenings – above pubs, in little arts venues I'd never heard of. Which meant that we mainly saw each other after school and at weekends. He would sometimes make me a meal and ask about the baby. I would congratulate him on a gig and sometimes give him directions to an audition. Only once had I ever heard someone with him: a woman's laugh; but she was gone by the morning and I didn't want to know the details. Not in my flat.

I had forgotten what day Brendhan was meant to land; perhaps I'd never been told. But one Wednesday morning, Oliver appeared in the doorway of the kitchen early. He still never came out of his room in less than boxer shorts and a shirt but his feet were bare.

'Hey, how are you doing? How's the bump?'

'We're both OK, thanks,' I said, absentmindedly putting a hand on the side of my stomach, where I imagined my baby's back to be.

'Good. I'm going to meet Brendhan tomorrow for dinner if you want to come? Some place in Chinatown.' Oliver was biting the skin next to his fingernail again and there were bags under his eyes.

'Ah.' I thought of the bus. The ache in my legs. Sitting at a table while my mouth filled with the sour wash of hunger. 'Would you like me to come?'

'Yeah, I mean, whatever, but if you don't fancy it . . .' Oliver looked somehow shrunken. I thought of his story about the knife and the frying eggs. I thought of the man I'd seen on the phone. His thick neck and meaty hands. Oliver was nervous. I felt sorry for him. Like me, he was the little sibling but, unlike me, he seemed scared of the older one. He wouldn't have asked me, surely, otherwise.

'Then, sure. What time are you meeting? I might as well come in straight from work.' The jolting number 55 as it wheezed through traffic. The stop and start that twisted my stomach into vomiting. The heat of the engines and people's breath.

'Like, seven? But if you wanted, I could move it earlier?'

'No, seven is fine.' Seven was midnight.

'I thought maybe we should invite Rita.'

'Really?'

'She might not be my biggest fan but she is your sister.'

24

The restaurant had high ceilings and plastic plants. The smell of ginger and meat was almost overpowered by the aftershave of the waiter who met me as I came through the door.

'Hi, there should be a table for seven o'clock under the name Oliver?'

'Yes, come this way.' The waiter was wearing a very small, very tight waistcoat. As he walked, his shoes made a clip-clop noise against the tiled floor.

We walked past large family groups: children drawing on iPads, tissues, bags, adults talking over their heads. I was surprised by the places Oliver knew in this city after just a couple of months. I knew he'd been getting a lot more work than he'd first expected; that's partly why he'd stayed. Maybe all those producers and directors and TV people had been taking him out for meals in Soho. He'd been meeting cool people and doing glamorous things, while I'd stayed at home and grown like a volcano.

'Here you are, madam.' The waiter gestured towards a table in the corner, under a red wall hanging.

All I could see was a square back. Actually square, like an oven, under a black shirt. Peeping round the edge of the back was Oliver, also in a black shirt, drinking a beer.

'Hello,' I said, and felt my arm rise up into the air to wave. I was less than a metre away from them.

'Nancy! Hi.' Oliver stood up to greet me but it was impossible to hug or kiss because of the back. The back blocked us almost completely. 'Nancy, this is Brendhan. Brendhan, Nancy.'

The square man grunted as he stood up and slowly turned around to face me. His face was a deep, rusty brown and his greying red hair, swept off his face, was thick and long. 'Nancy! Good to meet ya.' His hand was the size of an oven mitt, with smudged tattoos across his knuckles. 'Why don't you plant yourself down here and we can get cracking.' He pulled out a chair as if it weighed less than a cup.

'Thanks.' I looked at the gap between the table and the wall. 'I might have to go here, by Oliver. I'm not sure I'd fit in there,' I explained.

'Ah, yeah, how many weeks along are you?' asked Brendhan, and the way he looked at my belly made me feel bovine.

'Thirty-one,' I replied, banging my bag into the table so a wave of beer slopped against the edge of Oliver's glass, threatening to tip it over.

'Ah, has the little bastard finally moved down so you

can breathe again?' As he sat down, Brendhan made a noise like an old sofa.

'Ummm, perhaps.'

'I always knew when Cherie was in the final trimester because she could suddenly shout at me again.' Brendhan's laugh roared out across the whole restaurant.

I smiled and turned to Oliver. 'I did invite Rita but I doubt she'll come. She hasn't replied to my message.' I took a sip of water. It was room temperature and tasted slightly of lemon.

'Rita?' Brendhan leant on to the table. As the sleeves of his shirt rode up, I saw two patches of thick, orange hair. I thought of the bracken at the end of summer in the Lake District. I thought of pine needles and nettle stings. 'Is this the brick shithouse of a sister I've been hearing about?'

'That's me.' I looked up to see Rita in a pair of black dungarees. Her hair was loose and she was wearing a silver nose ring. My heart leapt. She looked beautiful. I had missed her.

'Shit,' Oliver said under his breath.

'Well, from one shithouse to another' – Brendhan stood up and thrust his meaty paw at Rita – 'it's good to meet you. I'm Brendhan. But you probably guessed that.'

I could see some kind of struggle happening across Rita's face. Like she couldn't quite decide where to set it.

'Actually, I thought you were the waitress.'

Brendhan threw his head back and laughed like a petrol-powered mower. I could see the black teeth crowded in behind his gold one. Then he slapped his hand down on Rita's shoulder and said, 'Good to meet you, Rita.'

I was amazed she had come. Maybe Rita had wanted to make a scene; to shame Oliver into leaving London. Maybe she was itching for a confrontation. Maybe she was curious. What I really wanted was for her to be worried about me: protective, jealous, even possessive.

'So, you're the brother of the brother?' Rita pulled out her chair and hovered behind it as Brendhan sat down. I knew her. She wanted to sit down last. She wanted to be taller than him. Even just for a minute, she wanted to be able to look down on this sun-baked giant.

'I guess you could say that.' Something seemed to be wrong with Brendhan's neck; instead of turning just his head to look at you, he rotated his whole body. I thought of the grey columns of kebab meat in takeaway windows.

'And are there any more of you?' Rita asked.

'No.' Oliver had been looking at Rita with a hard, steady gaze. He was neither hostile, nor friendly. He didn't lower his eyelashes or rub the back of his neck. He wasn't using any of his charm on Rita this time. Maybe he was too stressed to bother. It was almost ugly.

'When I found Oliver on that DNA site—' I began.

'Must have bust your gusset!' Brendhan interrupted, then slapped the table, clearly delighted at his own joke. I winced. The atmosphere around the table felt tight and stiff and hard; wound taut with unsaid thoughts and vicious suspicions. And here was this man, this bear, so unpredictable and explosive and dangerous. If I could just keep it polite – if I could just make things seemly, maybe we'd all get out of here unharmed.

'Would you ladies like anything to drink?' The waiter was back, appearing at the table as if from nowhere.

'I think we'll have a bottle of the . . .' Rita scanned the wine list. She was doing that very specific combination of geography and maths that a wine list demands. 'Château Les Moines. And' – she looked around the table – 'four glasses.' I was annoyed that Rita was taking over.

'Rita, I'm not—' But Rita put her hand on the inside of my elbow and I stopped speaking. The touch of her, after all these months, was like being thrown against a wall. Like the taste of my own blood, like getting back into bed after a long train journey.

'Could we also have a very large jug of water for the table and a bottle of sparkling?' Rita continued. 'And no ice or lemon near any of that. Thank you so much.'

'I'll have another of these, if you're going by the tap, mate,' Brendhan said, passing his glass over his enormous shoulder to the man behind him.

'And for you, sir?' The waiter turned to Oliver with just a hint of a smile.

'I'll be good with the wine, thanks.' And for a moment, I wondered if this was Oliver's way of drawing a line of separation between him and Brendhan. If he was trying to communicate something to me.

A damp silence descended. To talk about blood and love and fathers would be too big a leap right now. So I turned to Brendhan.

'So, Brendhan, are you going to watch one of Oliver's gigs while you're here? Or have you already seen it in New Zealand?'

A flicker of discomfort crossed Brendhan's face. The same look crept over Oliver, as though in a mirror.

'Ah, well, living up on a farm, you know, I don't get to the city as much as some folks,' Brendhan answered, rubbing his great meaty hands together. I realized I had accidentally turned their estrangement into small talk. Of course Brendhan hadn't seen Oliver's show. They hadn't spoken in years. Why had I asked that?

'Nah, truth is, I found my wife, Cherie, in a pretty compromising position with the woman who sells us our salad seeds.' The woman? Every time I'd heard this story I'd just assumed the seed-seller had been a man. Brendhan smiled. 'Right there on the kitchen floor, next to the chook feed.' Out of the corner of my eye, I saw Rita's eyebrows rise. 'Anyway, she told me last month that she's filing for a divorce. Wants to take the kids to live with her new lover down the coast and so I'm probably going to have to give up our block.' Brendhan ran his top teeth over the short stubble below his bottom lip. 'What with all that going on, I kinda fancied getting away for a bit. So I thought I'd take you kind folks up on the invitation.' He leant towards me and out of the corner of his grizzled mouth added: 'Even if you didn't really mean it.'

'Your wife's gay?' Rita cut in before I could start my half-hearted denial.

'I guess you'd say she was always a queer one.' Brendhan smiled again. I felt my knees press together.

'Is that meant to be a joke?' Rita looked like vinegar.

'Well, I'm not exactly laughing at the situation myself,' Brendhan replied. 'Why? Are you a lesbian, Rita?'

'Yes, I am.' Rita picked up her fork and started pushing the prongs into the tablecloth. My God. I looked at Oliver but he seemed to have turned inside himself. He was looking in the direction of Brendhan's neck, completely still. His hands in his lap.

'Well then, you might understand it.' Brendhan scratched the back of his head. 'I knew Cherie had had girlfriends before we got together.' He smiled. 'So had I, matter of fact. But when we got married I thought that meant we'd both cut out any other shenanigans. You know, forsaking all others and all that.'

'When did you get married?' Oliver's brown eyes had come back into focus. He turned his head a little and I could see the angle of his profile. He was like a bird, inspecting a nearby beast.

'Back in 2012,' Brendhan answered.

'Did you invite Ma?'

'Nah, mate. No family.' Brendhan had turned away from Rita to field his brother's questions. 'You could have come, I guess, but it was mainly just local folks and a couple of guys from my Bluff days.'

'But not your dad?' Oliver's question was cut over by Rita, asking in a sharper voice:

'So the fact that your wife slept with a woman isn't the reason you're getting a divorce?'

Brendhan looked back to Rita. 'Of course that's the reason. At least, that's her reason. I don't want to get divorced at all.' I felt a pull in my chest. Gamar. 'But she's met someone she wants to be with more than me and I just have to bite the nettle and suck it up.' Brendhan laid his palms open on the table. 'If that's not mixing my metaphors.'

'But if she's gay . . .' Rita looked ready to continue but Brendhan ground his enormous body round so he was facing her, knees square, shoulders down. It was hard not to feel threatened by his size.

'Well, I guess I'd just hoped that she could love me the way I loved her.'

By the time the food came, Rita and Brendhan were talking aggressively about nitrate fertilizers. I worried they were arguing – their conversation definitely had the cadence of an argument – but as far as I could tell, they were actually just agreeing about the threat to rivers and wells very loudly. Rita was sitting back with her arms behind her head, framing her face with her clay-brick biceps. Brendhan was using a chopstick to scratch between his shoulder blades.

I had ordered bean curd with ginger and spring onion. More onion. The plate was slick with a shiny brown oil. It coated the rice, made everything taste of bitter allium. Oliver was eating king prawns with cashew nuts. I hadn't eaten a prawn since finding out I was pregnant; I longed for one. Probably because I'd been told I couldn't have them.

'How did your gig go in Camden?' I asked, sipping my fizzy water. I felt a tightness in my side that didn't seem to shift, however I sat. Perhaps it was trapped wind.

'There were a couple of women, absolutely soaked, who kept asking if I was from the Strokes,' said Oliver.

'Soaked?'

'Yeah, drunk.' Oliver took a sip of wine. 'Which is always tricky in a small crowd because you never know if they're going to try and throw the whole gig off course.'

'How do you handle hecklers?'

I could tell from his face that this was a boring question. Oliver had probably been asked it in every interview he'd ever done. But then, when had he ever asked me about teaching?

'Ah, it's different with different crowds.' Oliver stood his chopsticks up on his plate like legs.

'Like what?' I wanted him to give me a line. To make me laugh. I wanted to laugh off this brown, oily tension clinging to the table. Between Oliver and Rita. Oliver and Brendhan. Me and Rita.

'Oh, like, if it's a guy, I'll ask if he took up rugby as a way to cover the brain damage.'

I winced. Opposite me, Brendhan was eating spare ribs and honey sauce with his bare hands. Pieces of chilli and drops of sauce were slopping down his fingers, which he occasionally rubbed on his shirt. And yet here was Oliver, talking like a Neanderthal. I didn't like this side to Oliver – the one I'd seen in flashes on stage. The version of him that seemed desperate to be the alpha male. Although, looking at his big brother, I could guess where that urge had come from.

'Whenever we went to restaurants, Dad would tuck his napkin into his collar, like a huge tie, to make us laugh,' I said, a little too loudly, talking into the middle of the table.

'Not every time,' Rita corrected me. 'He wasn't a clown.'

'Well—' I tried to assert some authority against Rita but was interrupted.

'I don't reckon my dad ever went in a restaurant that had napkins,' said Brendhan, his beard glistening with oil, 'unless they were made of paper.'

'Was he funny then?' Oliver was looking at me, his eyes suddenly sharp.

'Who, Dad?' I glanced at Rita, then back to Oliver. I felt both of them willing me to tell a version of my father that they could recognize. And yet they were coming at him from different directions. 'Well, yes, quite.'

'He thought he was funny,' said Rita, 'which isn't always the same thing.'

'Oh, come on, Rita, he made us laugh loads, especially when we were little.' Rita's critical tone had made me spring to Dad's defence. Although perhaps I was defending Oliver. It was easy for Rita to sneer, but Oliver obviously wanted to hear more about Dad, wanted to understand this half of his genes. It made me feel sorry for him. Oliver had put a girdle round the earth. Oliver had come to England to try and find out what kind of man had made him because he wanted to know what kind of man he, himself, might be. 'He used to do lots of funny voices. A bit like *The Goon Show* – did you have the Goons in New Zealand?'

'Before my time.'

'They were sort of like Monty Python before Monty Python, and our dad . . .' The phrase tripped me up like a tree root. Who was I talking to? Who was included? I felt Rita's eyes on me. A tang of pain. I swallowed. '. . . loved Spike Milligan.' The blush was creeping up my neck. 'What was that thing he used to say? Rita?'

Rita was almost gleeful at my discomfort. She had also drunk three glasses of wine. 'I'm a hero with coward's legs.' I forced air out of my mouth as if laughing. 'He did have real chicken legs, actually,' Rita added, looking across the table at Oliver. Was this her attempt at including the cuckoo? Bringing him in on a collective joke against our father? Or was she merely marking out her territory?

'Yes, and he insisted on wearing shorts all the time,' I said. 'Particularly in his studio, when he was painting. Even in the cold.' I had probably said this to Oliver before. How do you conjure a dead man? His spice rack; the sound of him adjusting a belt; white spirit and oil paints; Brian Eno; the way he sipped his too-hot coffee: short, short, long.

'So does it get real cold over here?' Maybe Brendhan had noticed Oliver's hunger. Maybe he felt his brother's drift towards another nest. 'Up in Kerikeri we never really dip below ten degrees. 'S why it's so good for growing.'

'Last winter I had ice on the inside of my windows,' said Rita.

'Only because your boiler had broken.' Was I, in fact, the jealous one? Rita was clearly trying to impress Brendhan; perform some rugged version of herself for his delight. And she was still being very cool towards me. Was that why I was challenging her? Maybe I just wanted to puncture this swaggering, brutish act she was putting on for Brendhan. Why was she doing that anyway? Because he was also the big sibling? Big and broad and practical? Or, I thought, looking at the way Rita was holding her shoulders, turning away from Oliver, was this her way of hurting the younger brother? Was she being friendly to Brendhan in order to further ostracize Oliver?

'It was minus three even in London,' Rita replied. 'Up in Scotland it was, like, minus fourteen.'

'No, thank you,' said Brendhan, slipping his middle

and forefinger into the gap between shirt buttons to scratch his stomach. 'Too cold for me. Tamanuiterā.'

'Since when did you start dropping in Māori gods?' The way Oliver looked at Brendhan – the belittling sneer – made me push my elbow hard into the table. I didn't like where this was going.

'You what, mate?'

'Tamanuiterā? I doubt there were many people calling up the sacred sun god down in Bluff.'

'Careful, little brother.'

'You're Pākehā,' Oliver said, with apparent satisfaction.

'What's Pākehā?' asked Rita.

'White people,' answered Oliver, smiling. 'Like me and Brendhan.'

'No way.' Brendhan bristled. 'Ma is Māori. So are we.'

'She's only half.' Oliver picked up his wine glass. 'Look at us! You're bloody ginger, mate. You're probably more Scottish than you are Māori.' Oliver intentionally mispronounced the word Māori. Brendhan pushed back his chair, knocking his plate with a big meaty elbow, causing one of the water glasses to fall over. He stood over Oliver.

'Don't call me a Pākehā and I won't knock your teeth out.'

Awful silence. I pushed the prongs of the fork into my open palm. The pain in my stomach was still there.

'Cool it down, Brendhan.' Brendhan swivelled round to look at Rita. 'You're not the only mixed-race person at this table, you know.'

25

By the time the dessert menu came, I was exhausted. My mouth tasted of batteries and a shelf of acid was sitting in my gullet. I thought about breech deliveries. I pictured myself standing in the birth suite with a pair of pink, squirming legs hanging out of me. A squid crawling from my body. For as long as I could remember, images like this had arrived in my mind without warning or intention. In primary school, I'd pictured slicing my eyeball open with a paper cut. Or pushing my friend into the road. Tiny films of murder, violence and pain would play out in my mind before I had a chance to intervene. They had frightened me then. I had learned the word schizophrenia. I had worried, as I would worry and worry again, that I was losing my sanity.

Until one evening, when I was about twelve, I had told Dad one of my films: a particularly troubling image of holding Rita's head down in the bath. I admitted, through quivering lips, that I'd pictured the bubbles stopping and the tension in my arm going soft. I had watched his face for horror. I waited to be told I was dangerous, insane.

But instead Dad had just smiled, his eyebrows sad. That was just an intrusive thought, he'd told me. They had a name and happened to lots of people. In fact, they happened to him. He had a whole series of paintings inspired by his intrusive thoughts, he went on: legs burning in a fire; teeth being hit by a hammer; pushing a buggy into the river. The last one had unsettled me. Had I been the child in the buggy? Had he pushed me along the South Bank picturing my buggy tipping into the choppy brown filth? Still, I had been relieved to learn I wasn't the only person haunted by these slivers of horror. And now, every time I imagined pushing a kebab skewer through my belly button or pictured someone stamping on my pregnant belly, I could tell myself that they were nothing more than a blip – a psychological hiccup over which I had no control.

'You all right, Nancy?' Brendhan was looking at me. 'You're looking a little ... ah ... crook.'

'Yes, fine. Just a bit of heartburn, I think.' A gnawing, wrenching pain that seemed to be creeping down my belly. Was this heartburn? Perhaps.

'Ah, jeez. Cherie had that awful. And how far along did you say you were?'

'Thirty-one weeks,' I repeated.

Brendhan was beaming, his earlier set-to with Oliver apparently completely forgotten. 'You got a picture?'

As I took out my phone, Brendhan started waving enthusiastically at the waiter. I didn't hear what he said – I was looking at the black and white scan picture of my baby, their face lit as though from an overhead spotlight. This was them at twenty weeks. Their skull was a hard, dark shadow. Their body too tightly squeezed to see. When I finally looked up, the waiter was approaching with a small glass of cloudy-looking water.

'For you, madam,' he said. 'A first for us, I must say.'

'It's just baking soda,' said Brendhan, leaning forward on to the table, his giant shoulder pushing into Rita's arm. 'Perfectly safe, but works wonders on that stomach acid.' Brendhan laughed, pulling a hand through his ginger-grey hair in just the way Oliver ruffled his own.

'Are you sure it's safe to drink?'

Brendhan nodded, sucking a lungful of air through his teeth. 'Yep. Baking soda is high alkali so when it comes into contact with the stomach acid it just sort of neutralizes it. Stops the stinging.'

Instinctively, I turned to Rita for confirmation.

'Well, from a chemical point of view that makes sense,' she said. 'I'm sure you could google it but there's bicarbonate of soda in, like, scones, so I don't think it can do much harm.'

'Thank you, Brendhan.' The taste made me shiver. It was neither salty nor sweet. Rather, it was like drinking chalk. In fact, it tasted exactly how I remember drinking the glass of water that Dad kept his watercolour brushes in. Why had he let me do that? Drink a glass of diluted paint? Or had he just not been looking?

'I'm going outside for a smoke.' He didn't exactly

stomp but Oliver was clearly feeling left out. I knew that Rita would find that kind of petulance disgusting, particularly in a man. For the last few minutes I had felt Rita finally, perhaps, thawing towards me; and I didn't want Oliver to kick a dent in it by going off in a sulk.

'Excuse me,' I said, standing up.

In the street outside, cabbage leaves and crumpled plastic bottles stuck to the pavement. I quickly found Oliver, pulling on a cigarette.

'Are you all right, Oliver?'

'Yeah.'

The smell of the smoke was like hot tarmac, sweet chemicals. The sharp stabs in my side were easier to ignore out here. 'What are you looking at?'

Oliver took the cigarette between his teeth, suddenly looking like a guitar player, and pointed at the tall red-brick building opposite. 'Just that. I still haven't got used to having such old buildings everywhere.' His consonants were a little soft. 'Like, you know, New Zealand is the most beautiful island on earth.' He took a drag. 'But there is something pretty awesome about walking down a pair of nine-hundred-year-old steps or standing in front of a four-hundred-year-old building.'

I nodded. 'Is it weird having Brendhan here?'

He shrugged. 'It's weird seeing Brendhan full stop.'

As I moved my foot, it stuck ever so slightly to the ground, as though it were laminated. 'Families are weird.'

'Sure are.' Oliver tapped his ash on to a paper cup

someone had put on top of the bollard. 'You know, Nancy?'

'Yes?'

'I know I haven't met the guy but this Gamar fella' – Oliver sniffed – 'he doesn't really sound like he's up to much.'

'Mmm.'

'And, like, I know you want him to be a dad to your kid' – Oliver looked down at the floor – 'but it doesn't look like he's going to do that any time soon.' The sadness I felt at this was tinged with embarrassment. I didn't like being pitied. Even by Oliver. 'But, like, I could always help out.'

I looked over at Oliver. His eyes were like beach glass. Was he drunk? 'What do you mean?' The unswallowed acid was still resting on my chest.

'Ah, I don't know, but I reckon I could make a pretty good, like, duncle.'

'Duncle?' I laughed. So he was drunk. This was just the kind of grand, gallant gesture that drunk men liked to make in order to feel heroic. This, or something petulant like punching through a window.

'Yeah, you know. Like part stepdad, part uncle.' And yet, Oliver's voice didn't sound slurred by drink. 'I could take him to the park, help you with the cooking and cleaning, do some babysitting.'

Him? So he had decided I was having a boy? I looked down at Oliver's hand, nervously tapping his cigarette. I remembered him crouching by my bed that awful night, as I'd waited, frozen in fear, for the baby to move. I remembered him feeling the baby kick in the park. The smoothies he made me and the scan picture he'd stuck to the fridge and the way I sometimes caught him looking at me as I rubbed my back in the afternoon.

But really, did I need this man to babysit my child? Was that where I had come to? Not a father but a duncle; a man who looked like my father but knew nothing of our real family; a man with no partner, no children, no home. A man who had come to stay for a few nights on my sofa and never left. I felt a twinge across my belly. A hard, painful stab. God, being pregnant was horrible sometimes.

'Where's all this come from?' I asked, buying myself some time to marshal my thoughts.

'Ah, you think I'm being corny. But I have been thinking about it.' Oliver looked at me. 'Seriously. When you had that nightmare? And I felt the baby kicking afterwards? I mean, it was crazy but it was also pretty amazing.' Oliver's expression was serious. Not joking but tender. I remembered what Mum had said about Dad loving pregnant women and unease crept across my shoulders. 'And just being in the flat together – doing the dishes and hanging out at the weekend. It's been pretty great,' Oliver went on. 'I think.'

I thought of Gamar. I pictured his angry pacing. His closed eyes. Punching the back of the sofa. Him telling me I would be a bad mother. I thought of the way he had once kissed me. Stroked my stomach. Lifted me on top of him. I thought of his hands on my waist and his smell on my sheets. I remembered the empty sound as he'd closed my front door.

'Thanks, Oliver,' I replied at last. There was so much more to say and yet, in that moment, I couldn't find it. We both sat for a few seconds. Then, with the sticking sound of my feet following me across the pavement, I walked back into the restaurant.

'Ah, Rita, you must be stoked about being an aunt.' Brendhan was grinning like a lion. I saw him look down at my sister's arm. 'Hey, jeez, you're pretty stacked.' As I took my seat, he gave Rita's bicep a squeeze. She would have found that repulsive. I waited for her cutting retort but nothing came. Brendhan looked at her shoulders. 'Seriously, I'd kill for those lats and traps. How do you keep so lean?'

In our family, Rita's body has always been something of an anomaly. I am small without being petite. Before I got pregnant, I had the kind of body that could easily fit into second-hand clothes and all hotel beds. Dad, with his thin legs and barrel chest, was never imposing in the way Rita somehow manages to be. He was the sort of man who you could imagine using his finger to eat hummus, big without being particularly strong. Marie-Louise, who was tall and lean as a rope, made a principle of never discussing people's bodies, except as conduits for their emotions: 'He has a lovely open face,' for instance, or, 'She has a lonely walk,' and yet I got the feeling that she looked at Rita's frame as somehow foreign. Mum constantly worried about the amount of exercise Rita did. Whether that was genuine concern for her joints or an ingrained misogyny that made her dislike muscular women, it was hard to tell. All in all, Rita's bulk and desire for tone singled her out from her immediate relatives. Even from me. And yet, the half-brother of her secret New Zealand sibling seemed to understand. I could see in her face that she was opening up to him.

'Thanks, mate.' Mate? 'I eat a lot of spirulina and follow a fourteen:seven plan.'

'Sounds technical,' said Brendhan.

'Why, how do you make gains?' asked Rita. I might as well have not been there at all.

'Aaah, unpaid manual labour.' Brendhan dissolved into another huge crackling laugh. 'Try getting forty head of cattle into a crush for their TB shots and you'll know you've done it.'

What was it about this man that had broken through Rita's antipathy? She could still hardly bear to be in the same room as Oliver and yet seemed to feel no ill will towards this lumberjack? Was it his size? His apparent total lack of inhibition? The fact that he had a bisexual ex-wife?

Or, I thought, playing with the tablecloth, was it just that Rita and Brendhan didn't actually share any DNA? Meaning there was no implicit expectation that they would have anything in common. His very existence didn't throw into turmoil the whole narrative she'd grown up with about what her family looked like and who her father was. Unlike Oliver, with his nose and his hand gestures and his way of pursing his lips that was altogether too familiar and therefore too unsettling. Brendhan was safe, which meant Rita could relax.

'Brendhan, do you know what happened between our dad and your mum?' Never one to skirt around a question, Rita had outdone herself. Brendhan looked at her and frowned, slowly. He ran his hand along the tabletop, like a carpenter checking for splinters.

'Well—'

Suddenly, pain like a carving knife tore through me. I clutched my stomach.

'Nancy? You OK?' Brendhan was halfway out of his chair.

I couldn't answer. My head was still bent over, a curl of pain and fear.

'Oh my God.' I could hear the panic in Rita's voice as her chair scraped across the floor.

'Does it feel like something squeezing your lower back, or just kind of a ripple across your abdomen?' I could smell Brendhan's yeast breath on my face and feel Rita's hand on my neck.

'A ripple.' I took a deep breath. 'It's hard and sharp.'

'Right you are.' Brendhan sounded nonchalant. 'And does it last a couple of seconds or less?'

I grimaced. 'It's sort of been there, on and off, all evening.'

'All evening?' Rita's hand tightened a little around my hair.

'Don't stress, Rita. It just sounds to me Nancy's having some Braxton Hicks,' Brendhan said. 'It's no biggie. Cherie had them for near four weeks before Manahira, my oldest.' I looked at him. 'It's just your body's way of limbering up. Kind of a preview, as I understand it.' Totally unselfconscious, Brendhan picked a piece of pear off my plate. 'You might just have overdone it a bit today, ya know?'

'If you're in pain we should go to A and E.' Rita's tone cut through Brendhan's laid-back, man-of-the-soil routine like a knife. Maybe she was right. Did I really want to trust my health to a farmer? 'You should be in a hospital.' But then again, something about Rita's big show of alarm felt competitive, bossy. As usual, she was telling me what to do.

'Nancy?' Oliver must have come back in. 'Are you all right? Do you want me to ring the midwife?'

The feeling pulled through my front again. Was it pain? Or just discomfort.

'No. Don't call her.'

'Oh, for God's sake, don't be ridiculous.' Rita had moved in front of me, blocking out Oliver. 'This isn't one of those things you can ignore, Nancy. It's not like a broken bathroom tile, it's your health. You *have* to see a doctor.' The acridity of the wine she'd been drinking was in her voice. Rita was overreacting. She was enjoying the drama. She was telling me off.

'But if I go into hospital I might be waiting around all night,' I said.

'True enough,' Brendhan said, his mouth still full. 'All she needs is to cool off and lie down.'

'She's not a cow, Brendhan,' Rita snapped.

'Listen, Nancy. I've ordered us a cab.' Oliver was talking from behind Rita, and using a special calm voice almost certainly designed to wind her up. 'It will be here in five minutes. If you want, we can go to Homerton or just straight home. Whatever you want. No sweat.'

My stomach clenched. Something was definitely wrong. Who should I follow?

26

The waiting room smelled of fluorescent light bulbs and grinding teeth.

It had been thirteen hours since I'd left the restaurant with Oliver, telling myself that perhaps these twinges really were no more than Braxton Hicks. Somehow, Rita's panic had put me off making a fuss. The more she told me to go to A and E the more I'd resisted, choosing instead to go with Brendhan's reassurances and Oliver's offer of a lift. But as the pain continued through the night and into the next morning, I'd started to worry. Brendhan might know about bovine mastitis and barley harvests but why was I putting my faith in the advice of a man with dice tattooed on his neck? I felt wrong. By breakfast, unrested and looking like dental adhesive, I had called the midwife. This time I had got through to Alwen, who had told me to go in to the hospital and get checked. 'And Nancy, love, don't walk. Just get a taxi.' I snuck out of the flat, trying not to wake Oliver. I hadn't wanted him to watch as midwives (or so I'd imagined it) pushed their fists inside me and palpated my stomach. I thought about calling Mum but was somehow more scared of her panic than my own.

'Rita?'

'Yes.'

'I'm at the hospital.'

'Oh my God. What's happening?'

'I don't know. I'm still getting these pains – I don't think they are just Braxton Hicks. The midwife told me to come in and so I'm here now. I'm just waiting to be seen.'

'Where are you? Which hospital?'

'Homerton.'

'OK. Who's with you?'

'Nobody. I didn't want to deal with Mum and I didn't tell Oliver.'

'Nancy!'

'What?' I could hear her sucking her teeth.

'Nothing. Nothing. OK, I'm coming. Keep an eye on your phone.'

'I'm at the maternity unit. It's Section D.'

'I'll find you.'

I had forgotten to bring a book and the only food in my bag was a small packet of Haribo one of the children at school had given me. The idea of eating a green foam ring at nine in the morning made me feel queasy. School had been lovely when I'd rung to explain; the head told me to take as long as I needed. She'd had three children, one of them an emergency caesarean. Like so many other women, she carried the kindness of experience.

On the wall, a big television was playing a cookery programme, where the contestants had to make a meal using five mystery ingredients. I watched the sharp knife, probably a metre long, slice through a piece of pink, veined salmon. I felt the pain in my stomach, sharp and ringing. There had been no blood. I hadn't been sick. And yet the cramping claustrophobia of pain had hardly lifted, even in my sleep.

'Mrs Obsedeilan.' A midwife stood at the door as a large woman in a tracksuit made her rolling way to the door, accompanied by a man whose bright white trainers made me think of travel fridges.

I thought of last night. Standing in the street with Oliver; the smell of cigarettes and onion. His awkward smile as he talked about Gamar. His offer to be, what, a kind of co-parent? Kind, yes. But was it real? And Brendhan. Shoulders like bus seats. The crackling, stick-breaking laugh. Did he know more about their mother than he'd let on? Through the discordant swirl of pain, I had been aware of a question from Rita. What had happened? What did he know? What could he, the older brother, actually remember?

I was staring, blankly, at a pan of frying spring onions when Rita came through the door. I knew it in the split second before I even saw her. Her movement, her smell, just the way the atoms around her spun was so innately familiar to me I could feel her body like a limb.

'Nancy, I'm here. I'm here. I'm sorry. I should never have let you go home with Oliver last night. I knew something was wrong.' I collapsed on to her shoulder; hanging all my weight on someone else for what felt like the first time in months. I felt her stroke my hair. 'It's OK. Don't worry. I'm here.' The cry that burst out of my mouth drowned the sound of coconut milk being added to spring onion completely.

'Nancy Albany.' It was a different midwife. She was small, with curly brown hair and two front teeth like computer keys. 'Sorry to keep you waiting. If you just want to lie down, we're going to pop the belts on here, to have a listen to baby's heartbeat and check for movements. Are you feeling much movement?'

Movements. I had been so focused on the source of this pain that I had stopped noticing the movement. 'I don't know.' Meaning no. Meaning probably. Meaning I am a bad mother already.

'That's OK. We'll soon have a listen.'

I was a captive, strapped to the bed. With the two belts across me I could hardly move. Bright blue light like a drill shone straight into my eyes. After a few seconds, the machine to my left erupted into life. Two needles started scrawling across a long, thin sheet of paper. What were they? Heartbeats? Movements? Contractions?

'Are you all right there?' The midwife was already moving towards the curtain. Where was she going?

'Yes.' Meaning no. Meaning please don't leave me.

'I'll be back in a few minutes.'

I felt my lip start to quiver. Pathetic. Needy. Don't leave me on my own.

Then I felt Rita slip her hand into mine. She leant forward, so close that I could feel one of her curls against my cold, damp forehead.

'Nice 'n' Spicy Nik Naks.'

I smiled. I was six again. Squirming on the back seat of our maroon Volvo, the seat belt cutting into my armpits. As the wires scrawled out their incomprehensible message and the buzzing light bulbs jarred against my eyelids, I thought of travel sweets and friendship bracelets, Blondie and dead legs. I turned my head towards Rita and whispered back, 'Findus Crispy Pancakes. Beef and Onion.'

She squeezed my hand. A tear fell from the corner of my eye, on to the blue plastic beneath.

'Does it really hurt?'

'I don't know.' I put my attention back on to my stomach, abdomen, spine, hips, ribs. 'It hurts but I think I was probably more just scared.'

'Of course.'

'So much of being pregnant is scary, Rita. I can't see anything in there. I don't ever know what's happening, what's safe. It's all hidden away.'

'Poor you.' And for the first time in months, Rita sounded like my sister again.

'I'm already nearly thirty-two weeks, Rita.' I looked down at my stomach. 'Some people give birth before that. They spend months in intensive care, with their baby in an incubator. I saw the ward.'

'When?'

'I did a tour a few weeks ago.'

'Who with?'

'Nobody,' I answered. 'I came on my own after work.' The glare of the hospital light shone off Rita's curls.

'Oh, Noodle, I would have come with you.'

I didn't want to say it but I said it: 'No, you wouldn't.' I wet my lips. 'You weren't . . . You were angry with me, for letting Oliver stay in my flat.'

There was an unhappy pause.

'I'm sorry,' said Rita at last. 'I . . .'

'No, it's OK. I'm sorry.' I reached for her arm. 'I've handled the whole thing badly. I've been clumsy. And selfish. And stupid.'

'Nancy, Nancy, stop.' Rita put her hand on my hair. 'You've got to stop talking like that – always criticizing yourself. It's not good for you. Or . . .' She stumbled. 'Well, or for the baby. It's living in there. Give it a break.' She ran her thumb along the edge of my hairline, just as Mum used to do when we were falling asleep.

'But you don't like Oliver.'

Rita sighed. 'I don't dislike Oliver.' I heard a click in her neck. She was stretching it out on one side. We used to call it doing a Mr Miyagi: making her neck crack when she was stressed. 'I don't even really know him. I just . . .' I opened my eyes and watched her. 'I wasn't ready for all this. Dad. The test. Some big secret. Him. I'm still getting used to the fact that Dad is, like, dead. I don't want to have to question everything.'

'I know.'

'And . . .' Rita pulled her hand into her lap and started to pick at the skin on her knuckle. 'And I was a bit jealous.'

'Really?'

'You and he seemed to get so close, so quickly. I mean, he's been the one around, while you've been pregnant. He moved in with you. You went to his gigs. Met his brother.'

'You met his brother too.' Stupid Nancy. Why be petty? Rita was apologizing. We'd nearly done it.

'OK.'

'No, Rita, I'm sorry.' I brought my hand up to my mouth. 'I shouldn't have said that.'

'Well—'

'I get it. I completely get it. It's just, well, when Gamar dumped me I was so alone. Reets, I was so sad and so lonely. You were angry with me; Mum was upset. I'd just started to feel pregnant and I was alone in the house. Gamar didn't even answer my messages. I was so . . .' The words started to melt into cries. I covered my eyes. '. . . sad.'

'Oh, Noose. Noose, I'm sorry.'

'And then Oliver turned up. And he cleaned the flat and cooked for me and when I told him I was pregnant – well, actually, he was a bit weird about that. He asked me if I'd done it on purpose.'

'He what?'

'But then he apologized,' I added quickly. 'And anyway, it's just sort of helped. Having him around. And, Rita, it's weird but because he looks so like Dad—'

'But Nancy, that's what's so weird. He looks so like Dad.'

I tried to nod, with my head on the blue plastic bed. 'I know. I know. But sometimes it means that just having him there, watching him rub his big toe along the back of his calf – it reminds me of Dad. And that, well, it makes me feel less lonely.'

'Hello, Nancy.' The midwife walked quickly up to the bed and started reading the printout, puddled on the floor beside me. 'Well, from what I can see here, the baby isn't in any distress. A strong, steady heartbeat and plenty of movement. Your urine sample has come back clear. Your proteins are a bit high but it looks from your notes like you've had Group B Strep so that would explain that.'

'Yes and I've got low Papp-A,' I said, readying myself to launch into the catechism of my pregnancy: the familiar chant of infections and measurements and tests.

'Right. But you had an extra scan at thirty weeks, did you?' The midwife glanced at the notes on the whiteboard above my head.

'Just before, yes.'

'And they checked the umbilical vein?' Rita squeezed my shoulder.

'Yes, that was fine. But the blood flow from the placenta was a bit slow on the left-hand side.'

'OK. But they didn't refer you for any further ultrasounds?'

'No.'

'OK. And you've been sleeping on your left-hand side?'

I nodded. Instead of looking at the midwife, Rita was smiling at me, but with her brows pulled together in concern.

'Yes.'

'And are you taking aspirin?'

'Yes. Once a day. Well, at night.'

'OK, Nancy. Let me just have a feel.' The nurse reached into a box, wedged on to the trolley next to the monitor. 'Oh, hold on. We're out of gloves. Just wait there one minute.'

'Jesus.' Rita exhaled when the midwife had disappeared around the curtain. 'I had no idea you had so much stuff.'

'What do you mean?'

'Well, that you were having such a hard time. So many problems.' I frowned and Rita tucked a piece of hair behind my ear. 'Sorry, I don't mean problems. Just there are so many things to think about.'

'Yeah.' I ran my hand under the waistband of my knickers, feeling the taut foothills of my belly. 'It makes you realize just how shit our biology curriculum was at school. Honestly, I've had to learn all this stuff. Before, I don't think I even really knew where wombs were. Or what they looked like.'

'I could have explained some—'

'You weren't speaking to me.' I'd done it again. Pushed unhappy accusations into this reconciliation.

'I'm sorry.' Rita took my hand again.

'No, I'm sorry.'

There was a moment when neither of us said anything. I heard doors swinging shut somewhere out of sight. A machine beeped. A phone rang. I lay still.

'We're both shooo ssshhhuoooory,' Rita whispered into my ear. The long, Californian drawl, the whistle in her teeth, the warmth of her body next to mine. As if we were kids again. It was perfect. Perfect.

27

The midwives decided to keep me in for twelve hours. Although there was nothing evidently wrong, they wanted to 'monitor the situation'. Which made me feel like a hostage crisis. A bomb threat. I was a global atrocity; they were weapons inspectors. I was also grateful.

Rita went to my flat to pick up a bag of stuff: a phone charger, paracetamol, apples, lip balm, a book, aspirin, a sandwich, even a toothbrush and knickers. I wrote the list on to her phone, hoping that a message from some new girlfriend would pop up as I typed; that I could get a glimpse into her life without having to ask. It would be the first time she had broached my flat in nearly six months. Oliver would be there, I had warned her. Rita had shrugged.

'And how is the pain now, Nancy?' A midwife with thick blonde hair and a large mole on her chin appeared by my bed.

'It's definitely getting better.' Was it? Or had the estrangement from Rita finally started to wash away? Where did pain in your stomach end and pain in your heart begin?

'Any change in your discharge?'

'No.'

'And you're feeling movements?'

'A few.'

'OK. I'm just going to do a quick blood pressure and temperature check.'

There is a term: white coat syndrome. I'd heard about it on a podcast but now was scared I'd develop it; that the moment I saw someone in a white coat, holding a piece of medical equipment, my blood pressure would start to soar. Would I be forced to spend the rest of my pregnancy in a hospital bed, alone and twitching?

'That all looks fine at the moment.' She looked at a clock on the wall. 'The doctor will be doing their rounds at about four p.m.' Then at my notes. 'If everything is all right then we should be able to discharge you this evening. You came in at' – she scans – 'eight a.m.? So you would be due to leave at eight. If there is any change, though, between now and then, we'll keep you in overnight.'

I just nodded. What could I say? Please don't send me away? Show me my baby? Let me see that they're really OK?

I was pretending to be asleep when Rita came back. I didn't want to talk to the woman in the bed next to me. She kept letting out these long, metallic sighs and hadn't turned off the keypad tones on her phone. I am not good at small talk. Dad had been able to chat to everyone; people on buses and in waiting rooms. Not by asking about traffic or football or how long they'd been waiting; instead he would turn to an utter stranger and say, 'How's your day going?' People loved it.

'I think I got most of the things you said you needed,' she said, dumping a cream tote bag on my bed so distended by its contents that it looked like a maggot. 'Oliver and Brendhan were both there.'

I readied myself for the attack. But Rita just sat down on the purple, wipe-clean seat and started reading my notes.

'Did you tell them what was happening?'

'I said you were in the hospital but that it wasn't early labour or anything.' Rita was frowning a little and the line between her eyebrows was exactly like Dad's. 'Brendhan started saying something about placental abruption but I think he was just trying to show off.'

'No, they did say the placenta was a bit weak.' I pulled out an apple, my charger and an enormous red box. 'Rita? Is this?'

'A packet of femidoms. Yes.' Rita looked like a child who had just done their first wheelie. 'Extra-large.'

'And . . .'

'A copy of *Angling Times*. That's right. I stopped at Chatsworth Road for some essentials.'

'Rita, is this vodka?'

'I just wanted you to make a good impression on the staff. And other patients.'

After about five minutes, a porter came over and warned us to keep it down. Apparently, some of the other patients didn't like the sound of laughter.

28

I knew something was up, the moment I stepped into the hallway that evening. Rita had held back, to hang up my bag. There was a smell like hamsters. Sawdust. And the pile of books beneath the coats had disappeared.

'Rita, what's going on?'

But she just smiled and walked towards my bedroom. The television was on in the front room and I could hear that particular nasal drone of sports commentating.

'Oliver?' I came into the doorway of my bedroom. There were shelves. A whole wall of shelves. I opened the door further – it didn't catch on the floor but just glided open. My clothes were in a laundry basket. The door to my wardrobe was hanging straight. And closed. 'Rita? Oliver?' I came out into the hallway. There was a lampshade in the kitchen. I glanced into the bathroom and saw that the hole above the shower rail was gone: tiled over. The hot tap over the sink wasn't dripping. And all my cosmetics were in a basket on the windowsill.

I felt the baby nudge a little: an electric pulse across the bottom of my abdomen but no pain. In the front room, I heard the snake hiss of a beer cap being pulled.

I didn't know what to do with my face. This wasn't a romcom. I was puffy and hospital grey. Oliver was not my boyfriend and Rita was not my best friend and Brendhan was a stranger with gold teeth. For a second, I thought about walking straight into my bedroom and just shutting the door. Crawling into a worm cast of my own bed and going to sleep. Then I heard someone open the oven and a red smell of oil and tomatoes and basil met me.

'Darling, I've made aubergine parmigiana. You didn't have any lasagne sheets.' Mum's voice. So Mum was here too. 'I had to do something.' Anne came striding out of the kitchen, drying her hands on a tea towel. 'Rita said not to come to the hospital because you were already on your way home, but I've been so worried.' She wrapped me up in her arms and kissed the top of my head.

'I did text you from the hospital,' I said, speaking into the fold of her blue cardigan.

'I know, I know. But ever since, well, you know.' Mum shook the hair off her face. 'I just can't bear the idea of anyone else getting hurt or anything.' The ambulances that came for Dad. The slow walk of the paramedics back across the beach. The awful wait. 'But you're like me. You're tough. And Rita said there's nothing to worry about.'

Was I tough? Rita was the tough one, not me. I cried in the shower and couldn't open jars and loved men who abandoned me. I didn't feel tough.

'Here she is, great with child.' Brendhan's face came around the living-room door. He had paint in his hair and a pencil actually tucked behind his ear.

'Brendhan,' I said.

'Brendhan and I are going to leave you three to catch up.' Oliver pushed past his brother and into the hallway. Brendhan smacked a giant hand across his back.

'That's right. Me and this fella have an appointment down the road with about six litres of ale.'

I smiled. I felt my shoulders soften. I was home. And, even if we didn't really look like one, I was with my family.

29

A week later, Mum invited me over for a barbecue. This was slightly odd because, as far as I was aware, she didn't own a barbecue. Nor did she particularly like meat. And at thirty-three weeks pregnant, I didn't relish the thought of standing around for two hours to get salmonella. When I mentioned this to Oliver, he told me that he had received the same invitation. Rita replied saying that she was bringing a Greek salad and that Brendhan was going to make something called 'mussel fritters'. So Brendhan was coming? And had told Rita?

The kitchen table had been dragged out on to the grass and a large roll of kitchen paper was slowly unspooling itself across a plastic tablecloth. Buster and Shadwell were dancing across the flower beds, nipping and twirling. It was mid-June and already sweat was trickling down the inside of my shoulder blades. Mum seemed to have bought twenty-four white batch rolls, which she'd left in their packets, and a tub of margarine. Never in my life had my mum bought margarine. There was also a carton of orange juice and two bottles of white wine in a recycling tub full of ice on the ground.

'Mum, is everything OK?' I looked over at the studio. There were no lights on inside but I could see that the surfaces were almost clear.

'Yes, fine. Why?'

'You've just' – I looked at the margarine – 'gone to a lot of trouble.'

'What do you mean trouble? I'm not trying to make any trouble for anyone.'

'No, no, I . . .'

But she was already heading back inside, flicking a tea towel over her shoulder, like an irritated head chef.

I took my shoes off and walked across the grass. There was a bush covered in yellow flowers in one of the beds. This, I had been told, was St John's wort and beneath it lay the decomposing body of our old cat, Finchley. I touched one of the flower buds, teasing it open with my fingers. Inside, the firework of yellow stamen was curled in on itself, small and moist. Not ready to come out.

'Ah, the old hypericum? You feeling blue or something?' Brendhan's chainsaw voice rang out across the garden. I turned. He was carrying a box of small fat beer bottles in one hand and a large Tupperware in the other. The Tupperware seemed to be full of sick.

'Sorry?'

'Hypericum – St John's wort? It's meant to be an antidepressant, or so I'm told.' Brendhan put the beers down on the table and scratched his chest with his now free hand. 'Personally, I prefer my antidepressants with a side of Jack Daniel's and Led Zeppelin.'

'What's in the box?' I asked, trying to keep the squeeze of revulsion out of my voice.

'Mussel fritters, mate. Took me a hell of a time to find good mussels in this town, though. I ended up having to ask some South African guy where I'm staying. He sent me to bloody Billingsgate Market. I had to go back the next day because by the time I rocked up the first time it was already closed.' Brendhan laughed, then ripped the top of the beer box off in one swift move. 'You fancy a beer, Nancy?'

The way he said it was so airy, so unconcerned that for a mad moment I considered saying yes. Until I remembered the hospital bed and the belts and the scrawling heartbeats.

'Thank you, that's really nice, but I think I'm going to stick to soft drinks.'

'Fair dos. With Manahira – that's our oldest – we did all that. No drinking, no soft cheese. Cherie even started buying pasteurized milk rather than using our own from the goats.' Brendhan bounced his toe on the ground and I noticed he was barefoot too. 'But then with Tehine, we kind of let things slide: the odd beer, poached eggs, you know.'

'And was she OK?'

'Hine? Man, she can split logs quicker than me. And she's got a mania for numbers. I used to get her to race the checkout at the dairy – add up the groceries before they were scanned and then tell me the total, you know?'

I found stories about laid-back parenting as unbearable as the neurotic ones. Mothers who gave birth at home while watching Arsenal vs Wolves; parents who cycled their six-month-old across France; women who rubbed whisky on teething gums. When every prawn smelled like potential salmonella and my nights were haunted by thoughts of cold, blue babies, I didn't want to hear about breastfeeding in the mosh pit at Glastonbury.

'I'm very scared of doing something wrong.' The words fell out of my mouth like pebbles: solid, uncomfortable.

Brendhan looked up. His face softened. 'Course you are, honey. It's heavy shit.'

'I asked Rita to pick up some more coal,' Mum said, stepping out into the garden with a large bowl of salad. 'She made this.' I presumed this comment was aimed at me. I had brought nothing, bar a box of baklava, while Rita had made a healthy, delicious salad. Wasn't it nice to always do the right thing? Wasn't it a shame I was such a lazy, childish mess? Isn't it funny how two sisters can be so different? 'I'm not sure where Oliver is.'

'He had to pick something up in town this morning,' I explained. 'So I said I'd meet him here. He knows the time.'

'Well, as long as he hasn't got a better offer,' said Mum. I raised my eyebrows at Brendhan but he pretended not to pick up on Anne's mood. 'Now, Brendhan, how are you going to cook these fritters of yours?'

'No worries, Anne.' Brendhan gave Mum a grin like a drystone wall. 'I even brought my own tin foil. Once the coals get hot, you can leave it all to me.'

'Well, I did buy some free-range chicken.'

'Good on ya. Our chooks lay their eggs in the girls' slippers.' Brendhan's smile faded. 'I mean, they did. Before all this.'

I wanted to pat his thick shoulder: to offer some comfort to this unbrother of mine. But I felt too embarrassed. Too awkward to reach my arms out, push my belly into his, to touch him with my skin. I thought of Dad. He had always hugged his male friends, even when we were little and Jim Davidson could make jokes about poofters on Saturday night telly. Even when the friends were 48-year-old boarding-school graduates who played golf and only read Lee Child novels. Perhaps Dad didn't worry about rejection like I did; maybe nobody had ever shamed his affection.

'Yeah, I can take care of the food and the fire while you ladies relax and talk about mastitis or something.' He was trying.

Rita walked into the garden a few minutes later, carrying the largest sack of coal I'd ever seen. She'd thrown it casually over one shoulder and was drinking a can of Old Jamaica ginger beer with her free hand. The whole look, this whole performance of machismo, was, I knew, entirely to impress Brendhan. While Rita had immediately painted Oliver as a fraud, she had just as quickly deemed Brendhan an ally. I could understand it; she and Brendhan were both older, both had complicated relationships with their mums, both loved the outdoors. It was just a shame that Rita had been so wary of Oliver at the beginning.

'It smells of the sea out here,' she said, dropping the coal on the patio and cocking her head like a bird.

'That'll be the fritters, girl,' said Brendhan. And once again, she didn't pick him up on it. 'Bet even that French mother of yours never cooked you a mussel fritter.' He put on a deep, twanging voice. 'This'll be a proper feed.'

'Afternoon.' Oliver walked into the garden fifteen minutes later. He quickly took a seat under the plum tree and started rolling a cigarette.

'Howdy, young fella,' said Brendhan, wiping his hands on his shirt.

Anne was buttering rolls, her head down, eyes on the table. I was sitting on a garden chair that had come from my grandmother's house in about 1992.

'Before we eat,' said Mum at last, 'there is something I wanted to say.' She put her fists down on the table and, just for a moment, I thought of a silverback gorilla. 'Oliver, can you come over here, please? When you've finished your cigarette.'

'What's going on?' asked Rita. But Mum held up her hand. There was an awkward pause. Eventually, as

Oliver took his seat, she started to speak. Slowly and deliberately.

'When we were going through Clive's studio, I found something.' I flicked a look at Oliver. He was frowning. 'Now, there's something that I have never told you two before.' Mum was looking at me and Rita. I bit my lip. 'That was the decision I took as your mother.' She steadied her voice. 'And as a wife.' The words were falling around me like drops of rain. A change in the weather. A storm approaching. 'However, something has come to my attention that has made me reassess that decision.' I watched her mouth draw down into a hard line. I clenched my knees together.

'Your father.' We waited. 'Your father had an affair,' she said at last.

'What? And you knew?' I blurted out.

'I asked him to never give me the details,' said Mum. 'He told me when you were about six months old, Nancy.' I felt my breath get shallow. 'He apologized and begged for my forgiveness and promised it would never happen again.'

In the silence that followed, I heard hissing. The barbecue. Fire. Brendhan was still at the barbecue. He alone seemed unsurprised by what he'd just heard. I looked across at Oliver but he'd put his head down, so all I could see was the curtain of dark brown curls. Rita was standing, like concrete, looking at Mum.

'As I say, you were a baby, Nancy, and, Rita, you were only four, and at the time I did not want it to break up our family.' The air in my throat had turned to dust. 'I believed it to have been a slip-up.' Mum's voice was steady but her chin was quivering. 'We went to Relate and worked through it. I never heard from the woman and, although I could never quite trust your father again in the same way, I believed that we came to an understanding.' A single tear breached the corner of Mum's eye. She wiped it away. 'We found a way to carry on.' My fingers were going numb. Dad. A cheat. Relate. An understanding. An affair. 'However, on going through his plan chest, I found something that may have bearing on the current situation.' She pulled out an airmail envelope. It had a blue rectangle in one corner. By air mail. *Par avion.* 'This letter.' The envelope unfolded and on it I could see loopy, tangled handwriting.

'"To my Picasso."' Mum stopped. She cleared her throat and tried again. Surely she wasn't going to read this – whatever this was – out to us? '"To my Picasso. I am writing to let you know that you have a son."' Thunder through my body. '"He is a beautiful, healthy boy and I have called him Oliver."' I looked at the blue veins that threaded up from Mum's knuckles. The gold wedding band. The liver spots like smudged freckles. I couldn't move. '"I am not going to ask you for money and I'm not going to attack your reputation, as an artist or"' – Mum paused – '"or a man."' Her voice rose like an animal in pain. '"But I think you should know that, over here …"' I looked between Mum and Rita. Rita was still frowning, but she had brought her hand up to her neck. Mum took a deep breath. '"... under the Southern Stars, there is a child with your blood running through his veins."'

Dad. Cheat. One of my teeth hit against another. A son. His reputation.

Mum gave a long sigh. 'I'm not going to read the rest, if you don't mind.' She passed it across the table to Oliver. 'You can, of course.' She touched her forehead. 'I have no idea if he ever replied to this letter or if there were others,' she said. 'I'm afraid this is the only one I've found. It was hidden – in a brochure about the Cotswold Wildlife Park, in fact. I suppose he counted on me never going through his desk.'

Suddenly there was a roar of blood in my ears. The Southern Skies. My Picasso. Your blood. He had known. Dad the doting husband. Dad the gentleman. Lies and lies and lies until one day he plunged into the sea and died.

'Nancy?' Oliver was crouching next to me.

His cold, white hands. The hours he spent in that fucking studio. His songs. The pencil behind his ear. Whistling along to Leonard Cohen. The bike rides. All those shows. The parties. Our teddies. Blue pyjamas. The camping trips. Ham sandwiches. The sea water in his hair. The smell of turpentine. The bruises around his forehead. Cigars. Champagne. Bedtime stories. The salt. My baby. Floating, not breathing, suspended in salt. Skulls.

'I'm sorry, Nancy.' I could hear Mum's voice and feel an arm on my back. 'It's OK, darling. It's all right.' And

I was falling on to her. Her neck. Astral face cream. I was being held. 'Shhhh, shhhh. Nancy, it's all right. It's a shock. I'm sorry – I shouldn't have told you like that. Shhhh. It's OK. Come on, Nancy. Quiet now, quiet.'

I was juddering. It was wet between my legs and on my face and in my armpits. Mum stroked my back and I cried. The roar in my head became waves. Waves crashing on pebbles. I tried to breathe. My Picasso. Your blood. A son. Dad. Dad. Dead. Dad.

'Nancy, I'm gonna take your shoes off.' Brendhan's voice. Someone pulling at my cheap white plimsolls. 'And, Anne, if you'll excuse me?' I tasted air; felt it on my face. 'Nancy. You need to drink this. Don't worry – it's not booze.' A glass was in my hand and on my lip. It was sweet. 'Right. Drink some more. That's it.' I opened my eyes and Brendhan was squatting in front of me. His shoulders were wider than my knees. 'Now, this is what I do with Hine when she falls off the shed roof. I want you to breathe in for four.' I watched as his punchbag chest inflated. 'Hold it for four.' I looked at his Adam's apple. 'And now breathe out for four.' Hops, yeast. The beer on his breath was on my face. 'OK, a couple more.'

I breathed in. I held it. I breathed out. I could hear the crack of fire. I could hear chairs being scraped and a plane overhead. I wiped my cheek with the back of my hand and smelled my own skin.

'Right, sorry about that, Anne,' said Brendhan, standing up. 'I didn't mean to push in but I wanted to get some water in her. Even if I don't really drink the stuff myself.'

I looked around. Rita was still standing, her arm on Mum. Oliver was squatting on the ground near me. Mum had her hand in her hair.

'Right. Before we go any further, let's sit down and eat something,' said Brendhan. 'Nancy, why don't you head to the dunny, sort yourself out. I'll dish up.'

'I'm not hungry,' Oliver said.

'Thank you, Brendhan,' said Mum at the same time. 'But I'm not sure I could.'

'Sure, but I think you should.' Brendhan was unperturbed. Brendhan, alone, seemed to have missed the explosion that hit the rest of us. He started clearing a space in the middle of the table. He let Mum pick up the letter and put it back in her bag, then moved the box of beers into the shade of the plum tree. 'Nobody wants bad news on an empty stomach.'

When I came back from the toilet, everyone was sitting around the table. Mum had refilled her glass of wine, Rita and Brendhan were drinking beers and Oliver had a beer, a glass of water and some orange juice in front of him. There was a plate already set out for me. Salad, chicken, French bread and a small round thing that looked halfway between a pancake and a bhaji.

'I'm not sure I can eat mussels,' I said, sitting down between Oliver and Brendhan.

'Nah, I checked your NHS website,' said Brendhan, his

mouth full of bread. 'Says as long as they're cooked through and piping hot. And, girl, that is one piping-hot fritter.'

Mum's news seemed to have buoyed Brendhan. While Rita and I crept away from the bomb crater of our childhood, and Oliver sat like a dog that had just been kicked, Brendhan was having a relaxing lunch.

'I'm sorry, everyone,' said Mum. She hadn't eaten anything yet but had her fork resting on a piece of tomato. 'I shouldn't have announced all that like that. I don't know why – I didn't mean to make it dramatic. I thought—'

'No, Anne, I'm sorry.' Oliver twisted the bottom of his glass of orange juice in a quarter-circle. His voice was rough. 'I'm sorry you had to be the one to pass on that news.' He was looking at Mum from between his thick, dark eyelashes. 'It must have been awful. And I'm sorry if me being here made all that . . . well.'

'I just don't understand.' Rita put her elbows on the table. 'Why . . . Why didn't he tell us? Tell you?'

'I don't know,' said Mum.

'How could he have done that?' Rita was almost spitting. 'Had an affair when you were pregnant. She already had a family. What were they thinking? How could he have kept it a secret?' I looked quickly at Oliver. 'Had he done it before?' But Rita didn't wait for the answer. 'And wasn't he worried we'd find out? That she'd turn up? Tell you? Didn't he care that he'd got someone pregnant? Didn't he do anything to try and make amends?'

'Maybe that's why he was on that DNA site,' said Oliver, still holding his glass. 'Maybe he'd got curious.'

'Well, it was a bit fucking little, a bit fucking late.' Rita smashed her fist down. 'Your mum was a single parent, wasn't she?' Rita turned to Oliver.

'Well—'

But before he could answer, Rita started again. 'She had to do everything while he ran away to live off his rich wife, as if nothing had happened.'

'I don't—' Oliver began to speak.

'I can't believe he knew!' Rita was almost shouting. I could see her eyes flicking across the table in front of her, as if trying to read a huge map. She was lost. She was losing it. 'The selfish, lying bastard.' Her anger had been let loose.

'Rita—' Mum tried to say something but, at the sound of her voice, Rita seemed to go on to another track.

'But, also, how? How did he get a woman in New Zealand pregnant? He never flew! He never went anywhere! He just slobbed around the house, doing his stupid art, while you did all the work.'

'I don't know,' said Mum quietly. 'I can't think how they met, or where. But then, I was working a lot in the run-up to Nancy being born. I missed a lot of things.'

The bread in my mouth felt like wood. 'Mum, this isn't your fault.' I felt the baby thrust a knee, or perhaps a foot, into my bladder. 'None of it. But why didn't you just tell us?'

'I did just tell you, darling, and look what happened.'

I felt a blush rise from my chest. 'You and Rita had just lost your father. Imagine if I'd told you then. Admitted that, for his whole life, Dad and I had lied to you.'

'He lied; you didn't,' I said.

'I covered up for him, darling,' said Mum. 'I made his secret our secret. And I'm sorry, Oliver. I really am.'

Oliver went to speak but Rita cut in. 'But why? Why did you go along with it?' she asked.

'With what?'

'All of it,' said Rita.

'Like I say, I didn't know about Oliver, obviously.' Mum picked up her fork, then put it down again. 'Or any of that. I didn't think he'd done it before; he wasn't unfaithful by nature. And as far as I knew, your father loved me and I loved him and we were a family.'

I winced.

'OK, but you did know he'd cheated on you,' said Rita, clearly so angry she couldn't see what her words were doing to Mum. 'Why did you forgive him like that?'

'Oh, I don't know. I suppose I loved him. And everything had changed after you came to live with us anyway, darling,' said Mum. 'We'd started to feel like a proper family.' She glanced up at Oliver. 'Sorry, Oliver – I don't mean—' But Oliver waved down her apology. Mum went on: 'You girls needed looking after and Clive was working on a show. I'd already decided that I had to be the sensible one; the one that held everything together. So I'd given up acting and gone back to the law and I think maybe Clive really struggled with that.'

'Acting?' I asked.

'Don't you dare blame yourself for this,' Rita shouted, but Mum chose to answer me instead.

'Yes. For a few years in my twenties I tried to get a career as an actor. Oh God, sorry, Oliver, I didn't mean to end up talking about this.' But Oliver held his hands up. Carry on. 'I'd already qualified as a solicitor. My parents insisted on that first. But then I took a few years out to try and, well . . .'

'But what happened? I don't understand?' Rita asked.

'Well . . .' Mum patted the paper napkin by her plate. 'When I met Clive, he had just had a show in Newcastle or somewhere and it had actually sold quite well. I thought he was talented and, well, I fell in love with him, darling. Then, when we moved here, things got a bit tight, so I went back to the law and, well, Clive . . .' She paused. 'I think, in a way, he felt overshadowed or something.'

'So he had sex with other women? To perk up his ego?' Rita's rage was painful just to witness. Of course she was angry. I was angry. But the way she was talking to Mum – it was unbearable.

'No, darling. No.'

'And treated you like – like a doormat?'

'Rita, don't talk about your mother like that.' Brendhan's voice was low and serious. Rita flashed him a look but said nothing more. 'Stepmother. Whatever.'

Mum shook her head. I thought I saw tears. 'When I found out I was pregnant, and when Marie-Louise agreed for you to start nursery here in London, Rita, I was delighted. I had always wanted a family and to be a mother and there I was. I thought . . .' She almost choked on the words. 'Well, I thought Clive would make a brilliant father.' There was an agonizing second before she carried on. 'And when he confessed to what he'd done, well, I tried to be the bigger person. It was hard and I hated it at times, but I also knew what we'd be throwing away if it went the other way.'

There was a pause. 'Do you think he was sending money to New Zealand?' I asked, surprised at my own question. 'Do you think he helped her at all?'

'I honestly don't know. But I rather doubt it somehow,' Mum said, looking again at Oliver, then at Brendhan. 'I'm sorry to be talking like this in front of you two.'

'Don't be,' said Brendhan. 'Not on my account, anyway. You all right, Ollie?'

Oliver nodded but said nothing.

'Your father never earned much,' said Mum. 'Nothing really, once you included his expenses and outgoings. He always chose his art over money.'

'Was that why you were always working so much when we were little?' Rita asked. 'Because you had to be the breadwinner?' Another layer stripped away. Another truth about our father laid bare.

'Yes.' Mum looked down at her plate. 'Yes, I suppose so. And that was rather a regret.' There was a tiny pause. 'I wish now that I hadn't spent quite so much time working and let Clive do all the fun stuff. But it meant we could live here and, well, I did like my work. Remember' – she inhaled slowly – 'I was the first female partner Rudge and Partners ever had.'

'Good on yer, Anne.' Brendhan was holding his beer bottle up as though in toast. He looked ridiculous.

'Thank you, ah, Brendhan,' said Mum.

'Ma always worked – she was a grafter,' said Brendhan. There was a horrible silence while we all thought of Anahera, cleaning floors and emptying other people's ashtrays to make some extra money. A secret buried deep within her. 'But I'm glad,' Brendhan continued. 'Me and wee Ollie here had to muck in with the chores while she was working. It's a good lesson for kids: that we all have to pull our weight.'

'But it sounds like Dad didn't.' I flashed a look at Rita as I said it, knowing she'd be thinking the same. 'It sounds like Dad did whatever the hell he wanted and left it to everyone else to clear up after him.'

'Well . . .' Mum began saying something.

'Nancy.' It was Oliver. Not Rita. 'We'll never really know what your dad was thinking.'

I looked at him. One of the collars of his black shirt was folded in on itself. He looked crumpled, emptied out. All those years with his mum, no money, no Dad, no security. And the man to blame had known, all along. He'd known about Oliver and never even tried to reach out to him. Poor Oliver.

'I never knew the guy, obviously.' Oliver's voice was

strange. He was trying to sound light, like Brendhan, but I could see he was upset. We could all see that. 'But it sounds like he decided to put you three first.' I wanted to hold Oliver against my cheek. I wanted to reach back and grab Dad by the throat. I wanted to undo all that pain.

'I'm sorry, Oliver,' said Rita. 'I'm so ashamed of him.' She sniffed. 'And, well, I'm sorry I gave you such a hard time. You know, at first. I didn't realize that you were a victim here, too.'

I reached for Rita's hand. I knew, with the certainty of siblings, that she was feeling all the things I was feeling. Betrayal, anger, confusion and a hot new punch of grief. We had just lost our father all over again. Two years after he'd died, two months after his son appeared, we had just learned that his life had been a lie. He wasn't a loving, kind man, but a selfish, childish failure. He had been weak. Lazy. He had fathered a child, failed in his career, lied to his family and forced his wife to provide for him. No wonder I had such trouble with men; I didn't understand them. I didn't understand them because the first one I'd ever loved had been living a lie. I had imprinted on a man who had betrayed us all; who cared more about his public face than private happiness; who used work as a means of escape and poisoned two families.

I thought about Gamar. His remoteness. His devotion to his job. His inability to commit. All this time, I had been trying to make impossible men love me because I had been chasing a mirage. A man who didn't exist. A lie. It was shameful to admit but I had fallen in love with the *idea* of Gamar: the international humanitarian doctor who would one day come home to change nappies and push buggies. I had created him in my mind. I had ignored what he said in order to hear what I wanted. That version of Gamar had never existed, just as my version of Dad had never existed. He was an artifice.

Brendhan sat up straighter and pulled his hands together, like a vicar about to address his congregation.

But Mum spoke over him: 'What happened back then is something that cannot be judged by the five of us, not here and not now.' She picked up the glasses hanging on a chain around her neck and put them on. 'The point is that now you know. Oliver, I'm very sorry if you came to London hoping to find a fortune or a father. It appears you are to go home with neither.'

30

A few weeks after that awful afternoon in Mum's garden, Rita texted me, asking what time I finished on Thursdays, suggesting we go for a walk in Epping Forest after work.
Just you and me?
No, all of us. The 'siblings'.
I wasn't entirely surprised by the suggestion. Ever since the barbecue, I'd been thinking of arranging something similar. Of course, I had talked to Oliver. That night, he and I had stayed up later than usual, drinking non-alcoholic beer and decaffeinated coffee: pretend versions of real drinks to talk about pretend versions of real men. Oliver had told me how Guy – Brendhan's dad – had made model aeroplanes. The little Airfix ones you give children at Christmas. I'd told him about Dad's canvases, which he'd stretched himself. I'd described how he would get so hot doing it that we'd often look through the window to see him topless, knee on the workbench, wrenching the thing into place. Eventually, Oliver had asked how I was feeling about Clive and I'd tried to explain the betrayal, the shame, the way I felt untethered to everything I'd thought I knew about

where I came from. Oliver said he'd always felt untethered. He'd never really felt at home with Guy, felt abandoned when Brendhan left, had never got on with any of Anahera's other boyfriends. He'd been a man with no idea how to be a man.

Now I wanted to talk to Rita. I wanted to hear what Brendhan thought. I wanted to pick over the strips of the past that we'd been handed and try to make some sense of it all together.

I could get to Chingford by about 4.30?

Overground to Hackney Downs, change, on to the Clapton train all the way to Essex.

OK. I'll text Brendhan. You ask Oliver.

The siblings. The 'siblings'. After the heat and weight of that South London afternoon, I was longing for the green quiet of the woods. Summer had sidled its way into London but I had been too occupied to notice. There were huge drifts of pollen across the tarmac paths in nearly every park; the skies were rose gold until nine at night; roses were now kissing the ground, bowed by their own weight. I wanted to feel the soft bounce of moss beneath my feet and to hear birds. Perhaps it was being pregnant but I had a thirst for space that felt somehow powerful.

Luckily, Oliver didn't have a gig that evening. Or a date. He had shown me some of the women he talked to on Tinder: sliver-thin waists, doe eyes, coral-coloured lips. So many of them. So many women in so many bedrooms, standing in front of so many mirrors and in so many bars. I'd thought how at odds his dating life seemed with our domestic one.

When he met me at Hackney Downs he took the rucksack off my shoulders without a word, and handed me a sesame snap.

'Good day expanding the minds of the next generation?'

There was sweat on my upper lip and some weight pulling on my lower back. 'Not bad, thank you. Felix Bridgewater tried to drink the inside of a biro and Seema Ghoshal told me I looked like I'd swallowed a sofa, but there were Party Rings in the staffroom.'

'And so the wheels of civilization keep turning.' As the train approached, Oliver put his body between me and the queue of people pushing to get to the edge of the platform. 'Hey, can I use that about drinking the biro?'

'Use whatever you like. Although I think Felix's dad runs an ad agency, so you might want to change his name.'

The train was cramped and smelled of the inside of other people's lungs. Oliver ploughed a line through to one of the priority seats for me, then started talking to a woman with oily blonde ringlets above my head. It was funny to see him like this – switching between modes. One minute my guardian, the next minute a shark. I watched the marshes flash below me, the River Lea blue for once. I gazed idly into the back gardens of Walthamstow, Wood Street, Highams Park, with their plastic slides and wooden planters and footballs. The pulsing in my back was still there, even sitting down. By the time we wheezed into Chingford, Oliver was giving his number to the woman with hair like Super Noodles and telling her to come watch him at the Bill Murray pub.

Rita was already on the platform with Buster; she must have taken the afternoon off work. As the throng of people in shirtsleeves and pointy shoes started to thin, I saw Brendhan lumber out of one of the rear carriages. He was wearing a vest and a pair of combat shorts and looked like someone about to set up a wall of amps at Reading Festival.

'*Ka pai*, that was one busy fucking train.' Brendhan gave Rita a high five that clattered off the walls. 'Little bro' – he turned to Oliver – 'looking fly as usual, you handsome bastard.' He dropped a paw on Oliver's shoulder and gave it a squeeze.

'Shall we go through?' I started walking towards the ticket barrier, my phone already in my hand. I wasn't sure I wanted to touch Brendhan's bare skin.

'I love those little blippety blips these machines make,' said Brendhan, behind me.

'Bloody hick,' said Oliver, but I could see he was smiling. 'You still unpicking the seams of your shorts to scratch your balls, Brendhan?'

'Watch yourself, runt. There might be bears in them there woods.'

We walked across the grassy plain towards the edge of the treeline in a jumble. Rita was throwing a stick for Buster and telling Brendhan about her new personal best for inverted push-ups. Oliver was typing on his phone, a sly smile at the corner of his mouth. A drone buzzed over us, operated by a man in a utility vest and baseball cap, standing next to a threadbare hawthorn bush. But as we stepped into the dappled light under the hornbeams and on to a carpet of yellow flowers, we all fell quiet. A bird called out its two-note song. Squirrels scurried up nearby trunks. The air turned green.

We walked on for maybe thirty seconds in that silence, coalescing into a square: Rita and I at the front, Brendhan and Oliver behind us, Buster sniffing for squirrels. Rita took my hand and squeezed it lightly.

'So, how are you feeling after what Mum said?' Rita was facing me but could have been addressing us all.

'Weird.' I looked back at her hazel eyes, her dark curly hair, her lips. 'Weird that Dad lied to us.'

'I know.'

'Lied to everyone.' I felt a stick break beneath my foot. 'When I did that test, I honestly never thought I'd find out anything like this.' I looked over at Oliver. 'I thought it would just be something fun – hair colour and stuff.'

'I wanted to find out about dementia,' said Oliver. 'So not exactly fun. But yeah, I didn't expect to find out all this.'

'Do you think your dad knew?' I asked. 'Your stepdad, I mean.'

'What, that I wasn't his? Nah. Mum never said anything, did she, Brendhan?'

But Brendhan had followed Buster off the path towards a moss-covered tree stump. I watched him drop down on to his knees and examine something, close to the ground. A mushroom? A plant?

'I just feel like everything I thought I knew about Dad was wrong,' said Rita. 'Instead of this lovely, fun guy, actually he was just a liar and a sleaze. He was a shit to our mum.' She turned to Oliver. 'And a shit to your mum, too. It's turned everything upside down. I grew up thinking Dad was the nice one and Anne was a bit grumpy.'

'You thought Mum was grumpy?' I asked, feeling a gentle pull in my back.

'Sorry, Nancy, but didn't you?' Rita replied.

I thought about it. It was Mum who had always told us off for leaving our dirty socks in the middle of the floor. Or made us take our dishes to the sink. Or went to bed at nine o'clock every night. I remembered her bottles of paracetamol and aspirin in every drawer.

'And all along he had this bomb just sitting in his studio, ready to go off,' said Rita. 'I mean, how did he know Anahera wasn't going to tell everyone? Or turn up?'

'Maybe he sent her money not to, secretly,' I said. It felt unsavoury to be talking about this in front of Oliver. The poor relation. The bastard. Being sent scraps.

'Maybe he *was* worried.' Rita looked at Oliver. 'I mean, we're talking about all this, but the point is, Dad was on that DNA site well before he died and never told anyone.'

The baby was lying heavy on my pelvis with a lilting, squeezing pressure.

'Nancy, you all right, *kō*?' Brendhan said, catching up. 'You getting tired?'

I stopped. 'Actually, I'm quite thirsty. Do you mind if we stop and just have a drink for a sec?'

There was a patch of grass and a pond to our right. A copper beech to lean on. I gratefully lowered myself on to the ground. Rita, I suspected, was annoyed by the interruption. Oliver started rolling a cigarette.

'You know what you were saying about your ma doing all the housework and earning all the money?' Oliver licked along the edge of the paper. 'Well, that's what being a single parent is. That's what Mum did, after Guy left.'

I touched my stomach. A single parent. A scaffolding of one. A whole family. Was I ready to be a single parent?

Brendhan thumped on to the ground beside me, like a redwood being felled. My mouth was sour.

'Oliver, can I please have my bag?' I started rooting through, looking for a packet of oatcakes. I pulled out my water bottle, a hairband, some Rescue Remedy, a matchbox and some tissues before finally finding the cellophane packet of slightly crushed biscuits.

Brendhan picked up the matchbox. 'Hey, this is a Kiwi brand.' I looked at the red and black beehive.

'That's one of Mum's matchboxes.' Oliver's voice was odd. He seemed to be speaking on the wrong speed setting.

'Your mum's?'

Oliver dropped his cigarette and came towards me.

'Yeah. She made a load of them for one of her shows. Don't you remember, Brendhan? She had them on the windowsills in the kitchen?'

Brendhan didn't say anything.

'Man, I haven't even thought about that kitchen for years.' Oliver dropped to his knees and snatched the box out of Brendhan's hand.

'Don't, Ollie.' A muscle in Brendhan's neck went rigid and, for a second, I worried there was going to be a repeat of the scene in the restaurant. But Brendhan didn't move. Oliver pushed the box open with his forefinger. And there, inside, was the petrol shell. A swirl of shiny blue, purple, green that I'd found in Dad's studio.

'It's a *pāua* shell,' said Oliver. Tiny pockets of silence dropped between each word.

'What's that?' Rita came to lean against the tree behind me.

'A *pāua* shell. They're a New Zealand thing. We used to find them all the time on our beach.' Oliver looked up at Brendhan but the big man was facing the ground. 'And . . . and Mum did a whole thing with them once. Made a load of matchboxes with *pāua* inside. Something to do with the ancestors, watching down on her as she broke the rules. She did an exhibition, didn't she, Brendhan?'

We were all looking at Brendhan.

31

'That's right.' Brendhan was running his thumbnail up the inside of a blade of sedge grass, scooping out the white pulp.

'You remember it, don't you?' Oliver asked.

'I remember her going away,' said Brendhan. 'Having a show abroad with her matchboxes.'

'In London?' Rita asked.

'Could be.' Brendhan flicked the pulp on to the ground with his thumb. There was a moment's silence.

'Wait. Did you know?' Oliver's voice sounded sharp.

'Know what?' Brendhan's hands fell still.

'That Dad wasn't my dad. Did you know all along?' Oliver was staring at Brendhan.

'Well . . .' Brendhan threw the strips of green on to the surface of the pond and took a deep breath. We waited. 'OK. Well, when I was real little, just started elementary school . . . Listen, Ollie, are you sure you want to hear this?'

I felt the lapping, watery feeling again at the bottom of my belly. It wasn't a cramp and it wasn't the ripping pain I'd had before, but it was noticeable. It was uncomfortable. Oliver looked like he might be about to falter. Then he pinched his cigarette out against his fingertips and nodded.

'Spill.'

'OK. I don't remember it really at all.' Brendhan flicked a piece of grass off his enormous thigh. 'Except driving Ma to Auckland in Dad's old ute. She bought me a cassette of Roald Dahl stories at the airport.' We all waited. 'And, well, Mum was going to London. I remember that because I loved Rollerball Rocco the wrestler and I knew he lived in London.' I felt the wave inside me. So that was it. Anahera had been in London. Dad had never left. It was all so simple. 'I think things were a bit rough with Dad – I was a little kid and probably pretty hard work. She'd been invited to be in a show. Something about a council? You know, I was, like, four.' Brendhan dug the heel of his boot into the moss. Nobody else spoke. 'All I remember is that for a while it was just me and Dad. Auntie Kiri, the neighbour, brought round an apple crumble. I don't know how long it was – I was a kid.'

I waited for someone else to break the silence. A small grey bird with a yellow belly landed on a branch on the other side of the pond. Dad. In London. A woman. A stranger.

'So?' Oliver prompted.

'Well, then she came back.'

'And?' Oliver asked.

Brendhan let out a sigh. 'OK. OK. Well, I remember Ma telling me I was going to have a little brother or sister. I don't know how soon after. But I was stoked, you know? I got given my own portable radio. And I said the baby could sleep on my bookshelf.'

'She was pregnant?' Rita asked.

'Must have been.'

'When did she tell you?' Oliver asked. 'Like, how long was it?'

'Ollie, mate, I said. I was, like, five. If it wasn't for the radio, reckon I wouldn't have remembered any of this.'

'But she definitely came to London?' Rita had come a few steps closer.

'Yeah. It was definitely London.'

'And you knew about this all along?' Oliver's face seemed to have folded out of shape. As though someone had hooked a piece of wire under his forehead and pulled, very hard.

'Ah, like, I didn't think anything about it Ollie. Not for years.' Brendhan hesitated. 'But then when I was, I don't know, sixteen, Dad told me he was leaving. Called Mum some pretty choice names.' Brendhan rubbed the back of his neck.

'Tell me,' Oliver said. He'd come up off his knees and was crouching on the ground. Facing Brendhan. Shoulders square.

'He called her a slut and a cheat.' Brendhan looked at the floor. 'Said he'd been bringing up someone else's child. He called you a little wop, Ollie, I remember that. Seemed to think your dad was some Greek waiter she'd met in London or something. Remember how racist he was about Greeks?' Brendhan looked up at Oliver, then quickly away.

I put my hand on my stomach. I couldn't feel any kicking but there was a squeezing feeling, just around my knicker line.

'Wait, you're saying that Dad left because of me?' Oliver's voice had a terrible copper note of pain.

'No, mate. No no no. It wasn't like that.' Brendhan pushed his hand into a fist against his leg. 'I reckon him and Ma had just had another bust-up and Dad got suspicious. He wanted to leave anyway. Things weren't good. You remember? The fighting, the drinking. They both worked but we never seemed to have any money. Dad slept on the sofa; Ma was doing shifts down at the pub so was always coming back late and pissed.'

I was watching Oliver lose his childhood. Just as he had watched us kick apart the man I'd called a father, I was now watching his early life turn to mud. A father who left. A mother who loved him. A brother who was just a half-brother.

'Why did you go with Dad?' Oliver asked.

'Ah, Ollie, I was fifteen.' Brendhan cracked the knuckles of his left hand against his right. 'I was in trouble just about everywhere up North. Dad told me I could drop out of school and start working. And, you know, I felt kind of weird about Mum too. Protective, I guess, of Dad. She'd made a fool of him. At least, that's what I thought.'

A family on bikes wheeled past us: a dad, a mum, two blond children, all in brand-new helmets and high-vis waistcoats. They were chatting animatedly, health beaming off their peach faces. None of us said anything until they had passed out of sight, behind a line of trees.

'Is that why you never came back?' Oliver asked eventually. 'Because you were angry with Ma?'

'I don't know.' Brendhan shifted on the grass. Oliver was still crouching in front of him. 'I guess I just kind of took Dad's side. And then pretty soon I'd moved out, started living on my own. Eventually I met Cherie and she convinced me to go visit but by then Mum had started going kind of soft.' Brendhan let out a sigh full of pain. To lose your mother twice. Once by distance and then by memory. To have a mother who doesn't know you at the door. To have a mother who doesn't remember she even has a child. It was so sad.

'Why didn't you fucking tell me any of this?' Oliver was almost shouting.

'Ahh ...' Brendhan seemed unable to answer. In the pause, I felt the ache in my lower back. I was tired. I'd just walked further than I'd done in weeks. My body seemed to be pulsing from the effort.

'Maybe he didn't want to upset your mum,' said Rita. Rita the big sibling. Rita the oldest daughter. 'I never talked about Anne to Nancy.'

'Talked about what?' I asked.

'Like, how she was always stressed,' Rita said. Aware we were cutting over a bigger conversation, I let it drop.

'Yeah, nah. I probably thought she'd told you. At first.' Brendhan was finally speaking. 'Then, when I moved North and started hearing about you from Ma, I didn't want to bring all that stuff up again. Then when you said you were in London, because of some DNA test, well, I thought you'd figured it out.'

'Is that why you came over?' Rita was looking at Brendhan.

'Maybe a bit. I guess.' Brendhan pulled up another piece of grass. 'That and my wife fucking some seed woman on my kitchen floor.'

I exhaled into the familiar joke. A release of tension. A chance to breathe again. But as I did, I felt a larger pull. This time, joining all the way under from my belly to my back. A heaviness. The lapping waves had suddenly become a riptide.

'Nah, honest, I thought you'd know. I thought that DNA thing would have done it. I thought that's why you'd come to London – to meet him.'

'But he'd died.' Rita, again.

'Yeah, so it turns out.' Brendhan started to split the reed from the bottom with his thick thumbnail.

'I can't believe you knew.' Oliver's eyes were glassy. He was holding himself very tight.

There was another pull inside me. Heavier this time. Not a yanking but a weight. The sort of weight that breaks cheap shelves. What was this?

'I'm sorry, Ollie.'

Oliver didn't reply. Perhaps he couldn't. Because to open his mouth, even for a word, would unleash all his pain.

'Does anyone want to carry on?' Rita edged a stone out of the moss with the toe of her shoe. Oliver looked up and along the path, now empty of other families.

'Sure.' Brendhan hauled himself up, then Oliver. For a moment, the two men were silhouetted against the sky like trees.

I started to stand, pushing up from the ground with my hands. I was so ungainly.

'Ah, Nancy, don't worry.' Oliver was beside me, wrapping a shirt around my waist. 'It's OK, nobody will notice.'

'What?'

'I think' – he lowered his voice – 'I think you might have had an accident.'

I put my hand to my crotch. It was wet. I slid my hand down further. The wetness was spreading down my legs.

'No,' I said. 'I'm not. I'm not weeing, Oliver.' I looked down at my leggings, now wet and black and shining.

'Brendhan?' Oliver turned to his brother. I watched Brendhan's face change. The smile seemed to slide down one side of his face.

'You had an accident, girl?'

'Rita?' I wanted my sister.

'Oh, Chunky, what's happened?' There was almost a chuckle in Rita's voice. What had her silly little sister gone and done this time? But I wasn't silly.

'Nancy.' There was a warm hand, a man's hand, holding the bottom of my back. 'Unless you've had an accident, I think maybe your waters just broke.' The hand made a small circle.

'Her waters?' I heard Rita ask.

'I'm not going to get down on my knees and give it a sniff but if that isn't urine then I reckon it's amniotic fluid.' Brendhan's voice rumbled up through my body. Amniotic fluid. Amniotic fluid. I looked down and saw the glistening damp, reaching my shoes. I couldn't feel anything. Amniotic fluid. 'That's fine. Nothing to worry about.' Brendhan took his hand away. 'It just means that, sometime soon, we might want to think about getting you back into town.'

Into town. I looked up and saw a sea of green. Huge tree trunks, like pillars. The sour leaves. Tiny purple flowers and spiky brown beech nuts.

'Rita, what are you doing?' Oliver's voice. I looked down again. Rita was squatting on the ground, beside my feet. Buster was running around us, dizzy with the excitement of this new turn of events. Rita was sniffing my trousers.

'It doesn't smell like urine.' Rita stood up without even using her hands. My sister is strong. 'Shut up, Buster.'

'Nancy, here. Drink this.' Oliver held out a water bottle. The water inside was cool. I felt another tugging weight in my back. Not crunching or churning, just a deep, fuzzy pull that I could do nothing to resist. I sucked in more air.

'When Cherie had Tehine, her waters broke down in one of the paddocks,' Brendhan said, scratching his beard. 'She didn't actually give birth until the next day but, still, I think we should get you out of this little wood.'

'Rita, do you think this might actually be happening?' I spoke almost in a whisper.

'What?'

'Do you think these are contractions?'

'What do they feel like?' Brendhan stepped aside; the others had started to crowd in around me.

'They're like . . .' I felt silly. What if they weren't contractions? What if I had just had an accident? 'A sort of pressure in my lower back?'

'What, not your uterus?' There was a haze of sweat across Rita's upper lip.

'No. A weight. Pulling on my back.'

'And how long have you been having them?' Brendhan asked.

'Well, actually.' I thought of the waves licking at my spine during work. Were they? I thought of my back, in the train. Had I? 'Maybe for a while. Since this afternoon,' I said. 'But when they got stronger, walking through here, I thought it was just from doing exercise.'

'You've been having contractions all this time and didn't even tell me!' Rita's voice was shrill.

Oliver put his hand on her shoulder and slipped his body between us. 'Rita. It's OK. Nancy's fine. Here, sis, have some water.'

'Tsssssh.' Rita's teeth were bared. 'Is that your one thing, Oliver? Offering water?'

I looked up at Brendhan. A dark silhouette, ringed by silvery red hair. 'Do you think they might actually be contractions?'

Brendhan scratched his chin. 'Sounds to me like they might be.'

My notes. The blue booklet, lying on the bed. The birth plan. Low Papp-A. Antibiotics. All the notes. I'd left them at home. It was early. Too early. I shifted my weight and heard the wet sucking sound of my shoe. The midwife had said that once my waters broke I'd have to go to hospital. There was sweat on my neck. Spit in my mouth. Wetness down my legs and into my shoes. I thought of Clive. Of his grey, swollen body in the water. All that water. Broken water.

'Now, I can carry you.' Brendhan's voice jutted into my thoughts. 'But I actually think you'd probably be safer walking.' Walking where?

'Walking? Where are we going?' Rita's voice was sharp. I could hear she was panicking.

'To the hospital.' Oliver stood in front of Rita, absorbing her shock before it reached me, full force.

'She can't walk all the way to Homerton!'

'No, Rita. It's OK,' said Oliver. 'We just need to get back to the road. I've ordered a cab. It's coming.'

32

As the next wave came, I rolled my head down like a bull preparing to charge. Oliver's chest. I buried my face into him, hard. I was scared. I was being pulled down into the ground.

'Don't worry, Nancy.' I heard Oliver's voice. Gentle. Confident. This was his talking-to-women voice. This was how he did it. 'You're all right. We're here. We're going to look after you.'

I looked into his face. Dad? I felt a hand across my cheek.

'Now, little sis, there's a tree root here.' I felt Brendhan's arm around my waist. Another beneath my elbow. For a second, the weight lifted from my bones. It was all soft. All green.

Walking could help bring the baby down, engage the cervix, bring on dilation. Did I want to dilate? I wasn't ready. I was only thirty-six weeks. The flat. No blankets. No bibs.

'Nancy, you're doing great.' Oliver's voice. On my other side; not touching but close. There he was again.

With his chin and his eyes. Where was Rita? Rita was meant to be there.

'Rita?'

'She's here, she's here,' said Oliver. 'She's walking right behind you.' I tried to turn but Oliver put his arm around me, blocking the view. 'She's a wee bit emotional just now. But she's fine. We're all fine. You're strong, Nancy. You're real strong.' Through the fuzz of this great, bursting body, I sensed that Oliver and Brendhan were guiding me forward. Past trees. Over soil. Out of the woods.

'Now, Nancy, your body knows just exactly what to do.' Brendhan's voice was like rust. 'I was there with Cherie both times. She had the girls at home. Your body won't do anything until you feel safe.' The sun danced across my skin. 'As soon as we get to the hospital, you'll be ready.' I sighed into the weight. Into the heavy, swelling weight. 'I've seen it with the cattle. They'll be pacing and pacing and then, suddenly, they're ready.' I was an animal. I could taste blood in my mouth. I could smell the men beside me. I was an animal.

I had to stop twice. Completely stop and just gasp. Fill my lungs with cold, silver air shivering off the leaves. Fill up this burning darkness and breathe out great spirals of light, going into the sky. I was a dragon. I was a volcano. I was about to erupt.

'Hrhrhrhrh.' It wasn't a moan but a sigh.

'That's the way, Nancy.' Oliver stroked the hair from my face. Rita, Oliver, Brendhan. I wanted my mother. How long had we been walking?

'They're still only eight minutes apart.' Oliver's voice was gentle.

I stopped. This wasn't a baby; it was a planet. The gravity of the whole planet was pulling down on my back, my pelvis, my bones. I was a tiny, teetering creature on top of this great planet of heaviness. Shudders of rock and bone and lava moved beneath my skin.

'There's the car park, Nancy.' Brendhan this time. 'And there are our cabs.' I opened my eyes. 'Now, me and Oliver, we're going to take you straight to the hospital. Rita's going to go to your flat and pick up everything. OK, Rita?'

I turned and saw Rita. Her face was a mask of tears. Frozen. Eyes wide. Rita was terrified. She had absorbed all my panic and added her own, too. So that's why they'd kept her behind me.

'Hey, man,' said Oliver, lifting his chin to the two taxi drivers standing beside their open doors, leaning against their cars. 'Sorry about the wait. It took us a little longer than—'

'No worries, pal.' I caught a glance of a dark, ferrety little man. 'I have bin liners in case.'

'Her waters already broke in there.' Brendhan nodded into the trees. 'So we should be right.'

I wanted to tell Rita to bring the blue book. I wanted to explain where I'd put a nightie and that I'd need knickers and how we didn't have a car seat and that I'd not got a bag and which was my toothbrush but I couldn't speak. I was hanging on to the edge of the car, just trying to resist this awesome force pulling me into the ground.

'Rita, sis, you've got this. OK?' I could hear Brendhan murmuring. 'You're a fighter. You need to be there for Nancy, OK?' What was he doing? 'Ring your mum in the car. And don't panic.' His voice dropped even further. I only caught snatches. '. . . at least another three or four hours . . . some snacks . . . all good.'

'OK.' Rita sounded like a child.

'Rightio. Don't forget a phone charger.'

'Homerton Hospital, please, mate.' I felt Oliver's hand against my back. For a second, the touch of someone else transported me.

'Press,' I gasped. 'Press my back.'

'It's OK. I have done this journey,' said the driver. 'With my wife.'

'Hear that, Nancy?' Brendhan laid his hand over mine and started to unclasp my fingers from the metal. 'We've got another professional with us.' Oliver had let go of my back. I was being dragged down again. 'Now, if you don't want to sit down you can kneel, that's fine. Face any which way. There's plenty of room.' Was he talking to me? 'Reckon you'll have to come back here with her, Ollie. No way we'll both fit.'

'Wait!'

Rita. She was out of the car and walking towards me. I could hear the scuff of her shoes on the gravel. I knew her just by the rhythm of her feet. 'This isn't right. She's my sister. I should be with her.' I felt a hand on my back.

Knuckles, pushing hard against the bottom of my spine, right where the pain was focused. 'Oliver?' Her voice was almost adult again. 'You go and pick up the notes. Take Buster. I'm fine. I just got a bit scared but I'm OK now. I want to be with Nancy.'

Something lurched up my throat. Vomit. I was going to be sick. I turned away from the car but managed to hit Oliver's shoes.

'*Ka pai.*' Oliver was trying not to sound angry. The air turned sour as it entered my mouth. 'They're not my favourites.'

I was kneeling on the back seat of the car, pressing my face against the cool glass of the window. The light outside was so bright. Since throwing up, the sweating, volcano heat had changed into something paler, sharper, calmer. I wasn't tired – I was translucent. For the first time in – what? hours? – the world outside had come back to me. I could hear the taxi driver's radio. I looked at the small, red-brick houses and realized that every single person who had ever lived there had been born. Every person who had made the bricks, fitted the windows, trimmed the hedges, had been born. Everyone in the whole world had been born. Being born wasn't just something we have in common; it was who we are. We are all born. I had been born. Mum had done all this once, just so I could be born.

'Tell Mum,' I was whispering.

'I have, Noodle. I've told her.'

'No.' I ran my tongue across cracked lips. 'Tell her that I love her and now I understand.'

'Understand what?' Rita was tapping on her phone, probably glad at last to be doing something.

'Understand what she did.' I sighed again into that cold, white light. 'And I love her. Tell her I love her.'

The waves pulling down inside my body were still there but I wasn't resisting them. I wasn't pinned down by them. I had let go utterly. I was on my way. My sister was there and Brendhan was there and there was no way back. I saw that now. Was I thirsty? Was I tired? I didn't know. I wasn't a body; I was motion. I was gravity.

'I'll just take you up to the door,' said the taxi driver and I felt the car vibrate beneath my knees.

'Thanks, bro,' said Brendhan. Brendhan. How funny that Brendhan was here. With his cow crush and his tomato seeds. For a second, I felt the stream of my thoughts slide towards Gamar. But no, I had to let that thought sink away, into the ground. Gamar was not here. I sighed, feeling a sharp, metal shiver run through my body. Gamar was never here. Someone would tell him, when they needed to. Rita could tell him. But he was not here. And because he was not here, he was not my family. I was resigned to that now.

'You have to walk in, I'm afraid,' the driver said and I could hear the smile in his voice. 'They don't let me drive into the birth pool.'

The car door beside me opened. Light. The world was so bright. Bleach. Tarmac. Aeroplanes. Glass.

'Right, Noo, me and Brendhan will help get you out.' I turned and saw Brendhan's stomach beside my face. His T-shirt had ridden up slightly and there was soft, white skin. He was a baby once, I thought. He was born. I'd never really understood it before but now I did. He, we all, had been born once too.

'Right, miss, let's get you to the pea-shelling section.' I was lifted out of the car. Two hands in mine. A mismatched paperchain. As I stood, the weight inside me came back, stronger this time. I was being pushed into the ground. I couldn't move. I don't know how long I stood there, being squeezed into the very centre of myself, but eventually I realized that the taxi had disappeared. We started to walk, smooth as butter, towards a glass door. Rita on one side, Brendhan on the other. Beyond the door was a golden pine desk. Its edges were round. Everything was round. I felt the hands on me start to push me forwards. Why were we rushing? What was the hurry?

Rita and a woman behind the desk were talking but I could only hear snatches: 'room available', 'assessment', 'monitor', 'dilation'. I stood, my eyes fluttering shut. Was I swaying? Perhaps. I was salt water. I was an ocean. Eventually, Rita turned to me and said, in a voice I knew from so many games, so many car journeys, so many plans: 'Nancy. You have to do a urine sample. I'll come with you. As soon as someone is available, they'll take a look at you, and give you a blood test. Then we can go into a room.'

She passed me a jar. I smiled and whispered back, 'The champion's cup.'

There was a string of red in the jar after I filled it. It looked like a tiny jellyfish. The whole thing seemed to sparkle with flecks of red and gold and white.

'Well done, sis,' Rita said, taking it from my hand. I didn't want to pull my trousers back up. I didn't want to add any pressure to my skin. 'Let's go and have a sit-down.'

Brendhan was looking at his phone in the waiting room. Through half-shut lids, I looked down at the screen. Two girls with long brown hair. On a beach. Holding a string bag full of shells. I started to drift away from the room. Shells. Shelling peas. I heard a phone ringing far away. Pāua shells. Power shells. The ocean. Fluid. Waves.

'Wanna sit down, kid?' Brendhan took my elbow but as I touched the seat it felt all wrong. I was too soft, too open for this brittle surface.

'The chair is very hard.' I almost whispered it.

'Here.' Rita was pushing something underneath me. 'Sit on my coat.'

I smiled, hazily. 'You never lend me your clothes.'

Something had changed since getting out of the car. It was now as though I was hanging, suspended, between two worlds. I was ceasing to be. I was exhausted, perhaps, but I had also surrendered. And I was finding this disassociation almost funny. Look at me: in a hospital, giving birth. As though that was something I was capable of doing. Look at us: three siblings with different parents. Mum would be on her way. Dad gone. What a huge genetic joke, to be making more members of this messy family.

After a few minutes, perhaps a few hours, I opened my eyes and saw Oliver. Funny. Oliver was funny. He was talking to a woman in blue behind the reception desk. She was shaking her head. Then Oliver reached across the desk and took the woman's hand. He looked at her, his head slightly tilted, and said something. The woman in blue, her hand still in Oliver's, looked over at me. Then back at him. Slowly, I watched her nod. She had an expression on her face somewhere between coy and confused; as though surprised at her own relenting. My blue book was in Oliver's other hand. The notes. The birth plan. The birth planet. I was a birth planet. I closed my eyes again. There was something hot against my knee. I looked down and there was Oliver, kneeling at my feet. He was holding something small and green in his hand.

'I found it when we were in the wood,' he said. 'In New Zealand, we say a four-leaf clover is good luck.'

'We say that here, too,' Rita replied. 'Here, I'll put it in the pages of my book for safekeeping.'

'Nancy Albany.' A woman in paler blue scrubs and white trainers was standing by the door. In response, I felt Rita and Brendhan lift me up, on to my feet. What had happened to gravity?

'I'm afraid I can only have one person in here while we assess her,' said the midwife. Was she a midwife?

'Rita.' My voice didn't sound like my voice.

'I'm here.'

'I want you,' I said.

The bed was blue and wipe clean with three seams across the middle.

'Just pop yourself down here,' said the midwife. She was small. So small that I felt like I was looking down the wrong end of a telescope. 'I'm just going to take some blood and pop this belt around you, to monitor baby's heartbeat.' How was this woman, with her Mini Milk arms, ever going to reach across my body?

'Why are you doing a blood test?' Rita asked. I was listening to everything now. I had become sharp. I was open. The fuzzy heat of the earlier contractions had gone and I was metallic.

'Oh, just standard tests. Blood group, HIV, iron levels.'

Iron, I thought. I was iron. I was a knight and these were my men. I was shining.

'Have you read the notes?' Rita and the midwife were talking over me. Rita was always talking over me.

'Don't worry, we've got them.'

'The birth plan.' I heard the panic at the corners of Rita's voice. 'We have a birth plan.' I remembered Rita's face in the woods, how Oliver had tried to hide her. The fear. And then I thought of Rita at Dad's side in the funeral home. She had refused to touch him. She had retched, later, in the street.

'We've got time for everything, don't worry.'

Rita squeezed my hand hard. Too hard. Another searing wave of pressure ripped through my body. My closed eyes were facing the glare of the ceiling light. How much longer was I going to have to lie like this? Pinned down. Strapped to the bed. Then, the galloping sound of a heartbeat erupted into the room.

'There they are,' said the midwife, reading the numbers on the monitor. 'And they sound fine. Quite fast but fine.'

I listened to the heartbeat. Thunder. The chase. A typhoon. As the gasping pain eased from my body, the heartbeat started to slow. It was no longer a heartbeat, not even a baby; it was the ticking of my body. It was the countdown to the rest of time.

'I'm going to do a vaginal examination now, OK?' said the midwife. 'Are you happy for me to examine you?' I nodded. I could feel the midwife's fingers in my vagina. I felt like the mouth of a river.

'Great, Nancy. So you're eight centimetres, which means we can get you on to the labour ward.'

'We wanted a pool.' Finally Rita spoke.

'Your partner wanted a water birth?'

'She's my sister,' Rita replied sharply. 'Not my partner. And she was booked into the birth centre.' I thought of dormitories: women screaming and thin curtains. The heartbeat on the speakers sped up.

'I see. OK. Well, we're not too busy today, so I'm pretty sure you can go into one of our birth rooms,' said the midwife, snapping off her gloves. 'Mum isn't high risk.'

Mum isn't high risk. Mum. Anne. I reached out for Rita's hand and put it on my forehead. I wanted her to stroke across my eyebrows, like Mum used to as I was falling asleep. But Rita just brushed the hair from my face instead and murmured: 'Don't worry, Nancy. Don't worry.'

'Are you OK standing up?' The midwife, the size of a sparrow, was undoing the Velcro around my waist. The clip-clop, clip-clop disappeared and for a second the silence was like a physical jolt. Like a missed step. Like a rolled ankle. God, I was tired. Tired and sharp and too tight all over. The lights were too bright. My mouth tasted of rust. But I was eight centimetres. I was being allowed in.

As the doors to the reception area swung open, I saw Dad waiting by the window. He turned and smiled, a curl of black hair stuck to his eyebrow. Dad. Dad was there. He was in Oliver and he was in Rita and he was in me. Which meant that, somehow, he could be in the room when his grandchild was born. Did I want him there? The man who had betrayed us? But then, he had made us. He had created the spark. He was a liar. He was my father. He was dead. But he was here. I could feel it. Oliver was here too. Oliver was real. Not a secret any more.

'Now, Nancy, you can have two birth partners in the room with you.' Another woman was talking to me now. She was curled over. Was I curled over? 'Anyone else can wait here, of course. Or our restaurant is open again.' I reached my hand out towards Oliver.

'Ah, Nancy.' He looked apprehensive. 'Don't you think Brendhan might be a bit, aaaah ... like ... You know, he's done this before ... and ...'

'That's right, bro.' There was a laugh at the back of Brendhan's throat. 'I've done it all before. Maybe now it's your turn.'

'My turn?' Oliver shot back at Brendhan.

'You don't have to have anyone else, Nancy.' Rita, this time. 'I'm your birth partner.'

Another wave shuddered through my body and I needed to take off my clothes. All my clothes. The damp leggings hanging from my waist were a vice. The seams of my T-shirt were slicing into my armpit. I needed to get them away. So without a word, and without letting go of Oliver's hand, I started to walk towards the door like a cowboy.

33

'Hello, Nancy, I'm Katie.' I was staring into the face of the most beautiful woman I had ever seen in my life. A woman with pale skin and freckles the colour of conkers. 'Are you Dad?' she asked Oliver.

'No, he's our half-brother. I'm the birth partner.' Rita started to rub the bottom of my back, although there was no contraction. 'But I'm single. I mean, I'm her sister.'

I had shuffled out of my shoes and was peeling off my leggings.

'If you want, I can ...' Oliver took a step towards the door.

'Now, Nancy, when did you last empty your bladder?' Katie's voice was close and I could feel her breath on my face. It smelled of peach yoghurt. 'If you're not feeling the urge to push yet, it might be an idea to try having a wee, make some room.'

'Stay here,' I said to Oliver, my fingers already pulling at my knickers.

On the toilet, something changed. Just behind my bum I was seized by a familiar sense of readiness, of anticipation. With my eyes truly open for perhaps the first time in hours, I walked back into the room. Rita was talking very quietly to Oliver beside a purple inflated ball. He was pale.

'Nancy?' Katie the beautiful midwife put her hand on my shoulder, as light as a bird. 'Can you feel anything in your bottom?'

'Yes.' How did she know?

She smiled. 'And are you feeling the urge to push?'

'Perhaps.' I could really hear this woman. And talk to her. Despite the typhoon inside my body I could engage my mind. I could see what was going on.

'OK,' said Katie. 'Sometimes being in the water actually slows things down for a bit so I want to make sure your contractions are really established. How about a go on the birth ball just while we fill it up?'

Walking towards the purple ball, I saw Oliver's eyes were wide, like a spooked horse. Was I bleeding? Was he frightened of blood? I looked down. With utter indifference I saw that I was naked. Small pearly beads of colostrum rolling on to my stomach.

'Nancy, we're just going to listen to the heartbeat.' No. No no no. I couldn't lie down again. Not the lights. Not the belts. I couldn't. 'It's OK, it's wireless. You just ignore me and keep going.'

White, blinding light pushed down through me. A tree cracked in my ear. The galloping sound was there again. Faster this time. Forward. Onward.

'Ngggaaaaaaaaannnnrrrr.' And suddenly, there was Oliver. In front of me.

'It's OK, Nancy, it's OK.' I pushed my head into him. 'Feel your body. Let it come. Just feel your body.' He kissed the top of my head. 'It's your body. You're all right.'

Another contraction, so close to the last that there was no time to breathe. The galloping sound was faster. Katie was there but I could no longer feel my skin. As the contraction seized me, I heard the heartbeat slow. The baby. My baby. I needed it to stay alive. I needed to stay alive. I tried to feel my body. I tried to exist. I buried my neck into Oliver. Everything else was obliterated.

'Nancy, I think you're getting close, my darling.' Katie sounded pleased. 'So let's get you on the bed so we can fit the cannula.'

'Caaaaaaggh.' I pictured the breath pouring out of my body. I felt another hand under my elbow. Rita was there. And Oliver. Mum and Brendhan were probably outside. My family had flocked to me. But I couldn't lie down. Not again. Never again on that blue leather bed. And so I just sank to my knees, leaving my hand on the bed, so Katie could insert her needle.

'Oliver,' I said, after a second. 'Rita.' A tiny smile. 'I'm not taking this lying down.'

Oliver laughed. 'Good one, Nancy.' His hand was somewhere on me but I couldn't quite tell where. 'Good on ya.'

My limbs seemed to have faded out. I was a tube. A wormhole. A portal between worlds. I could see a piece of plastic running into the back of my hand.

And there, next to my arm, was my father's hand. Oliver's hand.

'OK, Nancy,' said the midwife. 'Just because of this position, I'm going to bring the monitor in from beh—'

The rest of the sentence was lost in a sound like the tearing of metal. The noise, I realized, was coming from me. I was screaming. The urgency in my body was absolute. I was on the edge. I was teetering. And yet, even there, even peeping over into oblivion, I did not want to break apart. The baby needed to come out slowly. I did not want to be torn in two. I held back.

'That's OK, you're doing fine,' Katie said. A blast of beating heart filled the room again. 'Nancy, I want you to do short, shallow—'

'Can I push yet?' I gasped. My eyes were closed but I could feel the hopeful frown pulled across my face.

Katie stopped mid-sentence. 'Of course you can, Nancy. Of course you can push. If you want to.'

'Give it the big one, sis,' Oliver whispered. And so here it was. That pounding, familiar, irresistible urge. Here it was. To heave. To push. To expel.

'You can do it, Nandi,' said Rita, squeezing my shoulder. 'You can do it.'

I tensed my whole body, pushing my face into the bed. I turned myself entirely inside. I forced everything into a rock-hard stillness, until the interior of my body could finally dissolve. I imploded. Something rippled.

'Lovely, Nancy. I can see the head.' The head. The head. The head. The head. The head. 'On the next contraction,

Nancy, I think we can get the whole head out, OK?' Katie sounded calm. Utterly in control. Then, in a quieter voice: 'Birth partners, do you want to watch?'

'You're amazing, Nancy.' Oliver's voice was low. 'I won't watch. Don't worry. But you get that bloody head out. Get it out. You can do it.'

I sucked in every speck of air and, as the next contraction came, I clenched. Not my vagina but everything else in my body became a dense and immovable block.

'That's it, that's it,' Katie called out. 'Just one more—'

Suddenly, I could feel it. I could feel knees and elbows. I felt a body, passing through my body. With a slippery burst of power, I gave myself up to the world and gave my baby up to the air.

'I've got her,' Katie said. 'She's here. Nancy, your baby is here.'

I looked down between my knees and saw a tiny, purple person. Right there. On top of an NHS towel. Centimetres from the floor.

'Let's get you up so you can hold her.'

With no idea how it was happening, I rolled on to the bed. And there, on my chest, was a baby. A girl. Her face was stained with all the knowledge and all the pain of the world.

'Oh my God. I did it.' I looked up at Rita. And behind Rita, with tears in his eyes, at Oliver. 'I've actually done it.'

34

The door to the birthing room swung open and we looked up. Instead of a midwife, the person that toppled into the room, under a flurry of linen and carrier bags, was Mum.

'Nancy?' she whispered, moving quickly across the room. 'Oh, Nancy, I was so worried.'

The smell of Green Tea by Elizabeth Arden washed across my face.

'But where's the baby?' She whipped around like a gunslinger, knocking the side of my bed with her handbag. Then she must have seen Rita, in her bra, holding the baby. Rita's face was crumpled like an old Hula Hoops packet from so much crying.

'Oh, Nancy! Oh, Rita!'

'She's just asleep at the moment,' whispered Rita. A smile curled across my face. Everyone was whispering. In here, all was gentle and orderly and soft. Everything that needed to be said could be said in a whisper. I could have stayed in that room for the rest of my life.

'Oh my God, Nancy, she looks just like you!' Mum

dropped on to her knees beside the chair. 'But Rita, why don't you have your top on?'

'Skin to skin, Mum. It's meant to—'

The door opened again. This time it was Oliver, carrying a tray covered in five cardboard tubs, holding baked potatoes, beans, cheese and tuna. For a second, I thought they looked like skulls, broken open. And yet, my mouth had filled with saliva. I was ravenous.

'Oliver?' Mum's voice had gone tight. 'You wanted Oliver here for the birth? Rather than me?'

'Mum, I didn't know I was in labour.'

'Sorry. Sorry. I know.' Mum was still on the floor by Rita's chair. 'But when I saw Rita's message, I assumed you two were on your own here.'

I felt something tugging upwards, inside me. My body had broken into continents: limbs, pelvis, neck. And there, on Rita's shoulder, was the outermost part of me. A part that had, somehow, become detached. The baby started to cry and I was flooded with panic. My baby. She needed her mother. Her mother? But my mother was now standing between me and my baby.

'Reckon somebody's about ready for a top-up,' said Brendhan, coming out of the bathroom. Bulkily, unstoppably, he lifted the baby from Rita's chest and, holding my daughter's face down along his forearm, brought her to me.

'Brendhan?' Mum spluttered. 'What ... but ... you're ...'

'I was in the woods when Nancy's waters' – completely unselfconsciously, Brendhan pulled the sheet down from my chest and rolled the baby into my arms – 'broke. I missed the main show, of course. Half-brother's half-brothers have to sit in the waiting room smoking cigars and talking about horses.'

Very carefully, I lined the baby's nose up to my nipple, just as the midwife had shown me. I looked down at her grey, swimming eyes. Where was she? Her dark pupils were somehow empty. The twitching movements involuntary. So where was she, this child of mine? When would she arrive? The tugging at my breast was quick, urgent. She was hungry. I was hungry. And thirsty. Thirstier than I had ever been in my life.

Oliver came towards me with one of the potatoes.

'Water,' I said.

Like lightning, Mum was at my side, pushing an enormous red Nalgene water bottle against my mouth.

'Don't worry, Oliver, I can look after this.' She blotted out my entire view. I tried to swallow the lukewarm water without choking. The baby let out a small, musical sigh.

'Maybe us guys should . . .' Oliver gestured towards the door with his thumb.

Mum looked round. 'I'm sorry. Oliver. Brendhan.' She shook her head. 'Sorry I was sharp with you. I just hadn't expected you to be here instead of me.' Mum's voice was watery. 'But thank you. I can see that you've been looking after Nancy. You obviously helped.'

'No worries, Anne. It was an honour.' I saw a tiny smile creep across Brendhan's face.

'Well, see you later, Nancy,' said Oliver. I got the impression he didn't want to leave but I was too tired to negotiate. 'Well done.' Then, just before he reached the door, he stopped. 'What are you gonna call her? Our niece?'

I looked at him. This man who was not my brother, not my father, not a stranger and not my partner. I looked down at the baby in my arms. I traced the squashed-up brow and swollen nose. The dark wet curls stuck to her scalp. The familiar line of her chin. I thought of the way I'd felt Dad's presence during the birth. I thought of how my family had built around me like a buttress. I thought of the way I had been carried through the woods. Oliver. Clive. Love. Mother. In a voice that had been cracked open by love and courage and pain, I answered:

'Clover.'

35

I picked up the leaflet and read it again.

Jaundice is the name given to yellowing of the skin and whites of the eyes and is very common in newborn babies.

I had gone over these pages many times in the last two days. Every time, looking for something new: a passport home, a get-out clause.

It is usually harmless and clears up in most babies after 10–14 days.

We had been in the hospital for three days, my new, golden daughter and I. We'd spent our days shuffling down to the room full of disco boxes, where I'd placed her under the humming lights. The babies all wore sunglasses and nappies; a neonatal Ibiza on floor two.

I had slipped into a pale blue, postnatal haze in the hospital. My meals arrived on a trolley; biscuits and brick-coloured tea when I slept; nurses and midwives and doctors came and clicked Clover's hips and watched her feed and wrote things on pieces of paper I never saw again. I breastfed. I felt as if I were in an airlock, a waiting room, a departures lounge. Or no, I was on a train: a big pastel train called the NHS and I had to stay on that train until I reached my destination. The station called Normal Bilirubin Levels.

Rita had come on the first day with a bag of clothes and pistachio baklava and a copy of *Chat* magazine. Oliver had come too, with a bag of grapes and a book from my bedroom and a thermos cup. Mum had barely left. The way she looked at Clover was so intense it was almost threatening. As if she wanted to swallow her.

When the levels reach a level where phototherapy can stop, a blood test will be taken 12–18 hours after to make sure the jaundice has returned to normal. This last test may be done in an outpatient clinic.

There was no morning and no night and no afternoon and no day; there was just Clover. Me and my baby daughter, an eight-limbed, four-lung creature of milk and blood and heartbeats. I watched the velvet beating of her fontanelle and thought about the brain that lay just under the skin. How easy it would be to push my finger into it.

I was also punctured, frequently, by a single, uncontestable thought: I must not die. I had to keep breathing and eating and producing colostrum. Even as blood smeared out of me on to the enormous sanitary towels my mum had brought, I couldn't worry about myself. I was the one keeping us alive.

'Hello, Nancy. I'm Frances, the duty midwife today.' I was still holding the phototherapy leaflet in my hand, staring into nothing. 'How are you?' She was blonde and thickset, like a lasagne. I had not met her before.

'I'm . . . I'm fine, thanks.' It was like being at a twenty-four-hour job interview, on a plane, on your own.

'And how's Baby?' I was being scrutinized, I knew. They call it an assessment and it was. If I passed this, I might be allowed home. If I failed, I could – what – lose my daughter? Be locked away? If I opened my legs and screamed into her face, what would be the procedure? I had to be honest, but not too honest. I had to ask for help but not appear helpless. I had to show emotion but only the right emotions.

'She's fine. I fed her at five and again at six and at seven twenty.'

Clover was so small that she needed to be fed almost hourly. She shouldn't be here. She was too early for oxygen and nostrils and milk and fabric. It was my fault.

'Good. Now, I've had a talk with the doctor who's just come on duty and we've taken a look at . . .' She looked at the page. '. . . Clover's results and she's done brilliantly, bless her. So, we'll do a blood test on her today and keep you in for tonight but then, fingers crossed, you'll be going home tomorrow.'

My heart lurched against my ribs. Home tomorrow.

'Do you have someone who can take you home?'

I caught sight of a whiteboard above the empty bed opposite me. It had been cleaned but the marks and lines of previous patients' notes were still there, like ghosts. I saw one word: *tremors*.

'Aah, yes. I mean, yes.' I tried to sound like a mother. 'My sister can drive me. Or my mum.'

'Oh, lovely. You're all in London, is it?' I must have nodded. 'And do you live with anyone, Nancy? We do recommend having someone there for the first few weeks.'

Home. My flat. A flat with people hitting cricket balls against the wall. Hard, solid balls that would sink into the soft flesh at the top of my daughter's head.

'I . . . I live with my brother.' Banging doors, key fobs, cigarette smoke from Yvonne downstairs, the black mould in the bathroom, no cot, single glazing, the 253 bus, stairs, petrol, speakers, dogs.

'Oh, big family! Lovely.'

I wasn't ready. Suddenly, in the space of a breath, I knew I wasn't ready. I couldn't go back to the flat. Oliver on the sofa, the neighbours arguing, bleeding into my toilet. I'd thought I would have more time. I was supposed to have four more weeks to prepare. I'd been waiting for the nesting instinct. I had been waiting for Gamar to contact me. Just as Rita said, I had been waiting for things to happen to me. That old, bad pattern. I had expected things to get done; I hadn't been doing them.

'Hello, darling. Oh, hello, Frances!' Mum's sandals slapped against the floor as she came towards the bed. How did she know this midwife's name? Had I met Frances before? How many days had I been here?

'Hello, Anne.' Frances moved a little closer to the

curtain so Mum could start unloading her bag on to the bed. Flapjacks, the *Guardian*, lavender essential oil, reading glasses, a spinach and feta pastry, a sleep mask, a purple tube of lanolin, oranges, more sanitary towels, a flannel. Too much. Too much stuff.

'I was just saying to Nancy that after this morning's dose of phototherapy, we're going to do a blood test,' said the midwife. 'Then, hopefully, we'll be able to discharge mum and baby tomorrow.'

Mum and baby. Mumandbaby. Mumnbaby.

'Really?' Mum's voice sounded caught between fear and delight. 'Are you sure she's ready?' Then she shook her head. 'Of course, you know what's safe. Tomorrow! Nancy!' I said nothing. Mum's worrying had annoyed me. Her spilling bags of shit had annoyed me. Where was her faith in me? Why was she questioning the midwife rather than asking how I felt? Something changed. I wasn't just a daughter and a sister, but a mother. I was trying.

'I'm going to go to Clover.' I slid my legs on to the floor. My dressing gown had fallen open but I did nothing to adjust it. The soft mounds of my body still only felt partially my own. I couldn't think of them now. I had to get to Clover.

In the room, boxes and boxes of babies stood, at waist height. There were portholes in the sides of their cots we could push our arms through. Monitors blinked and whirred. The tubes, the clamps, the white medical tape. I smiled at the mothers. Clover was the third from the left. By comparison, she looked so big. At thirty-six weeks she was just one week pre-term; four weeks before her due date. In this ward she was Falstaff: round shoulders, black curly hair, organs you couldn't see beneath her skin. But she was small. So small. She was a universe in the bend of my elbow. Under the glow of the light I could see she was sleeping. I wasn't meant to take her out of the box except to feed and yet I was aching to hold her. She needed me. She needed me.

'Can I feed her, please?' I asked one of the special midwives with their different lanyards and quiet, neonatal voices.

'Again? OK. Of course. Here, take this chair. Anne and your sister can sit with you.' Anne? My sister? I looked around and saw Mum and Rita at the door.

As Clover was put into my arms, I felt the disorienting buoyancy of her tiny body. Where I expected weight there was just softness. Where I had expected density there was just tenderness. After a few seconds, I realized Mum was talking.

'Sorry, what were you saying?' I asked.

'Ah, I'll start again.' Mum smiled and reached out to touch Clover's foot. 'Rita and I have spoken to Oliver. And Brendhan.' Rita nodded.

'I think you should come and live with me, sis. Just for the first six months,' said Rita. 'But longer if you need to.' I dropped my eyes to Clover's sleeping face. The curve of her forehead was just like Rita's. Her glossy black curls reminded me of the baby photos I'd seen of my sister too.

'And I have offered Oliver the use of the garden studio,' said Mum. 'It has a sink and he can come and go as he pleases through the side gate.' Oliver. The garden. Rita's flat. A sink.

'That means you can let out your flat, Noodle.' Rita's voice again. 'You'd have another income while you're on maternity leave. And I could help out.' Paintbrushes, kitchen stools, a washing line. My head spun. An income. The bath. A changing table, fruit bowl, washing machine, coat hooks. London. Subletting. Every time I tried to grab a thought, three others slipped into its path. Pillowcases. Keeping-in-Touch days, this is floor two, clearing out under the sink, milk, heating. Could I sublet my flat? But it wouldn't be subletting, would it? It would just be letting. That's what Rita had said. I looked down to check that Clover was still breathing. Letting the flat. Letting it go. Letting go. And Oliver. In Dad's studio. Grass, paraffin heaters, Nescafé, my pelvis, the Northern Line, spare keys, the pear tree. So Oliver wasn't going back to New Zealand. Was Mum going to charge him rent? What about Brendhan? The words started to stick together in my mind, crawling down my head, ready to be spoken. I opened my mouth:

'What about all my stuff?'

'The others have packed most of that up,' said Mum.

'Which others?'

'Me, Oliver and Brendhan.' Rita wasn't exactly

whispering but her voice was soft and low. 'That's what we've been doing while you and this little egg yolk were in here.' She reached over to take one of Clover's hands. I sat, trying to shepherd all these skidding thoughts. My flat had been emptied? Or had my belongings been put in storage? I was moving in with Rita? Oliver and Brendhan had gone through my drawers. The things I'd bought for the baby – had anyone noticed them?

'What if I want to go home?' I asked.

'Then you can, of course.' Mum using her negotiator voice on me. 'You can see how you feel at Rita's and if it doesn't work then you can go straight back to your flat.'

I felt the fast, shivering tugs at my breast. I felt the cloud weight of Clover in my arms. I felt the aching tiredness in my back. At last, I spoke.

'Thank you, Rita. You're right, I'm going to need help. And the money.' I wanted to sound as authoritative as Mum. Despite my dressing gown and unwashed hair I wanted them to know that I was the one in charge of my daughter. 'And I would like to live with you. But maybe just for three months.'

I watched Mum and Rita pass a look between them. A look that said don't push her. A look that said she's very tired. A look that said we'll come back to this later.

'Of course, Nancy,' Rita said. 'Whatever you want.'

I closed my eyes and listened to the hum of the machines. The whispers of the other parents. The tiny murmurs of Clover.

'Where's my phone?' I asked.

'Here,' said Rita, reaching into her pocket. Before we left, I wanted to take a photo. I wanted to remember the single bed, the cot, the blue walls, my plastic bags of fruit and biscuits and nighties. I wanted to be able to show Clover her first home: Ward Two of an East London hospital. I wanted to remember the white light from the window and the yellow light that leaked through the swing doors. I wanted to take a photo of every mother I had slept beside because, suddenly, I knew I would never see any of them again.

There, at the top of a screen littered with white boxes, was a message from Gamar:

Rita has told me about the baby and that you're doing OK. She looks beautiful, Nancy. Not at all like me. Sorry I missed it but it sounds like you had a crowd. I'm in Uzbekistan now, working on their TB project. I get leave in three weeks. Can I come and see you?

36

The first thing I noticed about Rita's flat was the sound of trumpets coming down the hall. For a moment, I wondered if I was hallucinating; if I had started to warp the sound of Clover's crying inside my skull. Or perhaps this was a symptom of post-partum psychosis: a delusion of grandeur. Then came the gentle hum of synths. A warm, sunny sound of parties and red skies and burnt skin. A pulsing bass line; the echo of a woman's voice. Clutching the handle of the car seat, I realized that this was the first music my daughter had ever heard. The sterile, fluorescent world of the hospital was now being washed over with a mid-nineties rave track. I looked down at her small, still-golden face. Her eyes were marbles.

'Brendhan, can you turn that off?' Rita called out.

'It's fine,' I whispered.

'Clover's asleep,' said Rita, louder this time.

There was the scraping of chair feet on floorboards and there was Oliver, all in black.

'She's home! My little Pavlova!' He dropped to his knees and stared into the car seat like the first man to witness fire. 'Ah, Nancy, she's looking sweet.'

There was a clumping noise and Brendhan's hairy face popped round the corner. 'Ah, far out! Welcome home, Nancy. I'll go turn this down.'

Oliver tried to take the car seat from me but I wasn't ready to let go.

'Come in the kitchen. Are you hungry?' Oliver started to walk in front of me, still beaming. 'We've made you a bit of a spread, like.'

'Welcome Home Clover'.

Someone had cut the letters out of yellow paper and strung them over the dining table on a piece of garden twine. There was a plate that looked like the leaf of a cabbage, covered in triangles of watermelon. There were squares of cake, with chocolate icing and pink sprinkles. Sausages and white rolls on a tray. Even a bottle of cava in a mixing bowl, surrounded by ice. It looked like a children's party from a Shirley Hughes book. I made a noise like the air being squeezed out of a hot-water bottle. Tears burst from my eyes. Welcome home, Clover. But this wasn't my home.

'Ah, looks like someone's milk's coming through.' Brendhan walked over to me, cracking the tab on a beer can. 'Here, have this. It's non-alcoholic – although there's plenty of the real stuff in the fridge if you want.' He put the beer into my spare hand. 'Cherie's ma swore by beer when you're breastfeeding. She was Swiss and apparently they feed the stuff to their cows.'

'I've put your bags in your room, Nancy.' Mum's voice was sharp. She did not, it seemed, swear by beer.

'Why don't you give me Clover, and go and have a look?'

I didn't want to let go of the car seat. In fact, I didn't want Clover to be in a car seat any more. I wanted to hold her body against my chest and feel her heartbeat on my skin. I put the can down on the table, right on top of a paper napkin with a picture of a koala.

'I'll take her out,' I said, bending down. I tried to undo the clips and straps while my eyes were full of tears. Eventually, holding the back of her head like a bowl of water I was trying not to spill, I lifted my daughter up and on to my shoulder.

'Which room is ours?' I'd lost Rita.

'The spare one, of course,' answered Mum.

The room was green. It even smelled green. A sharp, Granny Smith smell of fresh paint, laundry powder and the tulips on the windowsill. Beside the bed was a cot. Inside the cot was an orange blanket that, with a flash of buried memory, I recognized from my own childhood. I had slept with it in my bed, beside a fluffy killer whale and a monkey in a pair of dungarees. All these things, these baby things, had just appeared in my life, wholesale. Rita's spare room had become a nursery. Was I the nurse? Then I realized: Clover had stopped breathing. Against my shoulder I could feel no movement, hear nothing. She had died and I had been too busy looking at tulips and blankets to even notice. I put my hand on her back. Through my panic, I tried to feel something. The rise and fall, her breath on my neck. At last, she gave a grunt and I felt her tiny ribs flare open. Open and closed. This frail travelling coincidence; who had called it that?

'Hey, Nancy.' I looked up. Oliver was in the doorway. Once again, I was struck by his hair, the colour of his eyes. He was so obviously one of ours. It was good to see him. 'Must be pretty weird, eh? Coming back here, rather than the flat.'

'Did you want to stay in the flat?'

'Ah, no, I didn't mean it like that, not at all.' He came and sat next to me, stroking Clover's hand as she lay against the crook of my neck. 'It's great of Anne to offer me that studio. I'm going to pay her rent and stuff. I'll be closer to the Tube. And I guess it's probably a bit more soundproofed, too. You know, in case.'

'In case you want to sleep with an opera singer?'

He laughed. 'Exactly.'

'So, you're staying in London, then?'

'Looks like it.' He kissed Clover's knuckles. 'Until the end of the summer, at least. Brendhan will be back in New Zealand and can keep me up to speed with Ma and everything. But, I mean it, Nancy. I would like to stay around. With you and Clover.'

Words. Sweet words. They were the words I'd been wanting to hear for months; the exact words I'd wanted ever since that confirming pregnancy test. Only these weren't coming from Gamar but from my brother.

'Gamar texted me.'

'Shit. For real? Is he coming here?'

'No. He's in Uzbekistan.'

'Classic.'

Even in moments like this, I found Oliver funny. I don't think a sense of humour is written in your genes, like a nose or diabetes. But it was true that he and I could now say things together that we wouldn't to other people. We could make jokes that others would shy away from. Maybe even Rita wouldn't dare to joke about Gamar just yet.

'He asked to see her.'

'In Uzbekistan?'

I smiled. 'What do you think I should do?' He was a man, after all.

Oliver wasn't looking at me. He was staring into Clover's face, despite the fact that she was asleep. The midwives had all explained that premature babies were sleepier than other babies. Secretly, I believed that she was just a very placid baby. She took after me, not Rita. She was happy just to be warm and loved and still.

'Jeez, I don't think I'm necessarily the best guy to give advice on relationships. Don't tell Clover – I don't want her to think that her duncle's a shitbag – but I once dumped a girl while siphoning petrol out of her mum's car.'

I sighed. 'So we're really going with "duncle", are we?'

'Sure are.' Oliver looked at me. 'Honestly? I think it's up to you. If you want him around, if he makes you feel good, then meet him. But if you're just doing it for his sake, or because you feel you ought to, or because a little bit of you still wants to get back together, then I'd steer clear.'

'Really?'

'Don't leave your front door open and then complain that you've been burgled.'

'Oliver! That's victim-blaming.'

'Ah, Nancy. Come on, you know I don't mean it like that.' He shifted round to face me properly. 'I'm just saying that if you let Gamar in, you're leaving yourself open to get really hurt again. Only this time, you're even more vulnerable. Because of Clover.'

'But he is her dad.'

'Well, so you say ...' Oliver's mouth twisted into a wry little grin. 'I know what you Albanys are like.'

'Are we making jokes about that too now?' I was almost breathless. It felt illicit to make a joke about Dad's infidelity. It was like putting my head out of a speeding train: reckless and thrilling but also incredibly dangerous.

'Well, I won't if you don't want me to. But I mean, I will probably talk about it in my next show.' Oliver pushed a curl off his forehead. 'So I'll need some jokes.'

'What? You're going to make a show about Dad?'

'Might be a bit tricky. Seeing as I never met the guy.' There was that naughty face again. 'But about the DNA test? Coming to London? Are you kidding? That's an award-winning show right there.'

I took a slow breath.

'Instead of going to therapy?'

'Hey,' said Oliver. 'If I need therapy then we all need therapy. But at least I get paid to air my dirty laundry.'

I wanted to lie down. I wanted to rest my head on his shoulder. I wanted to drink a pint of Guinness and wrap Clover in a hand-knitted shawl. I wanted to go outside and show her the leaves. I wanted to speak to my dad. I wanted to see Gamar. I wanted to swim across a frozen lake. I wanted to push Clover against my heart until she went back into my body. Instead, I said: 'Do you want to hold her?'

'For real?' Oliver's eyes sparkled.

'Yes. But really, you have to be very careful with her neck.' I felt my adrenaline start to rise again. 'She can't take the weight of her own head yet.'

'OK.'

'Have you ever held a baby before?'

'Sure.'

'A newborn?'

'I have.'

'Recently?'

Oliver put his hand on my arm. 'Nancy, it's OK. I don't need to hold her. She looks comfy where she is.' He stroked my shoulder. 'But I am going to go back in and eat one of those lamingtons before Brendhan swipes them all.'

'What's a lamington?' I said, not moving from the bed. But Oliver just winked.

*

In the kitchen, Mum and Rita were by the kettle. Brendhan was eating a piece of watermelon – drops of juice soaking into his beard. Clover moved, slightly, as we came from the hallway into the light of the room.

'Ah, she's a ripper, Nancy.' Brendhan was coming towards me, wiping his face on his sleeve. How many germs could one man harbour? I wondered. Should I keep my distance? 'Here, I got yous a present.'

He picked a blue pot off the table. There was a picture of pancakes on the side. 'Bicarbonate of soda. You'll thank me later.' I waited for the punchline but Brendhan didn't laugh. 'This stuff is like magic. Sick, spills, urine.' He pronounced it to rhyme with 'time'. 'You just sprinkle some of this over the puddle, wait for it to dry, then vacuum it off. I don't know how much I got through with Minnie and Tehine but it was heaps.'

The tears started to fall again. This time running sideways off my face, where I was supporting Clover. 'Thanks, Brendhan,' I said.

'No worries. And, mate – this is a big day. All that prolactin, it makes you feel nuts.'

'Prolactin?' It sounded like a yoghurt.

'Yeah, it's a hormone: stimulates your milk to come in after the colostrum. Same in cattle and sheep.'

'You really know about all this stuff, don't you?'

'What? Lactation?'

'No, babies. Fatherhood. Birth and everything. You're really confident.'

Brendhan came round the other side of me, away

from Clover. 'Nancy,' he said, quietly, and close to my ear, 'nobody has a fucking clue. All you can do is love them.'

And a quiet voice, inside my head replied: 'But how do I know if I love her?'

How could I? What did loving mean? Was it love that made me hold Clover to my breast and pour milk into her tiny, yellow body? Was it love that rested my hand on her chest in that blinking electric room to know that she was breathing? Because if by love we meant mutual affection, adoration, respect, understanding, then I did not love my daughter. I didn't know her. I didn't understand her. She couldn't even see me.

If by love we meant the thrilling pursuit of someone who makes you feel whole then, perhaps, we would grow into that. At the moment, all I felt was skinless, raw commitment. Total duty. Absolute purpose.

'Brendhan, Gamar wants to see her. When he gets back to London, in a few weeks.'

I felt his hand on my shoulder. 'Right.'

'What do you think?'

As Brendhan breathed in, I felt the thick slab of him expand against my side. 'Well, I reckon it's up to you, of course.' He hadn't finished. 'But, if she were my daughter, I'd do everything I could to see her.'

'I know.'

'I love my girls more than anything else in the world. I'd pull my ribs out one by one just to keep them safe.

That's why I'm going back to God Zone on Friday – I can't be away from them any longer.'

'But Gamar isn't like you.' I could hear the anger in my voice. 'He left. He said he didn't want to be a dad and just went. To Uzbekistan, apparently.'

'That's true.' Brendhan raked his teeth over some of the hairs around his mouth. 'Listen, Nancy. I grew up with my dad, I'm a dad, that's obviously going to skew my view of it all. But I reckon you should give him a chance. At least let him see what he's missing.' Brendhan gave my arm another squeeze. 'If he still acts like a cunt after that then, well, I'll break his knees for you myself.'

'Break whose knees?' Rita was holding a mug with a picture of Tina Turner on the side.

'Your man, Gamar,' Brendhan replied.

'What about Gamar?' Like a shrew, Mum scurried over to the table, taking a microsecond to check that my T-shirt wasn't blocking Clover's nose; just to check I wasn't suffocating my daughter.

'He wants to see Clover when he's next in England.'

'Does he?' asked Mum.

'When's that?' asked Rita.

'I think—' said Oliver.

'He said he's got leave in a few weeks,' I replied. There was a pause.

'So.' Rita looked at me. 'What are you going to do?'

37

'Hello.'

'Hi.'

'Come in.'

'Thanks.'

He was wearing black jeans and a pale yellow shirt. His dark, curly hair was cut tight to the sides of his head. His mouth was soft but unsmiling.

'When did you move in here?'

'Straight from the hospital.'

'Right.'

I turned and started walking towards the kitchen. I was wearing a red vest and a pair of Rita's softest denim shorts. It was the first time I had put on anything that wasn't nightwear or sportswear for three weeks. The waistband against my stomach felt like cheese wire.

'How was Uzbekistan?'

'Yeah, OK. I was doing a big project on TB.'

The door to my room – our room – was closed. I didn't want him to be able to see where I slept. I didn't want him to see Clover's sleepsuits. Not yet.

'Where is she?' Gamar looked around the kitchen as though for a wasp.

'Rita's taken her out for her nap.'

'I thought she'd be here.'

'I thought we should talk first.' In an effort to stop my hands shaking I walked towards the sink. 'Do you want some water?'

'Sure. I mean, yes, please.'

He was so beautiful. So painfully, achingly beautiful in that way that was both familiar and shocking. I knew every centimetre of his face and yet, looking at it, I felt as though I was seeing him for the first time.

'Nancy ... I know things are ... and I've been ... away a lot.' I pushed the tap hard, to make the water pour out at its maximum speed. 'But I want to give this a go. You know, try it.' The water bubbled over the ends of my fingers.

'Try what?'

'I want to try ...'

'You want to try being a father?' I was still looking into the sink. Outside the window, I saw a tree in a neighbour's garden. Its leaves barely moved. For a few seconds, nobody spoke.

'I am a father.'

'Are you?' Finally, I turned to face him. Sitting at the kitchen table, the last of the flowers from our homecoming splayed and overripe in a vase in front of him. I was angry. So angry that I wanted to push the roses into his mouth, to cut his gums with their thorns and choke him on the petals.

'Don't be like that,' he said.

'Sorry.' And then. 'But it's true.'

Eventually, I came and sat opposite him. I felt self-conscious. I'd put mascara on for the first time in weeks, maybe months, and didn't want him to know that I'd made the effort. I just wanted him to think I looked good. I just wanted to be able to control what he thought of me.

'I'd hoped to see her.'

'You can see her.' It felt as though someone was pushing a golf ball into my neck. 'Like I said, I'm never going to stop you seeing her.'

'Big of you.'

'What?'

'Sorry,' he said. But the sneer, that flash of hostility had been there. 'I didn't mean. I just—'

'How dare you?' I pushed my elbow into the wood of the table. 'How dare you act like the victim here?'

'I'm not.'

'Really?' I shot back. 'Because you seem to be making out that I'm the one who's stopped you seeing your daughter. When, if you remember, you left. You left the whole country.'

'That's not quite—'

My elbow rolled, suddenly jerking my body sideways. 'Please don't.'

'OK, OK. Whatever. We can discuss that another

time,' he said. 'The point is, I'm in London now. Like, properly in London. I've asked to be based here, so I can spend more time with you both.'

'What?'

'I've got a job at the London office. Policy stuff. Less field work. Like I said, I want to give this a go.'

How could this be happening? How were the very things I'd longed for coming out of his mouth at last? After I'd finally built up my carapace, created my family, he had turned up.

'But you didn't tell me,' I said.

'Tell you what?' He was almost smiling.

'That you were changing your job. Moving your life to London full-time.' I tried to steady my voice. I knew I was teetering on the edge of joy and despair. 'Didn't you think that might be something I'd want to know about? Have a say in?'

'What?' There it was again. The wolf flash of hostility. 'Are you saying you don't want me to be here?'

His antagonism yanked me back to myself. This wasn't right. He wasn't giving me what I'd wanted. This wasn't equality, a partnership, a family. He had done it. Unilateral action. One-point perspective. Secret, selfish, on his own.

'I wanted you to be here when I needed you.' Don't cry, I told myself. Don't cry. Don't cry. 'I wanted you to be here when I knew I was pregnant. Before that. I was so in love with you, Gamar. I begged.' Tears threatened to fall.

'You didn't—'

'I begged you to love me but you left.' I tried to breathe. 'You said you had no choice.'

'I said you'd given me no choice.'

'Exactly.' Finally I had got him to admit it. Hadn't I?

'I meant in having a family. You hadn't given me the choice.' I blinked. What was he saying? 'The chance to agree to it; to plan it. You never asked me. It was just there. What I wanted didn't seem to matter.'

A horrible sense of being flattened went through me. The bastard. He was blaming me. Even after all this, he still blamed me for getting pregnant. 'But, Gamar, that wasn't my fault!' Not again. I couldn't get dragged into this endless, swirling argument again.

'Listen . . .' He hesitated. Was he floundering? 'I had always told you I didn't want a baby.'

I wanted to scream. I wanted to push his face into the edge of the table so hard his cheekbone splintered.

'Gamar, I didn't make this happen on my own.'

'I know.'

'You say that but I don't think you do know.' I took a breath. 'Like, on some fundamental level I don't think you really do understand this. I can't just make a pregnancy happen on my own. Me and my womb. I can't. You did this, Gamar. You and me. But that does mean you.'

'Nancy—' He looked small.

But I wouldn't let him go. 'If you were so sure you never wanted a baby then why didn't you ever talk about contraception? Or come with me to the doctor? If you were so sure you never wanted a baby then why didn't you get a vasectomy? You work with doctors; we have a free health service.' It was the argument I'd been rehearsing in my mind for months. 'But, instead, I had to take it all on. All the pain and misery of not getting pregnant. Just so you didn't have to ever think about it?'

'I think "pain and misery" is a bit dramatic.' He was using his 'rational' voice. The one that made him sound like a *Top Gear* presenter. In that moment, I hated him.

'Do you? Do you really?' I blinked. 'Being depressed, getting fat, losing your sex drive, metal in your cervix, injecting yourself, swallowing hormones that make you insane, living in synthetic pregnancy for decades? And all because of you. Because you decided you didn't want a baby.' Thank God Rita had taken her out. I was losing it.

'I told you why,' Gamar replied.

'Yes, only after you'd actually got me pregnant.'

'What difference would that have made?'

'What difference?' I asked, almost shouting. I was getting drawn in again. Tangled in his non-logic.

'Yeah. If you're saying this was all my sperm's fault, then what difference would it have made if you'd known more about my past or my family?'

I got up and walked over to the sink. Gamar turned his body in the chair to follow me through the room. This, I thought, is how a mouse feels when it is being watched by a cat.

'Because then we would have been in a relationship,' I said. 'An actual, proper relationship. Don't you get it? If you'd actually been open with me and let me into your life, we could have been a real couple. I would have understood you. And we could have been equals. Instead, you always kept me at arm's length. You always shut me out. Never committed. Gamar, we'd been sleeping together for three years and you never once said you loved me. Do you have any idea what that did to my self-esteem?'

'Well, I just don't think . . .' In his slow, reluctant voice I saw it coming. I saw it on the horizon and I couldn't bear it.

'Please, don't say it.'

But he wouldn't stop. Looking up at me, his face pinched, he said it:

'I don't really know what love means.'

It was like my ears popping on a plane. The roaring pressure gave way to a thick, terrible silence. There he sat. This man who had walked out on me and then sloped back in. Not asking for forgiveness or love or commitment; just demanding a fatherhood that he felt was due to him. He didn't love me and he never had.

'Oh my God,' I muttered. 'See?' Then louder. 'See? You say you want to be a family. That you've moved back to London and all this stuff. But you can't actually commit.' I slammed the glass of water down on the counter, spilling it across my hand. 'You can't actually let yourself feel love.'

'That's not—'

'What is it? What is it that you're so scared of?'

I wanted my words to hit him like darts.

'Everything, Nancy. Obviously.' There. At last. I saw something in his face break. 'I'm frightened of everything.' He wasn't crying. But his lip wobbled. 'Life, work, money and where it goes, my health, the future.' I carried on staring at him. 'The planet, that I'll never see anyone, that she'll turn out like me or my mum or something.'

'But—' I tried to cut in.

'People who don't worry just never grew up.' The fragility had closed over, as quickly as it had appeared. Now he was back on the attack.

'Oh. So are you saying I'm naive?' I countered.

'No.'

'Because I've actually done this on my own.'

'Well, you had—'

'Yes, on my own.' I started to walk back to the table as I listed the things. 'The pregnancy, the birth, the nights, the feeding, the money, the endless, bleak days at home, the appointments, the planning.' I sat down, heavily this time. 'I've actually done it all, Gamar. If you think I'm immature, then you don't know what I've done. What I'm still doing. And I've done it all by myself, without you.'

'That's not true,' he said flatly.

'What?'

'You've not done it by yourself.'

'What?'

'From what you said, you didn't do it all on your own. Being pregnant. Labour. All this.'

The weasel. The absolute weasel of him, to try and turn my words against me. 'Well, no.'

'From what you said and what Rita told me—'

I interrupted: 'Rita?'

'She told me that she was there for the birth.'

'You've been talking to Rita?'

'She messages me.' He sounded almost smug.

'For God's sake.' The betrayal. I knew she'd messaged him after Clover was born but I'd imagined a quick, dispassionate statement of facts. Not back and forth. Not since.

'Don't blame Rita,' he said, delighted to be taking a moral high ground.

'I can't believe she's done that. She should have told me.' I was seething.

'Well, anyway, she said that during the labour that guy was there too.'

'What guy?' My breasts were starting to tingle. In the last few days, my milk production had gone absolutely berserk. Clover was feeding for hours, sometimes nearly two hours at a time, all night. And now my body was flooding me with milk that had nowhere to go. 'Do you mean Oliver? My brother? Yes. He was there.'

'So you weren't—'

'A man I'd known for basically three months was there for me when I needed him, Gamar. You weren't.' I swallowed but started talking again before he could begin to argue back. 'Oliver rubbed my back and helped me walk and talked to me in the hospital and stroked my hair. He got me water and held my hand. I had to rely on a man I'd barely met before, a man I didn't know even existed until last year, because you weren't there.'

'I—'

'You weren't there.' I screamed it. 'When I needed you. When I really needed you. You. Weren't. There.' And then I started to cry. I was so tired. No, I wasn't just tired, that first accusation thrown at all mothers. I was so disappointed to be having this argument that there was just no point holding it in any more. And so I cried until my tears splashed on to my huge, veined breasts. This wasn't the panic crying that sometimes seized me in the night, as I wondered what I'd done. This was crying to release. Crying out of heartbreak. Crying as grief.

'I'm sorry.' Gamar was beside me, squatting on the ground. He put his hand on the table. Not on mine but near it.

'OK.'

'I'm sorry I upset you.'

He couldn't do it. He couldn't really apologize. My breathing started to steady. I wiped my face. I noticed the staining on the front of my vest. I was leaking: milk, tears, all of it.

'Can I see her?' Gamar had gone back to his seat.

'I told you. When she gets back.'

'No, I mean, can I see your pictures? Now?' He put his hand forward, palms up.

'They're all on my phone.'

'Then can I see your phone?'

'No.'

In the awkwardness that followed, I stood up. My back ached and my front was now damp as well as sore. 'I'm going to make a cup of tea. Do you want one?'

'Ah, OK. Yes, please.'

Gamar didn't drink coffee and I was so scared of suckling Clover on caffeine that I'd given it up too, even though I would have loved the bump of it right now. That smooth, twinkling speed you get from a strong cup of coffee on a hot afternoon. But no. Baby comes first.

As I filled up the kettle from the tap, I started to regret crying. I had promised I wouldn't open myself up in front of him this time. But maybe I could get to him in return.

'How's your mum?'

'What?'

'I'm asking: how is your mum? Have you told her?'

'About the baby?'

'Yes. Have you told her about Clover? That you're a dad?' I saw something flicker across his face. Pain? Guilt? Shame?

'I sent her an email.'

'An email?' I clicked the kettle on, trying not to show my surprise. 'When did you last speak to her?'

'A few years ago.'

'Years?' Who was this man? This lonely, unloving man.

'Yes.'

'You haven't spoken to your mum in a few years?' I felt as though I were grinding an eggshell beneath my feet, making him vulnerable. But I also wanted to know.

'Not in person.'

'Why?'

'I don't know. I just ... She ... I don't want to talk about it.'

I wanted to talk about it. I wanted to prise his heart out of his chest and lay it across the kitchen table like a surgeon. I wanted to pick over it for all the scars and gaps and holes that he had tried to hide from me. For three years he had kept his family hidden from me, kept me hidden from his friends, kept his true self hidden from everyone; and it had left me ravenous. For details, for descriptions, for declarations. I wanted to know everything because anything short of total raw, meat-like exposure now felt like deception. And I was sick of deception. Perhaps that's what I'd learned; after discovering a brother and a baby within a month, I was sick for ever of secrets.

'I ...' But then I looked at him. At the bones on his shoulders, visible even beneath his summer shirt. I looked at the angle of his neck as he leant over the table. I watched his body squirm away from me and thought: what's the point? What could he possibly say now that would change any of this? Someone admitting to frailty doesn't make them strong; it just makes them a person.

Neither of us talked. A plane went over outside. I was waiting for the sound of the front door. It felt as though Gamar and I had been talking for hours, which must surely mean that Rita would be back soon.

'What's the best bit?' he asked at last.

'About what?' I came back to sit opposite him. As I sat down, I remembered the feeling of my nipple in Gamar's mouth. Of sitting on top of him as we had sex.

'About being a mum.'

'I don't know,' I answered. 'Right now, it's all hard.'

'What do you mean?'

'I'm exhausted, Gamar.' I sighed. I knew that everyone got tired. Of course doctors got tired. In a way, tiredness was almost as universal as birth. And yet this kind of tiredness was impossible to explain. He'd never get it. Rita didn't even get it. 'I get about three hours' sleep a night,' I said. 'But never in one go.'

'Maybe—'

I talked over him: 'I forget words. I'm always scared I'm going to fall asleep and drop her. She cluster feeds in the evening and screams in the night. I spend the entire time, like every other second, worrying that she's died or stopped breathing or is having a seizure. And there's this sort of hum, like a rolling spool, going on in my head of all the things I have to do. All the tasks; not things that anyone else would even notice but just the things that keep her alive. Changing her nappy, did

I wind her, when did I last feed her, from what boob, have I expressed enough, did I put her down on her back, when did I last trim her nails, what day is the midwife coming, did I call the nursery, when did I last eat, is that mastitis, when is her nap?' I wasn't shouting but my voice was loud. 'Everything, everything, everything. All day. And all night. It's all I can do.' I wasn't being dramatic. I wasn't looking for sympathy. I was answering his question.

'Nancy, I'm sorry—'

'Yeah, well, so am I.'

'What are you sorry for?' He looked surprised.

'I'm just so sorry that it turned out like this,' I said. 'That, despite all my hope and all that time and everything, this is where we are.'

There was a pause.

'Do you think it's really healthy to raise another girl in a house full of just women?' he asked. This was another attack. He was lashing out.

'Who said it'll always be just women?' I countered.

'What do you mean?'

'Well, I think one day, Gamar, I'm going to meet someone.' I tried to smile while saying this, even though the words felt like marbles in my mouth. 'And who knows, maybe we'll have more children? And maybe Rita will meet someone and have children. Or we'll both meet people who already have their own children and become step-parents. Just like our parents did.' I was talking but I couldn't quite feel my hands. As though I was being directed by some force outside of myself. 'But one day Clover will have half-siblings and step-siblings and cousins, as well as uncles and aunties and grandparents. She will have a big, complicated family and she will be at the centre of it. I want that for her.'

'A child needs two parents,' he replied.

I started to laugh. I couldn't help myself.

'What?' He was really sounding defensive now. Good.

'Well, that just seems a bit rich, coming from you,' I said. 'Now. Here.'

'Why?'

'Because if you'd really cared about her having two parents, then you wouldn't have left.' I felt the skin on my neck burning pink. 'If you'd wanted to be a father, you would have been a father.'

'But that's what I'm saying. I do want to—'

'No. You don't,' I cut in.

'Nancy.'

'She's nearly a month old, Gamar. It's been most of a year since I last saw you. My God, the times I imagined this conversation.' I pulled my fingers through my hair. 'How badly I longed for you to come back and say these things.'

'I am saying them—'

'But then,' I interrupted again, 'I realized family isn't about blood or genes or whatever.'

'I'm saying—' He went to speak. I put my hand up on the table, like a policeman stopping a car. I was going to speak and he was going to listen.

'What makes a family is looking after each other. Loving each other. Being there and being unconditional and being familiar. We were never that, Gamar. Not really. You were never that with me.'

'Nancy. Please—'

'I am going to be a mother and I am going to raise this baby. But I'm going to do it with my sister. And my mother. Maybe even with Oliver.' I swallowed. 'You can be involved, of course, but I don't need you.' I felt electric. 'I have my family.'

There must have been something in the way I said this, maybe the hand on the table, maybe the tone of my voice, maybe knowing that Rita was out with the baby, but all the fight seemed to just go out of him.

'OK.' He sighed. A clock ticked. A door outside banged shut. Then, eventually: 'Is there anything I can do while I'm here?'

'What, fix a tap or something?' I smiled, trying to show him that it was a joke.

'Well, yeah. I don't know.'

'You can take away my washing.' I crossed my legs under the table. Now that I'd laid down the law, I could try to relax.

'OK.'

'I'm joking, Gamar. It's OK. Rita has a system.'

'Of course she does.' He rubbed his open hand along the surface of the table. I wondered if he might be about to make another offer, maybe even a declaration. There was something humming there, between us.

'Listen. I'm not going to say that you can just turn up and start acting like her dad.' I put my hands on the table. 'But extra help would be good, especially when Rita is at work.' Slowly. Careful. Don't give everything away to him again. 'We could try you coming over, maybe once a fortnight or something, just for a few hours.' Could I trust him? Would he do what I wanted? He was a doctor, though. He must be able to look after babies. 'I'd be in the flat too but I could sleep. Or have a bath.' I felt the air quiver in my nostrils but kept my voice steady. 'If I feel comfortable with that, then we can take it from there.'

I looked up to see his eyes glittering.

'I—' He reached out to take my hand.

'No,' I said, sitting back. 'Don't.'

I heard a coppery wail. It was getting louder and more desperate. The tingling in my breasts became shooting pain. The key in the lock. The bump of the buggy.

'Hello?' Rita's voice.

But I was already up and running.

38

Rita and I were on the sofa, eating smoked almonds. Since having Clover, I finally understood Rita's obsession with protein. Only mine was being turned into milk, not muscle.

'Do you ever worry that you've forgotten Dad's voice?' Rita said, looking up from her screen. It was September now and the air coming through the window smelled slightly of woodsmoke.

'What?' I had been trying to book a baby swimming lesson on my phone for eighteen minutes but every time I tried to type in my details the page reloaded itself.

'I mean, unless you watched a video of him, could you actually remember Dad's voice?'

I thought about it. Could I? Really?

'I don't know,' I said. 'Maybe.'

'I'm not sure I could,' Rita said, taking another nut.

'But I don't actually watch videos of Dad really, any more,' I said. 'After it all came out with Mum, I actually thought about deleting them.'

'Really?'

'Yeah. But I couldn't.' I remembered the sight of his face. My thumb hovering over the picture of a bin. 'It felt weird. Like I was killing him. Again.'

'I never wanted to kill him. Again.' Rita smiled, acknowledging the ridiculous sound of this phrase. 'But God, I was so angry. About Anne, obviously, but also the way he'd treated Mum. And us. And Oliver's mum.'

I turned my phone off and put it down on the sofa. For once, Clover was sleeping in her cot next door, rather than in a sling as I walked up and down the flat. Buster was asleep in front of the window. It felt like the first time Rita and I had been able to talk to each other, actually talk, for months.

'When Oliver says about her being a single mum, it makes me feel so weird,' I said, sliding my hands under the waistband of my tracksuit bottoms and on to the still-soft flesh of my belly.

'Because you're a single mum?' Rita asked.

'Well, sort of. I mean, I'm not like Anahera. I don't have a husband, I'm not lying about who Clover's dad is, but yeah.' I licked my lips. 'I got pregnant by accident, with a man who didn't love me. And kept the baby.'

'Oh, Nancy.' Rita closed her laptop.

'I know.' I reached across and touched her arm. 'I'm really lucky too. I just wish ... Well' – I let out a long sigh – 'I just wish all the men in my life hadn't been such shits.'

Rita smiled. Then asked: 'Is that how you think about Dad? As a shit?'

I shook my head.

'Me neither,' Rita said. 'I mean, I think he did shitty things. I hate the way he made Anne be the boring parent while he swanned around doing all that stupid art. When he was carrying around this huge secret all along.'

'Did you really find Mum boring? And grumpy?' I remembered what Rita had said, that day in the woods before my waters broke. Before my uterus turned inside out and the whole world followed suit.

Rita looked at me. 'Well, she was quite strict. Remember how she'd make us clean the bathroom every Saturday morning before we were allowed to watch telly? And never gave us lifts in the car but made us walk back from the station?' Limescale remover and wet wool and lemon-fresh Ajax. Tired legs, orange lights, wet necks. I remembered.

'You still clean the bathroom every Saturday!' I said.

'True.' Rita grinned. 'But when we were little, Dad was always the one making milkshakes and playing loud music and getting out the dressing-up things. Like those clown trousers. You know, I think he actually sewed them himself, out of an old duvet cover?'

'Oh God!' I let my head fall back and covered my eyes, careful not to groan too loud, in case I woke Clover. 'Those trousers.'

Rita laughed. Then the laughing turned into a tearful sort of sigh. She pressed her lips together. 'I just wish I could remember all those lovely things – singing in the bath, tucking us in, calling us nicknames – without remembering that he was lying the whole time.'

'But was it lying?' I knew what she meant. It felt like lying to me too, but maybe that wasn't fair. Maybe there was another word for it.

'Well, it was lying by omission,' Rita answered. 'As Anne would say. Lying by omission in a pretty major way.'

I hummed a yes. 'I want there to be another word for having a secret that isn't lying,' I said. 'Because if he was just a liar then everything he did feels like a lie. Our parents' marriage, that house, our childhood.'

'Well, there are words,' said Rita, her eyes no longer swollen with unshed tears. 'Betrayal. Infidelity. Deception.'

'Treason!' I said in a mock-haughty voice. Like the Queen of Hearts. Casting judgement on an already dead man. Rita smiled.

'But actually, the more I think about it, the more I think that he did love us,' said Rita. 'And Anne. He did want to be a good dad. I think he could just, somehow, completely shut away this other part of him. This thing. My therapist calls it disassociation. Like, he could totally compartmentalize one part of his emotional life and ignore it. For years.'

I nodded. 'Yeah. I think I feel a bit the same,' I said. 'Like, Oliver was just this thing that he could lock away in a plan chest. I honestly don't know if he even really thought about him as a person. A boy. An actual man.'

'Except he went on that DNA site,' said Rita, picking up the bowl of nuts again. 'He might even have seen Oliver on there – we don't know.'

I swallowed. 'Does Oliver remind you of Dad?' I rubbed my right eye. I should really have been sleeping now; making the most of Clover napping. She'd be up at least three times in the night, I knew. But I didn't want to leave this conversation unfinished. 'Obviously he looks like him but do you think he behaves a bit like him?'

'What, showing off? Making jokes and stuff?'

'No, I mean more how he can separate things out too. Like, the way he is with us, with Clover and Mum – I think it's really different to how he is with the women he dates.'

'Pssssh.' Rita let out a sigh. 'I don't know. I'm not really au fait with dating men.'

'I know.' I twirled my ankle until it cracked. 'But you've seen the way he flirts, how he gets women to do things. Like how he got that nurse to let him into the hospital when I was in labour. But he never seems to have a girlfriend. He doesn't seem all that interested in settling down with anyone.'

'He has that line about being drawn to powerful women.' There was just a hint of a sneer in Rita's voice.

'Oh God, I know.' I giggled. 'It's so obviously a line.'

'Except he was actually brought up by his mum,' said Rita. 'She must have been quite tough to do that on her own. Maybe he really is more comfortable with women? Strong women? Even if he's not ready to settle down.' She shrugged. 'I haven't settled down and I'm older than him.'

'True,' I said and reached for my glass.

'Mind you, if he wants powerful women, he should go to Aynac. Try one of Marie-Louise's friends for size.' Rita was smiling but her face wasn't totally clear of sadness.

'Have you spoken to Marie-Louise much?' I asked. 'About it all?'

'No.' I thought Rita was going to stop there but eventually she spoke again. 'When I last spoke to her and told her about finding the letter, she just said she wasn't too surprised.'

'Really?' I felt instantly sad.

'I suppose, from her point of view, Dad got into another relationship pretty quickly after they broke up. Maybe she always thought of him as more of a . . . a . . .' She was searching for the right word. 'As more shady than we did.'

'I suppose.' I looked at the clock. Two seventeen. Clover would wake up soon and I needed to book this swimming lesson. And have a shower.

'The thing I think . . .' said Rita. She cleared her throat and started again. 'The thing I say to other people is that all families are complicated. I really do think that.' She stretched her neck to the side until it cracked. 'They all have these weird dynamics and tensions and secrets. If you spent any real energy looking, you'd find sordid and tragic stuff under everyone's floorboards. But our family has actually dealt with it. Not intentionally, necessarily. Not because we wanted to but because it all sort of just exploded in our faces.' She flicked her hand out like a bang. 'The DNA test, the website, Oliver coming over here, Brendhan, Dad's studio, the matchbox, Mum finding the letter.' Buster kicked the air in his sleep. 'And once it was all out there, we actually talked about it. We got to know each other and rallied around. And then, when Clover came along, and you moved in here, and Oliver moved to Stockwell, well, we've kept that going.' Rita shrugged, then reached over and squeezed my foot. I smiled back at her.

'I couldn't have a secret at the moment, even if I wanted to,' I said, spreading out my toes. 'I'm sleeping in my sister's spare room, I've got no love life, my ex comes round once a fortnight to change some nappies and empty the bin, and I'm so sleep-deprived I'd forget anything I wasn't meant to say anyway.' I laughed. Then I brought my hand up to my mouth as the laugh turned into a yawn. Rita patted my leg. And from the room next door I heard the first, burbling notes of my daughter waking up.

Epilogue

A warm yellow smell came off the river. Algae, reeds, sunshine, petrol. I looked at our reflection as we walked past the flats beside the River Lea. I looked almost normal. Almost just a woman. No bump, no sling. No buggy because it was being pushed by Rita, with Buster tied to the handle. Beside her was Oliver, walking with his feet slightly turned out, his hands in his pockets – a stance I could recognize even in shadow.

'Where did you tell everyone to meet?' Rita asked over her shoulder as we ducked beneath a green metal footbridge.

'At the bottom of Springfield Park,' I said. 'Under the trees, near the boathouse cafe.' I was enjoying being able to move like this, without Clover on me. I was unhitched. I could have walked all the way out of London along that river. On to Essex. Outwards to fields, hedgerows, reservoirs and horses. For the first time in months my back felt straight and the voice that whirred in my brain was quiet.

'What time?' said Rita. I looked at my watch.

'In about three-quarters of an hour,' I replied. 'I thought we'd need time to set up.'

'Will Maxine be there? With Arlo?' asked Oliver.

'I invited her,' I said. 'Why?'

'Oh, no reason,' he said. As we walked past a bench, I noticed a woman with a high blonde ponytail lift her face to him and smile, slowly. The woman next to her swivelled round to look too. Did they recognize him from some TV thing? Perhaps. But this was also just the way women followed Oliver, bumping around him like magnets. When he started to untie Buster's lead, I heard an actual sigh.

Mum was already there, shaking out blankets on to an enormous sheet of tarpaulin.

'Hello, darling. This is nice.' She half smiled, half frowned at a woman herding a gaggle of yapping, straining dogs past the edge of her territory. 'Although I did say you could have had Clover's birthday party in my garden. Then at least we would have had a toilet. And no other dogs.'

I put my arm around her and kissed her cheek. 'I know, Mum. But yours is just quite a long way to expect everyone to travel with small babies. And we can always use the toilets next to the cafe.' She nodded but I could tell she was still unconvinced. As usual, I felt both grateful and resentful that Mum was so involved, so willing to help, so quick to give her opinion.

'Buster loves babies, anyway,' said Rita. 'And he'll

stop any of the others coming over. You should have brought Shadwell.'

'Hmmm,' said Mum. Then turned to me. 'Are you expecting a lot of people, then?' She looked down at her baking tin, on one of the blankets. 'I haven't made a massive cake. Although Oliver said something about a watermelon?'

'That's right.' Oliver started ferreting around in one of the big blue Ikea bags he'd helped me and Rita carry over from our flat. 'I made it at Rita's before we left. Look.' He pulled out a big silver platter. On it was a tower of watermelon slices, topped with whipped cream, blueberries and sliced grapes. It was like a pink, bleeding parody of a wedding cake.

'Goodness me,' Anne said. 'And that's for the babies?'
Oliver nodded. 'I saw it on YouTube.'

'Well, you'd better put it away until the others get here or we'll be infested with wasps.'

Rita was leaning under the hood of the buggy. 'Let's have a smell of this arse, then,' she said, undoing the straps that crossed Clover's belly. Rita could never just leave Clover in her pram. Even when she was asleep, Rita would always be twitching to transfer Clover into her cot. I suspected that really, like now, Rita was just looking for an excuse to take over: to hold Clover, carry her, be in charge. It gnawed at me, this tussle for authority over my own daughter.

'Can't you just leave her in the buggy until we've

unpacked?' I said, pulling out a bag of chewable toys, fabric books, bits of fabric inlaid with mirrors.

'Sorry, she's out now,' said Rita, bouncing Clover against her hip. I had to admit, Clover looked thrilled to be up and about, craning her arms towards the blankets, the toys, the tub of hummus that she could already pull the lid off, unaided.

'She looks like a football casual in that outfit, Rita,' I said, watching her press her nose into Clover's bum.

'No, she doesn't. She looks smart.' Clover pushed a starfish hand into Rita's mouth and made a gargling noise.

'I can't believe Fred Perry even make baby clothes.' I smiled. 'I mean, it's got an actual collar.'

'It's better than all that Little Monster, Little Princess shit,' said Oliver, stretching a balloon, ready to inflate it. 'I'd rather Clover wore brown boiler suits until she was sixteen than some T-shirt that says "Sassy From Birth".'

I laughed. 'Well, there goes Rita's present.'

'I bought her a toolkit, actually,' said Rita. 'A toy one.'

'Hello, beautiful girl.' Mum walked over to Rita and kissed Clover's cheek; nuzzled the top of her head. 'Look at that hair. Just like Rita when she was little. Clive used to put coconut oil through to comb it.' Rita nodded.

'Ma just cut mine short with the bacon scissors,' said Oliver, bringing an orange balloon up to his lips.

'I've told Gamar we can never cut it,' I said.

'Is he coming?' Mum asked tentatively.

'No,' I replied. 'No. I've told him he can do something on the actual day. But I didn't want him here.' Mum nodded. I turned away: 'Rita, careful doing that, I don't want her to be sick before anyone has even arrived.'

Rita was throwing Clover up in the air and catching her. It was my daughter's favourite game and yet, somehow, when Rita did it, my baby looked like a medicine ball. It looked like cardio. Rita stopped and started nibbling Clover's tummy until she bubbled over with giggles.

'You wanting a bit of attention, are you, missus?' Oliver reached out towards Clover. 'I'll take her, Rita, while you put up the banner.'

'Are you trying to pose for when Maxine gets here?' Rita smiled ruefully at Oliver.

'What's that?' Mum asked, holding up a stack of small paper plates.

'Oh, I was just asking how things were in Casa del Shed,' Rita replied.

'Ah, great, thanks,' Oliver replied, studiously avoiding looking at me. 'I put in a security light on the side of the house and I've been looking after the veg patch down the back. All very wholesome stuff.' Clover slapped his chest with an outstretched hand.

'Mum said you're growing beetroot,' said Rita, unfolding a large foil banner with 'Happy 1st Birthday' in animal letters.

'Yeah, that's right. Brendhan gave me some tips, actually.'

'The garden is transformed,' said Mum, pulling out her phone.

'Really?' Rita smiled. 'And how is Brendhan?'

'Yeah,' said Oliver. 'He's back in Whangārei now. Got a little house, near Ma. Growing all sorts in his yard.'

'That's nice,' said Rita, and I really believed she meant it.

'And . . . how is your mum?' I was never sure whether we should talk about Oliver's mum. Especially in front of Anne.

'Ah, you know, she's all right. Not great,' Oliver said. 'She's not in distress or anything but she's starting to forget how to swallow and stuff.'

'Poor woman,' said Mum. In that moment, I felt prouder of my mother than at any time I could remember. There was still so much about Anahera and Dad that we didn't know. So many questions that now would never be answered. But Mum seemed to have found a way not only to accept Oliver into our lives but to find sympathy for his mother; for the other woman Dad had betrayed. Perhaps Mum had started to think of Anahera and Oliver as fellow victims. In his lifetime, Dad had committed the perfect crime; it was Oliver and I who had dug it up.

'Will you go back?' Rita didn't say it but we all finished the sentence in our heads: Will you go back when she dies?

'Oh, yeah, definitely. I'll probably go over in December, spend Christmas with her. Maybe meet Brendhan's girls.' Oliver bent over and blew a raspberry on the back of Clover's neck. I wondered if he was trying to hide his face for a second.

'A hot Christmas,' said Mum. 'That will be something, at least.'

'And with all that big TV money you can afford to, I suppose,' I said. Suddenly, Clover's face started to crumple. Her bottom lip went and I could see into her pink maw. Clover's mouth and Clover's throat and Clover's stomach and Clover's sleep were the scaffolding on which my life was now built. They were my master. I might dip into this outdoor world of parks and parties but the real world was her body and my body and the duty to keep her alive.

'Oh, sorry, chicken. Didn't you like that?' Oliver looked over at me, guiltily. Nobody likes to be the one to make your baby cry.

'No, don't worry. She's probably hungry,' I said. And she probably was hungry. You cannot give a baby too much milk or too much love. That's what the midwife had said during my last home visit, as I'd sat whey-faced and tearful on Rita's sofa. Just keep trying. Just keep doing what you're doing. Just keep going.

'Do you need a cushion?' said Rita, folding one of the blankets into a fat square.

'It's fine, it's fine,' I said, sitting down and lifting my shirt all in one smooth motion. As Clover latched on, Mum and Oliver sat down too and started to unpack more of the food. Rita went off to find a branch to hang the banner on.

'Hey, you're so good at that,' said Oliver, crossing his arms and nodding at Clover.

'Breastfeeding?' I asked.

'Well, yeah. But I meant all of it.' I watched Oliver start to tap his knuckles with his other hand. He did this, I knew, when he was about to say something earnest. 'You and Clover, you're doing great. You're a great little unit.'

'Thanks,' I said.

'You are,' said Mum, brushing a piece of hair off my forehead. 'You've done so brilliantly.' I felt the sun on my face and Mum's hand moving down on my back. 'It's hard to believe that this time last year we were all still reeling from that letter,' she went on. 'And you getting rushed to hospital and me not being there.'

'I'm sorry.' I sighed. How many times would I have to apologize for not having Mum at the birth? How long until she understood that I'd had no choice?

'No, no, I don't mean it like that,' Mum said. 'I just can't believe all that was only a year ago. I mean, it's less than eighteen months since you did that DNA test.'

'February last year,' said Oliver, opening a box of breadsticks.

I let out a sigh. I thought of the picture of Dad in the garden, in his red fleece. I thought of Mum, holding the *par avion* envelope in her shaking hand. I thought of Rita, changing Clover's nappy in the middle of the night in her head torch. Gamar and his narrow shoulders. Oliver's nose like an axe. Brendhan's woodsmoke laugh. Clover and her hazelnut toes.

'Well, I'm glad I did the test,' I said, looking down at my daughter. 'It's been weird – really weird – but I could never have had Clover without all of you here. I mean, literally. I probably wouldn't have got to the hospital in time without you and Brendhan.'

'And me.' Rita flopped down on a blanket next to Oliver.

'As I remember it, you were freaking out in a bush,' said Oliver, and Rita laughed.

'But we've got through the hard bit now,' said Rita, looking round at us all in turn. 'Our family.'

I looked over at the river: a vein running through the city. A carrier, a sewer, a garden. What makes a family? Was it blood or time? Was it in our genes or in the stories we told? Did we keep it in envelopes or blood cells or birthday cakes? Clover let out a small sigh and I looked down again at her body, curled against mine.

'Oh, the hard bit is just starting,' Anne said sardonically. Then her face smoothed out into a smile. 'But that's the good bit, too.'

Across the river, woven between two plants, was a nest. It hung, suspended, above the water. The biscuit-coloured sticks that held it together were surrounded by reeds, almost like arms. And inside, nestled on dry strips of grass, were four eggs. Pale, with specks on each shell. Inside, four chicks were held, warmed by the sun. Waiting for it all to begin.

Acknowledgements

Sometimes, writing a novel is like frying a pancake; the first one ends up in the bin. Thank you to all my friends for offering me sympathy, ideas and insight when things felt tricky. Particularly Becky Barnicoat, Josie Long, Miranda Ward, George Lewis, Hugh Warwick and Helen Lever.

Thank you to Andrew Hunter Murray – the most generous and most busy man alive – for his insight when I needed it most. Thank you to Daisy Buchanan for being the most supportive woman in the game.

Thank you to my agent, Zoe Ross, for her wit and wisdom. Thank you Olivia Davies for looking after me in the early stages. Thank you Transworld for giving me the opportunity to write another novel and to Sally Williamson and Cara Digby-Patel for all their editing help and guidance, and to Vivien Thompson for seeing the book through production. Thank you Marianne Issa El-Khoury for the beautiful cover and Becky Short for being a publicity powerhouse.

Thank you to Richenda Todd for her wonderful copy-editing and Clare Hubbard and Debs Warner for the proofreading. I wish I had your minds.

Thank you to the swimming women, the auntie army and the Larkrise Massive; without you, I'd never get anything done.

Thank you to the Bodleian Library for being the greatest place to read and write and think on earth.

Thank you to Xander from Caper, Elizabeth and Caroline at Daunt, and James at Blackwells for inviting me back to your bookshops. Without bookshops, there would be no books.

Thank you to Arvon for inspiring and supporting writers everywhere.

Thank you to the Early Pregnancy Unit in Rose Hill for looking after me during my darkest hour and for all the friends and neighbours who knew just what to do.

Thank you to Nick for being unflappable, always.

Thank you to my parents for always being my first and most enthusiastic audience.

Thank you to my big, complicated, international, generation-defying family. I could and would never put my actual family in a novel, of course; nobody would believe it.

About the Author

Nell Frizzell is a writer, journalist and *Vogue* columnist. She has written and worked for the *Guardian*, *VICE*, the *Sunday Times*, *Elle*, the *BBC*, the *Observer*, *Grazia* and the *Independent*, among many others. Her first book, *The Panic Years*, was an exploration of bodies, babies and the big questions facing modern life. Her debut novel, *Square One*, painted a humorous picture of moving home, fathers and daughters, and surviving heartbreak. She lives in Oxford, in a very small house full of pasta and bedding and bikes.